November 9, 2023

Dear friends,

In 2021, I read an award-winning story called "New Poets" in *Harper's*, about a young man who begrudgingly finds himself on a wild night out with old acquaintances, designated driver among drunks, feeling put upon and detached, an island unto himself. He is set apart from his present company and the mistakes of his past life by his newborn sobriety; appropriately, as he dries out that first summer, he is best known by his unreformed drinking buddies as Monk. I myself have never battled addiction, but like you (I'm guessing), I do love many people who have. And perhaps more importantly, I have known what it means to be in my midtwenties, standing at the precipice of the person I once was, contemplating the many miles I'd still need to traverse in order to become someone different, someone better, someone easier to love . . .

So moved was I by what I read in "New Poets" that in the spring of 2022, I flew to Los Angeles to find Michael Deagler. Luckily, he was kind enough to meet with me for coffee; luckier still, he agreed to let me publish his miracle of a debut novel. The book you now hold in your hands is the exquisite result of more than a year of our work together; it follows Monk as he returns to the scene of crimes he committed while blackout drunk, snapping back into consciousness and a painfully rude awakening. It is a millennial bildungsroman, a second coming-of-age story, about the particular aches that accompany not just recovery, but a quarter-life crisis. And it is the stunning first novel of a serious new talent in American fiction—a writer so special, so mature and accomplished, he has me going: Why me? Why am *I* the one who gets to tell you about Michael Deagler? Who died and made *me* his editor? *How lucky am I?*

So much of this novel tells how no person can ever really be an island; how we're not really grown-up until we learn to be in communion with others. And so, my friends, it means so much to be finally sharing *Early Sobrieties* with you. I hope you will love this novel as much as I do—and that you will reach out at the address below to let me know. It is an infinitely humbling, bewildering honor to find myself the editor of this beautiful book, and I want to thank you so much for reading.

Yours sincerely,

Deborah Ghim, Editor
ASTRA HOUSE | dghim@astrahouse.com
19 West 21st Street #1201
New York, New York 10010

EARLY
SOBRIETIES

ADVANCE READER'S EDITION

EARLY SOBRIETIES

A NOVEL

MICHAEL DEAGLER

ASTRA HOUSE
NEW YORK

Astra House
A Division of Astra Publishing House
astrahouse.com

ISBN: 9781662602245

Design by Alissa Theodor
The text is set in Warnock Pro Light.
The titles are set in Interstate Condensed.

For Ben Nangeroni, who told better stories

CONTENTS

EARLY
SOBRIETIES

ALL ADDICTS

Like all mailmen, my father hated James Farley, William Kendall, and Herodotus.

His reasons were self-evident. Farley was the namesake of the James A. Farley post office building in Midtown Manhattan. Kendall was the architect who inscribed the words across its frieze. Herodotus supplied the slogan: *Neither snow nor rain nor heat nor gloom of night stays these couriers from the swift completion of their appointed rounds.*

"I can tell you Herodotus never had a walking route in August." That was something my father liked to say. I could hardly disagree.

My father hated, in particular, the currency of these words among the general public. He hated how people would recite them at him as he struggled through Pennsylvania's sundry elements. How they thought they were being clever in doing so, or that they were sharing a moment of mutual understanding with their beleaguered letter carrier. They were fools. There could be no understanding. Only a mailman could know the trials of mailmen. Even I, a mailman's son, knew them only secondhand.

"It isn't an oath," my father declaimed at the breakfast table. "It has no official status. It's words carved on a fucking building. Nobody told Kendall to put them up there."

"You know what gets me about it?" I asked. I wanted to stand with him on the same side of an issue. "It sounds like it's going to be a couplet, but it doesn't rhyme at the end. Feels like a missed opportunity."

There was a lack of pride in the way he looked at me. "Have you found a job yet?"

I was living in my father's house again, and he was unhappy about it. I was twenty-six. By the time my father was twenty-six, he'd been with the post office for four years. He'd secured a wife and an apartment. He'd never been an alcoholic. He mentioned these facts with some frequency to accentuate the differences between us.

"I have a job. I'm freelancing. It's a gig economy." I'd told him so many times before.

My father was disinclined to believe me.

Other men my father hated were Patrick Sherrill, Cliff Clavin, and Charles Bukowski. He hated Steve Jobs, Jeff Bezos, and whoever it was who invented email. He hated people who thought the post office was a waste of tax dollars and the whole enterprise should go the way of the Pony Express. "What the hell do they think this thing is about?" he asked me over breakfast. "The government fights wars, paves roads, and delivers mail. Democracy or not, the government has always done those three things. It's been that way since the fucking Romans."

There was no mail delivery on Sundays, which was why my father was present for breakfast. I was always present. My younger brother, Owen, had recently graduated from college, and he, too, was

4

a presence, chewing his toast with the unconsidered confidence of a twenty-two-year-old.

"Yo, Dennis, we're going to the Inn tonight," said Owen. "Having a going-away party."

"For who?" I asked.

"For me. Moving to San Francisco tomorrow with my buddy Logan. We're gonna get tech jobs."

"You're moving to San Francisco tomorrow?" It was the first I'd heard of it. "How are you getting there? You're gonna drive?"

"Yeah," said Owen. "So what?"

"It's a long drive."

"Sure is."

"That's, what, three thousand miles," I said. "You're really moving to San Francisco? Tomorrow?"

Owen shrugged. "Can't stay in PA. I'll end up a mailman."

"I wouldn't let you become a mailman," said my father, who had jam on his nose. Another thing my father hated was the popular misconception that a job with the post office was a *good* job. He was happy to detail why it wasn't. Downsizing. Gutted benefits. Extended hours. Tracking devices in the trucks. "There's no future at the post office."

"Dennis, are you coming or not?" asked Owen.

"To San Francisco?"

"To the Inn. I need a ride to the Inn."

Since he'd learned of my sobriety, Owen had taken to treating me as his designated driver. My mother said he just wanted to spend more time with me, but I knew better.

"You know it's going to take like four days to get there," I said. "San Francisco."

"Yeah, no shit," said Owen. "We've got it all worked out. Are you coming tonight?"

"I don't know what I'm doing later," I said.

"You're not doing anything," said Owen. "You have no job, no girlfriend—"

"I have a job. I'm freelancing. It's a gig economy."

Owen brandished his toast at me. "Maybe *you* should become a mailman, huh? Show some initiative."

"Neither of you is becoming a mailman." My father said this because he cared about us. We knew that. "I'd rather you both ended up in the street."

\\\\\\

Like all paralegals, my mother wore her resignation on her shoulders. I could almost see it, tucked in beneath her tweed blazer. It lent a spruce dignity to her movements.

She did the work of a lawyer but did not receive the pay of a lawyer, or the prestige of a lawyer. She didn't live in the house of a lawyer, or have the family that a lawyer might have. She worked for a credit card division that had merged, over the years, from one bank to another, accompanied by layoffs her bosses promised would never occur. She had the dead eyes of a partisan who had survived one too many purges. She had coffee mugs stamped with the logos of her former employers, long-subsumed financial institutions like First Union, CoreStates, and Philadelphia National Bank.

If she'd been surprised to see me return after eight years out of the house, my mother never said so. For me, the narrative was one of utter shock and tragedy, a knee-capped bildungsroman: a bright-eyed young man from the suburbs goes down to Philadelphia and drinks himself into a series of increasingly dire circumstances until he is forced by a deficiency of skills and wits and second chances back to the Bucks

County subdivision of his youth. I could hardly believe it. Not so for my mother. On the day, six months prior, that I had walked in from the train station, duffel bag in hand, she merely looked at me as though I'd returned from the grocery store absent whatever item it was she'd asked me to pick up.

"I put your books in the basement," she said.

That was it.

Now she leaned against the sink, sipping steam as it rose up from her Wachovia mug, uninterested in making conversation on a Monday morning. Silence swung between us, in the morning and most other times as well. I struggled to remember if it had always been like that. Maybe I had encouraged silence in the past, facilitated it with my teenage hostility. Now I wouldn't have minded a bit of small talk.

"This is good coffee, huh?" I said. "You get this at Genuardi's?"

"The Genuardi's closed," she said. "It's a Weis now."

Other burdens my mother bore without complaint were the grocery shopping, the cooking, and the laundry. She bore gray hairs dyed brown to conceal her mortality from her bosses. She bore the expectations of her dead parents, Irish Catholics illiterate in affection. She bore her commitment to the improved fortunes of the next generation, slippery as they were with ingratitude, liquor, and folly. She ignored the weight of these burdens. She willed it away.

Owen stumbled into the kitchen, wobbly with the symptoms of his hangover. His face contorted in the morning light like he was an especially stoic prisoner released from an especially dark pit. I'd gone out with him the previous evening, to the Inn and half a dozen other places, though I'd spent most of my night smoking on sidewalks. It was his going-away party, I'd reasoned. I'd been obligated to see him off. Then the prick hadn't even had the decency to go away.

7

"You miss your ride to San Francisco?" I asked him.

He scowled. "I'm not going to San Francisco. Logan's an idiot. You can't just show up in Silicon Valley and get a job off the street. Those tech companies bring in talent from all over the world." He pulled a plate of leftover chicken breast from the fridge and jabbed meat into his mouth with his fingers. "I don't even know how to code."

"Maybe you can get a job in a mailroom," I said. "Work your way up. Show some initiative."

"They don't have mailrooms, Dennis. They're tech companies."

"I know that. I was throwing your words back at you."

"Nobody works their way up anymore," said my mother, speaking into the mouth of her coffee mug. "There are executives and there are stooges. If you're not on the executive track on day one, you're a stooge. I'd say you've got one year, Owen, to get on the executive track somewhere. If you don't find something by then, you'll be obsolete, because next year there's going to be a whole new class of college graduates even younger than you. Youth is the most sought-after commodity in corporate America and it depreciates quick."

Owen rolled his eyes and continued to fill his mouth with chicken breast. He'd retained the undergraduate's inability to consider notions that he found distasteful. "What about Dennis? Dennis is twenty-six and he doesn't have a job."

At twenty-six, my mother had been employed, full-time, for eight years. Through some long-lost alchemy, she'd transmuted herself from high school senior to wage-earning adult without a single credit hour in between. She was back at the office five days after she gave birth to me. I didn't think any of that explained the distance between us. I didn't believe in that sort of early childhood determinism. I spent a lot of time with my grandmother in those initial years. A kind woman. Never a harsh word.

"It's too late for Dennis," said my mother.

"Thanks, Mom."

"It's not the end of the world." She said it as though she might mean it. "I'd rather you freelance than work as a stooge."

"What about me?" asked Owen. "Would you rather *I* freelance than work as a stooge?"

"Just find an executive track job," said my mother.

Owen gnawed his chicken. He probably believed, in the raw atria of his heart, that our mother loved me more than she loved him. But I knew, deep in the pickled ventricles of my own, that love had nothing to do with anything.

\\\\\\

Like all recent college graduates, my brother was unsuited to most professions. He considered them beneath him, or beyond him, or outside his field of interest. If the purpose of a college education was to broaden the opportunities available to him as a worker, it seemed to me that he'd ended up substantially fussier than he'd been four years prior.

We were back at the Inn for Owen's second going-away party. I refused to buy him drinks, out of principle and out of penuriousness. I felt as though I were witnessing the festivities from the outside. I often felt that way, in relation to my brother's life. We had different interests. Owen played rugby in college. At the bar, he wore a rugby shirt with a Jameson patch on the chest. He had informed me recently that sobriety was for little girls and Mormons, and for that my father rewarded him with a snort of laughter.

Other things for which my brother was unsuited were magnanimity, mercy, self-awareness, and fraternal affection. He was unsuited for our small suburban town, where he would always be the son of my father, the son of my mother, or the brother of me. He was equally unsuited for the larger world, where he could not depend on even those meager associations. You had to know him to like him. If you knew him well, there wasn't much to like.

I felt secure in bars. Sitting in a bar somehow made me crave the booze less than sitting at home by myself, where I'd start to feel like somebody else's disembodied thirst. The only perilous moment was the initial step over the threshold, when I would see the whiskey bottles lined up on the shelves, coy and incandescent in their recessed light. But I could quell the impulse to partake after a second or two. For an addict, survival is inaction. I would concentrate on my hands. On my shoes. Find a seat. Find a drinking straw to drum across the thigh of my jeans. Jitter my leg into a state of equilibrium.

The new plan was for Owen and his friend Jason to move to New York and get finance jobs. "You gotta already live in the metro to land a job in Manhattan," he shouted to me over the din. "Jason's cousin works as a consultant or something. He's got an apartment in Murray Hill. Said we can sleep on his floor till we get settled."

"Sounds like an in," I said.

"New York, New York." Owen downed his beer. "Let's do a shot. You and me. I can't believe you won't do a shot with your own brother before he moves to New York."

"I'm concerned that you don't understand how sobriety works," I said. "I'm concerned about what that portends."

Owen made a face like he was hurt. "I'm trying to bond with you, you prick. You used to be fun. We used to have a good time."

That was ridiculous, of course. We'd never been close. We'd each wished to be closer, though never at the same moment. But childhood had ended—several times over, it had ended—and intimacy proved to be another of those comforts reserved for other people.

I smacked my palm down on the scruff of Owen's neck. I meant for it to sting. His shoulders shot up reflexively. "You'll do great in New York," I said. "You talk a lot and you aren't encumbered by empathy."

"Thank you," said Owen, resting a hand on my shoulder. "I think so, too."

On the drive home I stopped at the Wawa so Owen and his friends could piss out their lagers and replace them with meatball subs. I stayed in the car. It was my mother's car. I hated driving anywhere in my mother's car. I sat and watched the boys through the store's plate glass window. They were lit up like diorama models beneath the fluorescent lights, stumbling into one another as they awaited their hoagies. The faint melodies of gas station pop floated atop the nighttime silence of the suburbs.

I preferred never to go into the Wawa myself. I'd worked there back in high school and there were still one or two employees left who remembered me. My stint was during the ciabatta melt years, arguably the zenith of Wawa's culinary prowess. Roast beef. Italian. It all went downhill after they stopped slicing the meat on premises. That was how empires fell, little money-saving measures like pre-sliced cold cuts. It occurred to me that I could work at Wawa again. I could be the one stuffing sandwich rolls for drunks. But not at that Wawa. Not for those drunks. I would have to find a Wawa a few towns over, somewhere less trafficked by people who might recognize me.

Owen got back in the vehicle. He handed me a sandwich wrapped in crisp butcher paper. "Thanks for driving, Dennis. I got you this."

For a moment, my insides were wet with affection. That happened sometimes, since I'd gotten sober. Some tiny kindness would fill my skull with madrigals and pinkish light, and I'd temporarily believe that a whole litany of implausible and much-lauded concepts—serenity, contentment, love—might be real and accessible to someone like me.

11

Then Jason got in the car. "Owen, did you gank my fucking hoagie?"

\\\\\\

Like all addicts, I had trouble explaining my behavior. I didn't quit drinking when I totaled a car at twenty-one, or when I lost my first job at twenty-two, or when the booze killed my best friend at twenty-three. When people asked me what it was that finally did it, I claimed it was learning that my ex-girlfriend—the only girl I'd ever loved—had gotten engaged to a guy who was basically identical to me, minus the alcoholism. But that wasn't really the reason, either. It wasn't something big like that.

I went to the library, just to get out of the house. A fine, neutral place, the library. I wandered the antiquities stacks, scanning spines for the much-maligned anecdotalist of Halicarnassus. I'd heard Herodotus's *Histories* was the urtext of the genre. The first instance of a person sitting down and trying to make sense of all that came before him. Eventually I located a hefty copy, the faded letters of the title faint against the age-darkened cloth. I flipped briskly through its brittle pages. It occurred to me to search for the postal motto, but I didn't know the context in which the lines originally appeared. There was no listing for *post office* in the index.

"Is that Dennis Monk?"

At the end of the row, Maeve Slaughtneil stood with the leather strap of a messenger bag slung over the blade of one skinny shoulder. Maeve Slaughtneil, my classmate from grades one through twelve, whom I had not seen since high school graduation. She was a fixture of my childhood, in name if not usually in person. Our mothers had been friends, back when mine was young enough for friends to seem a necessity.

"Maeve," I managed. It was startling to see her there. "Been a while."

She smiled like she was delighted to discover me there among the ancients. "Still reading, I see." I told her I wasn't, really, and she said she wasn't either. She held up some DVD boxes. They were concert films, *The Last Waltz* and *Festival Express*.

Maeve Slaughtneil, in the flesh. She looked good. I'd never thought so before. In school, she'd been an awkward assemblage of teeth and hair and freckles, a caricaturist's sketch of a girl. Now she was transfigured, a whole different person, but still Maeve Slaughtneil. I'd been seeing things differently of late—old things that weren't as I'd remembered them—and it was starting to make me suspicious of every impression I'd had in my life.

"Are you back around?" I spun my finger in reference to the Ptolemaic universe that centered on our hometown.

She tilted her chin and didn't answer for a moment, as though I'd asked a question of far greater complexity. "I guess I am. Temporarily."

"Of course. Yeah, me too."

"You look good," she said. "You look the same."

"You look different," I said. "You look good, too."

I could never have anticipated how much Maeve would excite me. In just a few seconds I wanted her as much as I wanted anything, except the one other thing. It had been a while, for me. It had been a few years, in fact, since I'd been with anyone. The booze had drowned my sex drive enough that I was mostly content to handle it myself. But with the advent of sobriety, my long-dormant libido had sprouted overnight like a mushroom from a wet lawn.

Whatever Maeve Slaughtneil was thinking, it turned out to be very near to what I was thinking, and in what could not have been much time at all we had gone from discussing her stack of DVDs to walking through her garage and into her parents' house.

"Is that Dennis Monk?"

This time the question came from Mrs. Slaughtneil. That should have been enough to chase me back out into the street, but Maeve hurried me through the kitchen and down the basement steps, and I allowed myself to be hurried. Between the resultant sensitivity of my long drought, and Maeve's unforeseen, aggressive expertise, and the novelty of my partner and our location and general state in life, the rapture was over quick. Quick enough for me to wonder if it had really been worth the ramifications since, in my excitement, I'd bumped Maeve's head against the sharp edge of her side table, breaking the skin beneath her left eyebrow.

"Shit, I'm sorry," I said.

"Everything's good," she said. "There's tissues there. Hand me one."

As we caught our breath, I had my first real look around the basement. It seemed to have always been Maeve's bedroom. The vestiges of her teenage years were visible beneath a newer layer of storage. A beanbag chair sat smothered in spare quilts and winter coats. A stack of yearbooks and fantasy paperbacks propped up a box of Halloween decorations. The small white desk was tattooed on each side with pop-punk stickers, and the crowded shelf above it held a sloppily painted birdhouse. I recognized the birdhouse because I had one just like it. We'd decorated them in art class in the third grade. My mother kept mine in the hall closet, next to the box where she hid our Christmas presents.

There were a lot of Slaughtneils, I now remembered. Maeve's siblings were older. Gone. Married? Maybe. Like they were supposed to be.

I needed to get out of there. I'd made a mistake. There was something perverse about it, sleeping with Maeve Slaughtneil, just because I was bored and at home and didn't know what I wanted. She looked like the Maeve from childhood again, breathing there next to me, the gawky, freckled girl. All we had done with our quick, naked communion was blot out the truth for a moment, that we were stunted, immutable letdowns. Washouts. Duds. Maeve must have read all this, or something near it, in my face.

"What's wrong?" she asked. She was sitting cross-legged on the mattress, holding a tissue above her left eye. She brought it down to look at it, and I could see the smallest dab of red, smaller than a ladybug. I might have told her anything then, and she would have listened, I think. But I didn't get into it. We were, maybe, too alike for that.

"I feel like this is weird, right?" I said.

"So what?" she said.

"So," I said. "So I don't know. It's weird."

"So leave, then," she said. "You can leave if you want."

"I'm really sorry about your head," I told her as I slipped back into my clothes.

I passed meekly through the kitchen, where Mrs. Slaughtneil was ironing shirts with a pained expression on her face. "Tell your mom I asked about her."

\\\\\

Like all Irish Catholic families, mine was suspicious of admitted alcoholics.

Part of it was a kind of cultural defensiveness. Part of it was shame. Part of it was the implied accusation that the addicted party leveled at everybody else. Mostly, though, an admission of alcoholism meant that a frank conversation was about to be had, and an Irish Catholic family abhors nothing so much as a frank conversation. My family preferred to communicate our frustrations in parables, like "The County and the Roads That Haven't Been Repaved," or "Mr. Fitzpatrick and His Fucking Dog," or "How the United States Post Office Bowed to the Insatiable Greed of Amazon."

"They're starting Sunday deliveries for Amazon packages," said my father. "You believe that? Sunday. White trucks, blue uniforms, on the sabbath. Because God forbid Amazon's customers wait an extra day for their shit. The weekend is over, boys and girls."

He and my mother were seated at the kitchen table. I was preparing a pot of coffee by the sink.

"Plenty of people have to work on Sundays," I said.

"Yeah? Do *you*?" The question sounded a bit like a shout. My father told his parables in a loud voice for emphasis.

"With freelancing," I started to say, "you kinda work whenever there's a job," but my mother shook her head. I opted to proceed as a non-participating audience member.

"Keep the working man busy so he can't start trouble," continued my father. "Just like in the old days, in the sweatshops and slaughter-houses. Make sure people are too tired to do anything but go home and go to sleep. No energy left for reading or voting or organizing or speaking your mind. I'll tell you what, that's the fucking end of this fucking country. The camel's back just snapped under a truckload of Kindles."

Other suspicions held by my family included those toward corporations, Evangelicals, vegans, atheists, entrepreneurs, astrophysicists, and anyone who was good with money. Anyone, in other words, who could stake a claim on enlightenment. We didn't believe in enlightenment.

"I like to come home and have a beer," said my father. His declaration seemed to be inspired by nothing other than my continued presence in the kitchen.

"That's fine," I said.

"It helps me unwind." He and my mother were drinking no-longer-domestic lager from tall, slick cans.

"That's part of the appeal," I said.

"You didn't used to be such a scold," said my father.

"I'm just making some coffee." I tried to be forthright when speaking with my parents. Sobriety required candor. I had lost my right to parables. Fiction was more than I could be trusted with.

"Don't you have friends?" asked my father. "When I was your age, I was dying to get away and meet up with my friends." He winked at my mother. They were each other's only friend.

"Friends are overrated," said my mother.

"Mrs. Slaughtneil says hi." I watched the coffee trickle into the pot. I didn't even like the coffee. It was bad coffee.

"What does that mean?" asked my mother, as though I had spoken in code. "Is that a joke?"

"No, I saw her the other day. I was hanging out with Maeve, and I saw Mrs. Slaughtneil, and she told me to tell you hello."

My mother chewed on the inside of her cheek as she watched me from beneath weighted eyelids. "Maeve Slaughtneil is disturbed. What do you mean you were hanging out with her?"

"I ran into her at the library," I said. "What do you mean she's disturbed?"

"She's mentally ill. She disappeared for three years. She just got released from a halfway house. She's in her parents' custody, for Christ's sake."

"She's what?" Suffice it to say, I had not been aware of any of that. A side effect of my habitual blackout inebriation was that it had kept me beyond the reach of most social memoranda. "When did this happen?"

"She moved back home last summer," said my mother. "It's a real tragedy. She'll be the Slaughtneils' dependent for the rest of their lives unless they find a way to drug her back to normal."

Well, fuck.

Mentally ill *how*, I wondered? In a way that resulted in promiscuity? Could Maeve have been trolling for men at the library?

And what the hell was Mrs. Slaughtneil doing, letting her bring someone home?

The coffee machine entered its sputtering denouement.

"Christ," I said.

"They say mental illness emerges in your early twenties," said my father, looking at me as though he didn't believe it. "You know what else emerges in your early twenties? Being a bum."

"Or being a mailman," I said.

"Bingo," he said.

\\\\\\\\

Like all Pennsylvania towns, mine was founded with the best of intentions. It had subsequently fallen short of expectations and continued on in a state of gradual regress. Such was the fate of most Pennsylvania things and most Pennsylvania people. We liked to laugh at the Amish, but they realized long ago that if you ask for more than the minimum you'll end up disappointed.

I was at the Inn again for Owen's third going-away party. The latest scheme was for him and his friend Morgan to drive down to Corpus Christi and find jobs on an oil rig.

I failed to see the angle.

"Dangerous work pays a premium," explained Owen. "With my degree, they'll probably make me a foreman. Two weeks on, two weeks off. Work a couple of years, pay down my loans, get a nest egg going, invest that shit. Capital gains, Dennis. Earned income is for peasants."

"What if you blow up?" I was reasonably sure, by that point, Owen wasn't going anywhere. The occupational hazards of rig work seemed purely hypothetical.

"Who gives a shit?" Owen slugged his whiskey ginger. "We all go sometime."

Other failures of my hometown were the three empty storefronts in our strip mall, the blank billboard on the northbound highway, and the condemned farmhouse across from our subdivision. And me. And maybe Owen. He had chickened out of his New York plans. Our region's native inferiority complex had flared up and kept him home. At least that's how we had chosen to look at it. If something could be categorized as our collective failing, then it couldn't very well be blamed on us as individuals.

"You guys aren't doing coke in the bathroom, are you?" I asked Owen. From across the bar, I'd noticed Morgan and Jason taking frequent trips to the bathroom together. Morgan in particular kept thumbing his own nostrils.

Owen glared at me like I'd accused him of something obscene. "Of course not. Why would you ask me that?"

He didn't really look like he was on coke. "It's bad for you, you know," I said. "And unhygienic."

"You should talk," said Owen into his glass.

The funny thing of it was, I never did drugs. No pills, no powders, no psychedelics. I'd never fucked with any of that. I'd rarely even smoked weed. I'd heeded the warnings of my teachers, DARE officers, and syndicated sitcoms. I was sensible. I'd stuck to alcohol, a substance so wholesome they served it in church. Terrible luck, to be addicted to something like that.

"I don't want coke in Mom's car," I said to Owen.

"Dude, we don't have any coke." Owen stormed off to stand with his friends at the other end of the bar. A while later he floated back to me to let me know that Morgan and Jason didn't need a ride home.

At the end of the night, Owen and I sat in the car in the Wawa parking lot. I wanted to smoke a cigarette, but it was my mother's car, and only she was allowed to smoke in it. I could have smoked outside, but it was raining. I could have walked under the Wawa awning to smoke, but there were already a couple of drunks smoking under there. Drunks for whom I had even less patience than I did for my brother.

"Too bad Dad's asleep," said Owen, his voice sluggish. "He loves the rain."

"You know how it should go?" I asked, unconcerned if he followed my train of thought. Being a sober man among drunks is tantamount to thinking out loud. "It should go: *Neither snow nor rain nor heat nor gloom of night / stays these couriers from the swift completion of their FLIGHT.* Night rhymes with flight. Why would it be *appointed rounds*? It's some kind of misdirect."

"Well, it wasn't written in English," said Owen. "It probably rhymes in Latin."

"Or maybe," I said, thinking that perhaps life, in practice, was mostly about appointed rounds and not so much about flying. I left the thought unfinished.

Raindrops passed through the beams of light flaring from the front of my mother's sedan. We watched them dash themselves dramatically against the rough asphalt of the parking lot. I imagined being born in a cloud and plummeting through the immensity of the sky—thinking, yes, here we go, I must be headed somewhere spectacular—only to kamikaze into a convenient store parking lot among oil slicks and cigarette butts and wads of gum.

"Hey, Dennis?" asked Owen. "Why'd you stop drinking?"

How anticlimactic, for a raindrop. How on-the-nose.

"If you're gonna get a sandwich you should go in and get your sandwich," I said.

"I'm gonna go in," he said, but he didn't move. His head was tipped slightly forward like he might fall asleep.

"Hey, Dennis? Why'd you stop drinking?" I couldn't tell if he asked it again because he really wanted to know, or if he'd simply forgotten he asked it the first time.

"Just to live for a while," I said.

"So you like your life?" asked Owen.

"I didn't at the time," I said.

"But you wanted to keep living?"

"I guess I didn't want to get off before I saw everything there is to see," I said. Under the awning, one drunk shoved the other one. "Especially if there isn't anything else afterward. I'd feel pretty stupid then, wouldn't I?"

Owen seemed to turn the words over in his mind. "Hey Dennis?" He said it like he was beginning the conversation anew. "You remember when we were kids?"

I'd thought a bit about my childhood when I first got sober. Just the kind of thinking a person does. Looking for the cause, the beginning of it. There were a few things. But nothing that said, *Here, right here, this is where it started.* I could spend my whole life turning things over, but I didn't see the point.

Drinking had provided the welcome service of clearing my life of debris. It demanded so much time—getting booze, drinking booze, finding ways to get more booze—that the nonessentials were gradually scrubbed away. Hobbies first. Minor social obligations. Shallow friendships. Things I valued in the abstract for which I could no longer find the time. Books. Travel. The search for a significant other. I let my hair get long. I stopped observing every laundry day. Then it was jobs. Not good jobs, since I'd never had a good one. It was liberating to lose the kind of jobs I lost. I bailed on plans. I stopped returning phone calls. The people I didn't see every day I mostly ceased to see at all. I skipped showers. I didn't keep food in the fridge. I didn't get out of bed every morning, not if there was already a bottle on the nightstand. I didn't need to *be* anything. It was easy to let go of the future—it was strange how happy I was to see it go—but it took the past with it. Memories. Former selves. I had to lose them. They were too difficult to square with who I was.

"No," I said and turned the key in the ignition. "I don't remember."

\\\\\\

Like all histories, my family's seemed composed of a series of recurring mistakes that, while theoretically avoidable, tended nevertheless to repeat themselves. My grandfather was a mailman, for example. And my grandmother, the kindly woman who watched me in my youth, took gin in her coffee. And nobody was happy, as far as I've been able to discover. Not in the way that we define happiness today. They lived and died comfortably in disappointment.

Owen and I drank our coffee at the breakfast table. It was a Sunday, again, though my father was at work. There were Amazon parcels to deliver. The day was overcast but blessedly dry.

My mother leaned against the counter with her Wells Fargo mug. She wore a sweatshirt, one printed with the name of the college that I and Owen had attended. It wasn't a very good college. All of us knew it. Her wearing of that sweatshirt struck me as a bit like hanging on to a third grader's poorly painted birdhouse. She didn't do it because she was proud. For her, it was a gesture of solidarity. She bound herself to us because she was our mother. Others might see it as an act of love. But love, I was sure, had nothing to do with anything.

"Two weeks is a long time to be at work," Owen was saying. "Even if you get two off, afterward."

"It is," I agreed.

"And the pay's not that good, considering. I mean, for as dangerous as the work is."

"It isn't."

The light, in the morning, in the kitchen, was a thing I did not hate. There was something about the slant of it, the way the room seemed to glow from the floor upward toward the ceiling. I sometimes thought, in moments when I could sit in that kitchen alone, in the morning, with everyone else away, how tolerable it was. I thought that, if it belonged to a different house, I would have liked for it to be my own kitchen. My adult kitchen, the kitchen for the rest of my life. And to be honest, the other rooms of the house were not so bad, divorced from their associations. I could have lived there happily had the house been in a different town. Even the town itself would not have been so undesirable, for all its failures, if only it had different people living in it than the ones I knew. And even those people could stay, all of them, apart from my family. Really, even my family didn't bother me in theory, and I could conceivably have remained with them, if only they were different versions of themselves. But how simple it would be, I thought, to make the world tolerable—to make the world good—with only the smallest of adjustments. A shifting of the light, a rearranging of the furniture. A vaguely different shade for every painted surface. If the houses could all be turned a few degrees in some direction, and if the car interiors smelled faintly otherwise, and if the coffee was improved by a hair. I could have lived in a place like that. I really could have. I knew how fussy I was being, but everything was so, so close to good. Like a letter delivered only one house away from its correct address. Like someone you could almost love.

"So what now?" I asked Owen. "Where are you gonna go now?"

He shrugged. "I think I'll just hang around here for a while. Figure things out."

"No," said my mother. This surprised me, but it shouldn't have, because I didn't know her all that well. She looked at my brother, looked at me. Pleaded.

"You have to go now. You both have to go right now."

PAT'S, GENO'S

That summer, someone decided to erect pop-up beer gardens in the unused lots throughout the city, which offended me in a way that I found difficult to articulate. They were affected, trendy places with trendy beers for trendy people. Not my scene, even if I'd still had a scene. There was one in the lot across from Pat's King of Steaks, beneath a crumbling mural of Frankie Avalon and Fabian and some other teen idols from the early sixties. I was sitting at one of Pat's picnic tables with my friend Bors Spang, and those teen idols were staring me right in the face.

At some point everybody had moved to South Philadelphia. I suspected it was initially a practical decision. It was a reasonably priced section of the city, with neighborhoods that were more or less intact. There were bakeries, bars, sandwich shops. The row houses were quaint in a pre-war proletariat sort of way, with garlands of Christmas lights strung between them all twelve months of the year. Once the first hipsters planted their flag, South Philadelphia became the cool place to live, particularly east of Broad in the old Italian wards. But I don't have to explain to you how gentrification works.

My retreat to my parents' house, out among the cornfields and subdivisions of Bucks County, had lasted a little over six months. My mother tolerated me until she didn't. My sobriety was not something she was obligated to foster like the orchid of some out-of-town neighbor. Owen found an apartment down the road, but I decided to come back to the city. I tried to return to Kensington only to realize I no longer knew anyone in Kensington. Or Fishtown. Or Northern Liberties. They had migrated en masse to South Philadelphia. I followed. What else could I do? I was sleeping on Bors's couch, washing dishes three nights a week at a banquet hall in Pennsport, spending my free time rereading Patricia Highsmith novels and sipping water in bars.

Bors was manhandling a whiz-with-onions as he told me a story from a time he'd worked a construction job out toward the middle of the state. "Lancaster County, near all the Amish, right? So I was eating by myself in this little roadside diner when I was propositioned by an Amish man. He offered me two thousand dollars if I would be willing to impregnate his daughter."

"Oh yeah?" I wasn't eating anything. The evening was too hot. South Philadelphia always felt hot to me. That June was subtropical. The whole district went sleeveless. We sweated as a body politic, indoors and out. Yet for some reason, the food was all tamales and phở gà and giardiniera relishes. Burgers topped with sriracha and long hots. Cheesesteaks the size of dachshunds. Jalapeño-flavored craft beers that even I thought sounded disgusting, though I still wanted them badly. It was too much. I would have been happy with cigarettes and coffee—that duo of vices still available to me—but it was too hot for them as well. I was a man at odds with his surroundings. I was perhaps less bubbly than my usual self. "And why would he do that?"

"See, the Amish have been intermarrying for generations," explained Bors. "They're all cousins at this point. They need to expand the gene pool or their kids will turn weird. So these Amish fathers go out scouting for studs."

"Why wouldn't they just go to a sperm bank?" I asked. It was a poor question given the context of the story, but I was playing a very passive role in the conversation.

Bors blinked at me like I was an idiot. "They're Amish. They do everything the old-fashioned way. Which means I'd have to deliver the goods in person. Like, with my dick." Bors wore a thick blond beard that would have made a Viking proud. His was just the sort of look likely to impress a man attempting to breed a new generation of barn-raisers and buggy-drivers.

I shrugged. "So you said no?"

"Of course I did, Monk. Who do you think I am? Forget even, for a moment, issues of consent. Can you imagine trying to have sex with a farm girl in a bonnet while her kinfolk are standing on the other side of the door, waiting to pitchfork me in the spine if they hear a noise they don't like?" Bors grabbed a wad of napkins and scrubbed them around the periphery of his mouth. "The whole thing is a huge turnoff."

We were at Pat's King of Steaks because Bors was a Pat's man, if only as a vote against its competitor Geno's, which rose before us like a neon casino catty-corner across Passyunk Avenue. Bors refused to eat at Geno's because of the sign at the counter: *This Is America: When Ordering Speak English.* Geno's founder Joey Vento was a love-it-or-leave-it type who, after years of serving steak sandwiches to the people of Passyunk Square, had looked around one day and decided that the neighborhood had gotten a bit too Mexican. Of course, observant patrons might have guessed Vento's politics even before he hung up the sign. There was a photo under the restaurant's awning of him sitting astride a monstrous motorcycle with a stars-and-bars bandana tied atop his walnut of a head, grinning like he truly believed that his five-foot-nothing paisano frame would have received a warm welcome in the Confederate States of America. Joey Vento had died a few years back, but the sign remained.

At some point in my life, I had been a Geno's man. At some other point, I had been a Pat's man. At various times, if a person had asked me, "Pat's or Geno's?," I would have replied, "Jim's," or "Tony Luke's," like a smart-ass. Later, I would have said something about the illusion of choice, and worked it into some discussion of late capitalism, or the American party system, or existentialist literature. I was, at times, a bit insufferable. But all that was in the past. Now, I was a cheesesteak ronin, masterless and unaffiliated. Because at the end of the day, who really gave a fuck?

Satiated, Bors turned sideways from the table and stretched his legs, bare below his cut-off jean shorts, out into the thoroughfare. I noticed there was a bandage taped over a section of his left calf.

"Get clipped with a nail gun?" I asked.

Bors glanced down at his leg. "Nah, new tattoo, bro."

"Didn't you already have something there?" I couldn't remember what it was. "What was it before?"

Bors grinned and shook his head. "What would be the point of getting it covered up if I went around reminding everybody of what it used to be?"

I figured it had been some emo lyric, something too angsty and teenage for the man Bors had settled into. "What did you cover it with?"

"Flyers logo." Bors stood, collecting the detritus of his meal. "I think we ought to take this show across the street, Monk. Have some drinks out under the stars."

There were no stars to be seen. In the haze of city summer, the night sky wasn't all that much darker than its daytime equivalent, though it came in a wider assortment of colors—reds, purples, oranges, browns. That particular night it had turned sulfuric gray, like a boiled egg yolk oxidizing in the open air. Even so, it was preferable to a ceiling, and the beer garden was already filled with dozens of people drinking in the twilight, laid-back youngsters with disposable incomes lounging happily on benches and in Adirondack chairs, chatting with their bearded boyfriends, their nose-ringed girlfriends. Tattoos and plaid. Ciders and wheat beers. Why did I hate them? Demographically, they were my people. But as an individual, no, I was not one of them, because I was not bearded or nose-ringed or tattooed, and because I couldn't afford to live anywhere without somebody doing me a favor, and because I couldn't drink ciders or wheat beers or stouts or whiskeys or novelty jalapeño-flavored ales, couldn't luxuriate in the bonhomie of unaddicted summer.

But I didn't hate them. I was done hating other people.

We were standing at the outdoor bar for a whole minute before I realized that its tender was an ex-girlfriend of Bors's. One of the more significant ones. Lilah Noth looked spent. Fatigue shadowed her back and forth across the bar as she filled plastic pint glasses with cloudy hefeweizen. She was short, with inky black hair, and had that vaguely ageless quality that a server's uniform and cigarettes and years of working nights gives a person. Which is attractive, I think, at least to the sort of people that find city life attractive.

"What do you want," she said to Bors. She looked less than pleased to see him.

"What have you got in the way of a dunkel?" asked Bors. He planted his elbow on the bar, his chin in his palm, and looked at Lilah as though she were an object of great curiosity.

Lilah ignored him. "Dennis Monk?"

"Just water, thanks."

"Monk quit drinking," said Bors. "Six months ago."

"Seven months ago," I said.

Lilah placed a cup of ice water in front of me. She reacted to my words with what might have been the faintest bit of surprise. Or feigned surprise. "Did you? Good for you."

"Anything malty, really, would be fine," said Bors.

"I saw Cathy Tomlinson the other day," said Lilah. Cathy Tomlinson was a woman I was with for a while, before. One of the more significant ones.

"Around here?" I asked. "I thought she moved to Seattle."

Lilah shook her head. "She lives on Thirteenth, right on Columbus Square. Nice house."

"Oh yeah?" That was not far from where we stood. A quick walk. "What's her situation?"

"I think she's working for some nonprofit. We didn't talk long. She's living with her fiancé, if that's what you're asking."

"You know, what the hell? Dealer's choice," said Bors. "I'll take anything with alcohol. Some of us haven't quit yet."

Lilah gave Bors a look of revulsion that only years of intimacy could foster. I took my cup of water and excused myself.

I found one of a trio of unoccupied chairs set around a patio table and sat staring up at the deteriorating portrait of Bobby Rydell. The surface of the mural had eroded in several places, including most of Rydell's torso, exposing the underlying bricks of the house on which it was painted. At the next table, I could hear a young couple telling their friends about their recent forays into homeownership. How they had purchased a little row house on Manton Street and were restoring it themselves, putting in the hours on nights and weekends, while she did something at Jefferson Hospital and he was an accountant for the school district. It was labor-intensive, but it made them feel as though they were earning the right to live there (said he) and that it was an emotional investment in the neighborhood (said she). Their friends lauded their passionate industry.

A benefit of sobriety was that I felt superior toward anyone who drank, regardless of the other factors of their lives or mine. An unflattering quality, for sure, but an indispensable one, particularly if you don't have much else going on. I sipped my ice water. It was cold enough to hurt my teeth. I was jealous of everybody for everything. I was jealous of the Manton-Street couple for their house, their jobs, their drinks, one another. I was jealous of Bors for his vocational skills, his apartment, his lucrative fecundity. I was jealous of Lilah for her lived-in life, her thick-skinned competence. I'd been under the impression that I'd been building up calluses during my eight years of ceaseless boozing, but upon ripping away my whiskey bandage I found there was only new red skin beneath it. I was raw as an infant.

From my seat, I could see Geno's shining like a carnival ride on its slice of pavement. Xenophobia notwithstanding, I sympathized with dead Joey Vento. I, too, was afraid of change. And who wasn't? My fear, precisely, was of the times passing me by. I had no real misgivings concerning the gentrification of South Philadelphia. I just didn't want to be left out of it. My peers were raising up their futures like the Amish with their barns, while I was still out on the road like a tramp, alone and less than whole. I didn't want everyone to be all right until I was all right. I knew it was selfish, but that's how I felt. Self-awareness, for me, was recent, revelatory, and bleak.

Bors walked up, chugging something amber from a plastic cup. "Come on. She's being a bitch."

\\\\\\

We were up the block at the Birthday Bar, where decades of drunken embellishment had plastered the walls with photographs of native sons even more obscure than those on the beer garden mural. Joe Valino. Sonny Averona. Dom Irrera. It was a cramped, muggy place, one that still allowed smoking, and though the fumes were already thick enough to give me a nicotine contact high, I lit a cigarette for myself. I could never resist the opportunity to smoke indoors.

The special was a Yuengling Premium can and a shot of Windsor Canadian. Bors got to work pouring them into himself. With every round he ordered me a water, a gesture I appreciated, though I hardly needed so many. The accumulation of half-empty cups made it look like I was preparing a glass harp performance. We sat jammed in at a communal table in the corner, elbow to sweaty elbow with people not so different from those in the beer garden, though these variants smoked and laughed and drank like they knew something and yelled over the New Wave being piped at us through unseen speakers.

I had called Bors when I first got back to the city because I knew he wouldn't mind me crashing on his couch for a while. I had a handful of other people I could call, and I figured I'd have to call all of them before the summer was over. It would take a while to get something permanent together. I didn't want to put anyone out for too long, but Bors, at least, was hard to put out. There was a disciplined equanimity about him. Even at his most publicly intoxicated he rarely got worked up over anything. And yet he was clearly bothered by the encounter with Lilah.

"I was working with these Guatemalans a few years back," he said, "installing a pool up in Quakertown. Illegal guys. They offered to sell me their sister—like, to be my wife—for eight thousand dollars."

"Eight thousand." I whistled. "You'd need to impregnate like four Amish women to afford that."

"Yeah, I don't know what the angle was." He was starting to sound drunk. "You would think, like, if I married her, she'd get a green card, and she could stay in the country. So shouldn't they be paying me? I told them that, and they were like, *No, no, she cooks, she cleans.* And I'm like, I could find a wife for free, guys. If I wanted one. I don't need to pay eight thousand dollars. It just kinda seemed like a slavery situation, you know?"

"You really have an ear to the sexual black market," I said. "I never get solicited for these kinds of transactions."

"That's because you look like a grouch. You should try smiling sometimes." Bors flashed his teeth to demonstrate.

"Did you hear Lilah say Cathy Tomlinson was back in town?" I asked him. "Do you know about that?"

Bors's gaze fixated on the woman seated beside him, at the other end of our table. She was engaged in an animated conversation with a friend, but I couldn't make out its theme. She wore a t-shirt bearing the likeness of Flyers enforcer Dave "the Hammer" Schultz, and I realized that was what had caught Bors's attention.

"Excuse me," he said to her. "*Excuse* me." He repeated it until the woman acknowledged that she was being addressed. When she turned to look at him, Bors lurched up onto his unsteady feet. "Check this shit out," he said, or rather shouted, and brought his left shoe up onto the table, wobbling as he balanced on his right leg. His calf was exposed, the one with the new tattoo. He ripped the bandage from it in one swift motion. I imagined I could hear a tearing sound over the music. Beneath it lay a wound of red and black and orange, a Flyers logo stamped onto the shaved, pink skin of Bors's calf. Inflamed and lacquered with ointment, it gleamed like the eye of Horus. "Right?" he said to the girl, but she turned her face in disgust. *"Right?"* She and her friend decamped to a different corner of the room. "Hey, come on," Bors called after them.

He took his foot off the table and slumped back down. He finished his Yuengling slowly, like he didn't recognize the taste. Like the bartender had given him something he hadn't asked for. "I think I'm done with this city," he said after a minute. "I'm gonna go to Idaho. I told you I was out there last summer for lineman training? I left early. Shouldn't have left, man."

"What's out there?" I asked.

"Hills." He closed his eyes.

I stamped out my cigarette. I couldn't sit there anymore. "I'm gonna head out. I'll see you back at the apartment."

Bors smiled, his eyes still shut. "Sure thing, Monk. I'll be camped right here for a while."

Outside, the night clung to the rooftops, ogling pedestrians as they shuffled their way from house to bar or bar to house. The light and noise of the city, the glaring, the clanking, was a comfort to me. Back in Bucks County, the night was black and still and silent. It reminded me of the emptiness of space, the interminability of the cosmos. City night just reminded me of egg rolls and burnt coffee and misdemeanors, of all the things I didn't need but could procure with little effort. Distractions to carry me through the hours until the sun came up. Dawn always felt like a victory, one that I could celebrate with sleep.

The sun setting and rising provided me with a sense of progress, though I'd made none to brag about. My primary achievement of the previous seven months was racking up days, like a prisoner etching x's on a cell wall. My primary achievement of the eight years before that was disappointing everyone I knew. Or, no. That wasn't quite it.

What I'd done was spend eight years lowering people's expectations of me, to the point where they could no longer be disappointed. People gradually ceased to take an interest in my life until they had no reason left to think of me. The dead lived on in the memory of the living, but there were plenty of living people who no one else ever thought about.

\\\\\\

Three-story row houses dozed all down the 1300 block of 13th Street, their upper windows thrown wide to catch whatever breezes might be blowing west from Camden. A breeze would need to travel far, high across the swollen Delaware, over the piers and roofs of Pennsport and through the swishing trees of Columbus Square. It would probably blow itself out before it got there.

The block was quiet. It was close to midnight. A Tuesday. There was no way to know which house was Cathy's, so I walked down the street until I found one that struck me. It had shutters on the windows and a freshly painted blue door, with gardening pots lined up before it on the pavement and, planted near the curb, a snowdrop tree. I knew it was a snowdrop tree because there was a little sign stuck in between the flagstones that identified it as such. It was a young tree, thin-trunked, fifteen feet high, but it wasn't difficult to picture it growing large enough to shade the whole front of the house in the sweltering summers to come. It was a suitable house, the kind I could have imagined for Cathy. The kind I could have imagined for both of us, at some earlier point in time, if I had ever thought to imagine it.

She answered after a few rings. Her voice was dense and low in a way that suggested she'd recently been asleep. "Dennis?"

"Cathy!" I said. "This might sound strange, but I think I'm outside your house."

"What?"

"You're on Thirteenth Street, right? Across from the park? Look outside."

I stared up at the open windows of the second and third floors of the snowdrop house, waiting for Cathy's face to appear at one of them. They remained empty in the hot night, like a series of abstract canvases painted one unvarying shade of black.

"I don't see you," came her voice on the phone. "Are you fucking with me?"

"No, I'm out here. Wait a second." I backed into the street and scanned the windows up and down the block. I saw a face peering cautiously out of the second floor of a house five or six doors up the row. I'd picked the wrong address. Guessing was never a strength of mine.

"Here I am," I said, walking up, waving. She offered a timid flutter of fingers. In the dark, I had trouble making out her features. Her hair was shorter than it had been, her neck looked longer. But the way she held the phone to her ear was familiar, somehow. The way her elbow cut in toward the center of her chest. She leaned against the window frame. We regarded each other for the first time in a long time.

"Wow." She was still speaking into the phone. She wasn't going to shout down to me. The whole block could probably hear our conversation as it was. "There you are."

"Come downstairs," I said.

"I'm not coming down. What are you doing here?"

I didn't have an answer for that. "How are you?"

"You're drunk."

"No."

"Be honest."

"I am. I quit." I'd wanted to tell her since it had first been true. "Seven months sober. I kicked it."

"Are you sure?"

I'd lied about kicking it before. "What's that supposed to mean?"

I tried to get a read on her reaction to my visit. She didn't appear to be smiling, but it was difficult to tell. She hung back, concealed in the shadow of her room.

"Dennis, we haven't talked in two years and you just showed up outside my apartment in the middle of the night. That's not exactly sober behavior."

I was growing self-conscious there in the dim light of the lampposts. I had unwittingly placed myself on display before all the denizens of 13th Street. "I heard you lived here. From Lilah Noth."

She cleared her throat. "And so, what, you've come to apologize?"

"No. No, I'm not in a program. I quit on my own. This isn't an apology."

She laughed. "Of course."

"Look, I've got a clean slate, you know?" I spread my arms wide to show how free I was. "The way I was, that's over. Gone. It feels great."

"Well that's pretty convenient, isn't it?"

"What do you mean?"

"You just get to decide that you're absolved?" Her voice was rising, but she checked it, found her steadiness again. "Look, I'm happy for you. I've always wanted you to get to a good place."

I really wished I could see her face in the light. If we were just face-to-face, if she could just see the clarity in my eyes, I knew she would understand that I had changed. "Come downstairs."

"We're not just going to be friends, Dennis." She was almost whispering into the phone. "The way you were . . . that hasn't gone away, not for me."

I stared up at her, but I couldn't think of anything else to say. I hadn't anticipated how easy it would be for her to rebuff me. We'd been very in love at one point.

I heard a man's voice in the background, groggy and interrogative. "I have to go," said Cathy. She pulled her head back into the house, and the line went dead. I stood in the middle of 13th Street and felt the eyes—real or imagined—of a block's worth of nosy, judgmental people peering out at me through open windows. I crossed to the sidewalk and started to leave, slowly at first and then quickly.

Before she left me, I remember Cathy complaining that I was motivated by hate instead of love. I think she meant it in the carrot-and-stick sense. The honey-and-vinegar sense. Like how I didn't try to quit drinking when I loved somebody. How I only did it later, when I hated myself. Most of the motivation for getting sober came from the belief that it would immediately solve the bulk of my problems. Depression. Anxiety. Indigence. Loneliness. Obesity. The bruxism that ground away my tooth enamel every night when I passed out. It was true that each of those things decreased in severity once I stopped getting sloshed, but none of them fully disappeared. I wasn't reborn as a seventeen-year-old with a decade's worth of unblown opportunities lined up before me like freshly wrapped Christmas presents. I was still twenty-six. Still broke. My old flames had moved on. My tooth enamel did not grow back.

I wondered, had I known all this, if I'd have been able to make it through the early days. If I'd have still thought it was worth it.

\\\\\\

I was wandering back toward the Birthday Bar when I spotted Lilah Noth loitering in the golden light beneath the Geno's awning. She was smoking a cigarette and seemed to consider her own, long shadow as it stretched before her across Passyunk Avenue. She might have been the subject of an Edward Hopper knockoff, preoccupied and elegantly alone. She spotted me approaching from half a block away, and she watched me until we were standing next to each other, as if we'd agreed to meet at that exact time and spot in front of the Geno's board of police department patches from across the country.

"He's not still around, is he?" asked Lilah.

"Bors? I think he's at the Birthday Bar."

"Your friend's a real asshole, you know that?"

"I guess he is, yeah." I tended to think that people are many-splendored, but that was usually a useless point to make.

Lilah gave me a quick once-over. "What happened to you?"

"Oh, who knows?" I was beginning to feel like an idiot. "You said Cathy Tomlinson was living on Thirteenth, so I just went over there to reconcile, and now I'm back here."

Lilah's eyebrows crept upward. So did the corners of her mouth. "It's kind of late at night for that, don't you think?"

I nodded slowly.

"Well. I do regretful shit all the time." She stamped out her ciga-rette and stepped under the heat-lamp glow of the awning lights. "I'm getting a steak."

"Are you a Geno's girl?" I wouldn't have picked her for one, but it was a hard thing to guess about a person.

"Duh," she said. "My dad used to take us here when we were kids."

"The sign doesn't bother you?"

Lilah swatted the idea away with a flick of her hand. "You expect these third-generation cheesesteak jamokes to take orders in Spanish? They barely speak English."

She bought her sandwich and we sat at an empty picnic table. As she tore into the steak with her teeth, globs of cheese and onions dripped from the roll's crevice and pattered against the wrapper. She nodded at it, offering me a bite, but I shook my head. I wasn't in the mood for anything. "So how's the not drinking?" she asked between mouthfuls.

That was just what I wanted, for someone to ask that exact question, if only as an acknowledgment of my Herculean task, how exacting it must be on my emotional state. I'd been preemptively composing an answer. "I feel like I've spent the last eight years on a cruise ship," I said. "Like, it was awful, and gross, and expensive, but I was drunk, so it didn't matter. And the whole time, I was just throwing things off the side that I didn't think I needed. Life jackets, suitcases, deck chairs. Just hurling it all over the railing. Then, in a moment of—I don't know—insanity, I jumped off the back of the boat. Jumped right into the ocean. The shock of the water cleared my head, and that felt good, for a minute. But now I'm just treading along in the wake of the cruise ship. And I'm starting to get tired. And all I can do is grab onto the things I dropped overboard, the deck chairs and suitcases, just to keep myself from sinking."

Hearing it out loud, the analogy sounded less profound.

"I've never been on a cruise ship," said Lilah.

"I haven't either," I admitted.

"My dad quit drinking, though. A couple of times."

"Yeah?" I'd found that the children of alcoholics tended not to be as sympathetic toward alcoholics as you might assume. "What's his current status?"

"Dead," said Lilah, her mouth filled with steak.

"Ah." I tried to remember if I'd known that about Lilah. I thought that I had encountered her father once, at a restaurant, but maybe he had been a stepfather. "I'm sorry to hear that. How long has it been?"

"Last week. Last Friday."

"Your father *just* died? Shit." I reviewed the night's events to include this new information. "Does Bors know that?"

"He knows," said Lilah.

"Wow. Damn. I don't know what to say."

She shrugged, chewed. "Yeah, well."

"We don't have to talk about it," I said. "How did he die?"

Lilah rested her sandwich on its wrapper. She picked up a napkin and balled it thoughtfully between her palms. "He quit drinking again, and his body chemistry got out of whack or something, from the withdrawal, and his heart stopped. Last Friday, they think. He was living in this shithole in Norristown, and there was nobody around to help him. The mailman found him Saturday."

"Wait, you can die from withdrawal?" I asked.

"Yeah, dude. Delirium tremens. How do you not know that?"

"I don't know, who tells you that?" If I'd known it might have killed me, there was no way I would have quit.

Lilah nodded solemnly. "That's how Modest Mussorgsky died."

"Who the hell is Modest Mussorgsky?" I tried to remember how I had felt my first week sober. I'd felt like shit, but I'd always felt like shit. I'd felt like shit every day for years and didn't even realize it. In my second week, I'd relearned what it was to not feel like shit. Health became its own inebriation. I would just lie in the sun on my parents' lawn, unpained.

"A composer," said Lilah. "But if it's going to happen, it happens like two days after you quit. You said you've been sober for six months?"

"Seven," I said. I breathed the scent of fried onions deeply through my nostrils, detained it in my lungs. "Jesus. Fuck, Lilah. That's awful about your dad."

"It is what it is." She sounded tired of the whole thing. "I mean, if he had kept drinking, it just would have been a heart attack or a stroke or something, this year or the next one or the one after. He wore out his body and it caught up with him."

She stared down at her steak, like it had spoken to her, and then let out a sharp, heart-halting sob. It was so loud that I glanced around despite myself to see if anyone was watching. But that was it as far as lamentations. She grabbed the wad of napkins and raised them to her nose. She sniffled.

We sat in silence while she took another tiny bite of the sandwich. She set it down on the wrapper and pushed it away.

"You sure you don't want any?" Her voice was even, as if the outburst hadn't occurred. "I'm not going to eat it."

"Save it." I meant to sound encouraging.

"What are you, new? These things don't keep for shit. They're inedible after forty-five minutes."

She got up and dropped the bundle with a thud into a garbage can. She lit a cigarette and cast meditative glances up and down the block.

I figured it might be best to push the conversation away from death and its related topics. "So where are you staying now?"

"Titan Street." She nodded in the direction of the river. She brushed a strand of hair from her eyes. "You want to see it?"

I watched her face to tell if she was asking what I thought she was asking. She exhaled her smoke at me, cloaking me in burned air.

"Yeah," I said. "Of course I would."

\\\\\\\

Her room was in the back of a first-floor apartment. The heat of the day had not yet dissipated, and the air in the place was stickier than the air outside. Lilah switched on an oscillating fan and lay on the bed in the dark. I crawled next to her and kissed her mouth. She smelled like sweat and beer and grease, nicotine and synthetic lilac. I didn't want a world that smelled any other way. I peeled off my t-shirt. I lifted my hand to her breast. She removed it, pressed back on my chest with the lightest touch.

"I changed my mind," she said.

"Huh?"

"Sorry. My head's in a weird place." She reached for a lamp on the table and startled the room with light. It exposed me, sweaty and underdressed.

"Um, yeah, no problem." I tried to project indifference. I wished I hadn't taken off my shirt. I retrieved it from where I had tossed it on the floor and hung it over my shoulder.

I was horrendously sweaty somehow. The room was suffocating. Equatorial. I stuck my face up against the oscillating fan and sat like a Rodin nude, skin glinting in the light.

"You're hogging that," said Lilah.

I pressed the knob so that the fan blew its breath across her. She lay on her back with her eyes closed like she was contemplating sleep. It struck me as too intimate a pose for me to see her in. She reached again to the bedside table. "Do you smoke weed, or is that out of bounds?"

I shook my head.

She pulled a ten-inch green bong from behind the lamp. "I'm gonna smoke. You can bounce if you want. This place gets pretty baked out."

"Okay. Yeah." I fumbled back into my shirt, wishing I had just gone back to Bors's apartment. Or stayed at the Birthday Bar. Or done any number of things differently, which might have spared me the humiliations of that and other nights.

I paused in her doorway. "Well."

"Congratulations," she said.

"For what?"

"For not being Modest Mussorgsky," she said, toasting me with her bong. It reminded me of the kitschy glassware people used for tropical cocktails. "You lived, I mean. Nice job."

I hurried out of the apartment, jerking at my t-shirt collar to pump air down my chest. On the street, I felt immediately hungry. Hungry

like I hadn't felt in weeks, not since before I'd come to South Philadelphia. I walked west until I found myself back under the late-night
lights of Geno's. I ordered a steak with whiz and onions and handed
over a ten for the pleasure.

The girl at the counter was younger than me, slouched against
the window in a tank top and Phillies cap. Our Lady of Guadalupe
was tattooed big and bright up her right arm from elbow to shoulder.
An aurora of stylized red fire framed the Virgin, her cool blue cloak
spangled with a hundred pinprick stars. Her eyes were downcast, away
from the world, as though to look upon it would bring her a sorrow
greater than all that she had already endured.

"Yo," I asked the girl, "do you speak Spanish?"

"Not on the clock," she said.

"Do people ever speak Spanish to you?"

She snorted and handed me my order. "Napkins and condiments
to your left."

I took the sandwich across the street and stood against the fence of
Capitolo Playground, where the young men of Passyunk Square played
basketball in the evenings. The courts were empty. I jammed the sandwich into my mouth, feeling bits of steak and onion leaping out the
back of the roll, splattering wetly on the sidewalk by my feet. I was rav-
enous. I'd never been so hungry. The heat inside my gut was the heat
of life. A heat that demanded to be fed, to burn, to spread as far and
wide as it could before death came and snuffed it out. I hated death.
Death was all I hated. I would flee from it forever. I would do whatever
I needed to keep it far away from me.

Halfway through, I started to feel full. I swaddled the remainder of
the steak in its logo-checkered wrapper, snug as a cocoon. As I walked
into the night I wondered if it was even possible to find a motivation
other than hate.

Soon I stood again in the middle of 13th Street, and I pitched the wrapped, half-eaten sandwich up through the second-story window where two hours before I had seen Cathy's darkened face. I made it on the first try. The cheesesteak was soundless as it sailed through the air, floating like a snowball into her room, among her books and clothes and furniture. As I turned and ran, I imagined that I heard it smack against some surface, knock some vulnerable object clattering to the floor.

I knew that no one would chase me as I tore up 13th Street. I ran simply because I could, because my legs still worked and it felt good to move them. I knew that the sun would rise before too long, that I would sense I'd had a part in its rising. And I knew that Cathy Tomlinson would wake and find half a cheesesteak lying like a dead pigeon on her floor, next to a shattered flower vase or water glass, and that she would know instantly who had thrown it there. Perhaps Cathy would notice that it wore a Geno's wrapper, and to her that would signify a certain type of vandal, one who might or might not fit with her conception of me. She would try to remember: Was the Dennis Monk she knew a Geno's man? Was he a Pat's man, or a Jim's man, or a Tony Luke's man? Was he the sort of man who believed that we had no choice at all? She would think of me, of all of me, and in her memory I would live.

SOUTHWARK

It began in an almost romantic way. I met Maureen Muehl by accident along Washington Avenue, in the early afternoon of a muggy day right in the June of it all, when she was half-flushed from the sun, and I was fully flushed, having spent the morning trying to find a decent place to read on various abandoned piers along the river. She was wearing skinny jeans and a billowy shirt. She was carrying a floor scraper.

It wasn't the first time I'd met her. I'd known her in college, though I hadn't seen her since. That day, on Washington Avenue beneath the lone surviving tower of the Southwark Plaza housing project, we were strangers again. I was a stranger to everyone, myself included. I was only just remembering how to walk in the clear-headed light of day, still enamored of every breeze that moved my hair or carried the smell of grass or rain or roasting meat. Maureen was coming from whatever adventures had befallen her in the last half-decade, something involving a guy or a job or the lack of either, or a convoluted family incident, or maybe a trip somewhere that had gone painfully awry. She was coming from *life*, and life turns us all into strangers.

I was happy to run into her. I would have been happy to run into anyone from college, not because I had a job or a wife or even a permanent residence, but because I was seven months and seven days sober, and I had been a drunk long enough that being seven months and seven days sober was sufficient to make me feel, on that blessed afternoon, like an unqualified success. Maureen, too, looked successful. She stood there on the sidewalk with the easy confidence of someone holding a purchase from a hardware store. Her very bearing suggested credentials. After we hugged, I could do nothing but rest my hands on my waist and hope that my bearing, too, suggested something.

"Are you tearing up a carpet?" I asked her.

"I am, yeah," said Maureen, with an eagerness that caught me by surprise. "You don't happen to know how to do that, do you? I'm a total carpet virgin. The Internet said I needed one of these things."

"It's a pretty simple job," I said. That was just an assumption. I'd never torn up a carpet. I'd only recognized the scraper because my friend Ivan—the guy who owned the futon on which I was at that time sleeping—kept such an instrument in his foyer. For protection from intruders, I think, as much as anything else. Ivan sold home security systems door to door across the poorer and more paranoid of the city's neighborhoods. I'd been bunking with him since Bors lit out for Idaho.

"Oh, maybe you can help me?" asked Maureen. "If you have time? No. I'm sorry, Dennis, you're probably busy. Are you busy? Maybe you could just get me started? I'd pay you. But that's super presumptuous of me. I'm sure you have somewhere you need to get to?"

She'd offered me an out. I should have accepted it, since I was misrepresenting my expertise and since pressing on would almost certainly reveal as much. But I could've used some cash, and I didn't have anywhere to be. And there was something magnetic about Maureen, the way the city's heat had dampened her forehead and neck and the visible triangle of her chest. And I thought I could tear up a carpet easily enough. Maureen's enthusiasm was infectious. It made me believe in myself.

"No need to pay me," I said, because you have to say that.

Maureen lived a few blocks south of Washington Ave in Pennsport. She had recently bought the house at a good price for the neighborhood, which was quickly becoming another charm in Philadelphia's hipster bracelet. The new gentry strode the blocks like consignment-shop conquistadors in their beanies and lip rings and flannel. I knew them. I had grown up with them in the suburbs, where we were too young for those specific affectations. I had attended college with them and witnessed their bohemian rebranding. The dudes, in particular, confounded me. They were the sons of lawyers and pediatricians who aspired to look like the sons of miners and farmers. Or, better yet, the sons of no father at all: primordial men who had sprung fully formed from the earth itself, who had walked out of the woods with an undercut and a five o'clock shadow, smelling of pine and smoke and the vernal soil. I envied them, those confident pseuds, since presenting such a curated persona to the world was surely better than proffering my own flawed, mostly authentic one.

"Fun neighborhood," I said as we walked.

Maureen smiled. "It's cool, right?"

She lived on an elbow-shaped alley that ran for half a block off 3rd. Her place looked modest from the street, a two-story red-brick row house with unadorned white lintels above the windows and door. The interior was in a state of transition. One wall was exposed brick, another half-painted plaster, white replacing blue or blue replacing white. The rooms were crowded with boxes and errant objects that hadn't yet found permanent homes. The shelves and cabinetry, as spare as scaffolding, looked like they had been hung an hour before our arrival.

"It's small," said Maureen. "I probably shouldn't have bought it, honestly. But I figured it's an investment."

Maureen worked for a pharmaceutical company in Center City. Her position involved business-to-business transactions, her explanation of which I hadn't fully comprehended.

"It's great," I said. I meant it. There was nothing I wanted more than a little house to live in while I figured things out. The fact that Maureen had pulled the trigger on one made me esteem her all the more. I was still grappling with my memory of Maureen from school, where she'd never struck me as someone capable of financial responsibility or domestic commitment or serious employment. Though no one else had, either. I'd never expected anyone to actually grow up.

"The floors down here were carpet-free." She tapped the dark wooden boards with the handle of the scraper. "It's upstairs I need to fix. There's a really awful green shag up there." I followed her to the second story to observe the offending material. It looked like sheet moss, coating every floor but the bathroom's and threatening to ascend the walls.

"I'm a little afraid of what I'll find under there," said Maureen.

"You mean, like, creepy old photographs?" I asked.

"No," she said. "Like, laminate."

She led me to the back bedroom, empty of furniture. Maureen had already acquired the rest of the tools for the job: pliers, a utility knife, a stubby crowbar. I picked up the crowbar and felt the weight of it in my hand. Just holding it gave me an unearned sense of efficacy. I crouched down to investigate the fissure where the carpet met the wall, cognizant of Maureen's eyes on my movements.

"I think you start in the corner, don't you?" she asked.

"Definitely." That sounded right. I shifted a few feet toward the back of the room, where a delta of green shag met the right angle of the wall. I fit the claw of the crowbar between the carpet and baseboard. It caught on something and I yanked. The carpet leaped upward with unanticipated ease, heaving an exhalation of gray dust that powdered my eyes and nostrils. I allowed myself one deep, masculine cough and yanked again. Once I had a wall's length of carpet detached, I folded it over and looked down at the exposed tack strip and padding beneath it. I peeled back the padding, hoping to find wood. Maureen crept up for a look.

"Oak!" she said, and I believed her. "Just like downstairs. It's beautiful."

I rapped my knuckles on the wood and nodded. "That's oak alright."

I sliced off the free section of carpet and padding with the utility knife to give myself more room to work. After half an hour of yanking and slicing, I'd made it to the door, which had to be removed from its hinges. Maureen said that was enough for one day. She ordered us dinner while I washed up in the bathroom, discreetly hacking carpet particles into her sink. As we sat in her cluttered kitchen eating pad thai and drinking seltzer from Maureen's soda maker, we agreed that I would come back the next day to finish the job while she was at work, if it wasn't too much trouble and only if I had the time.

"I've got the time," I said, because I did.

Her smile enticed like rice noodles and tamarind pulp. "I'll leave a key in the mailbox."

\\\\\\\

I returned in the morning with a dust mask and gloves and a shop vacuum that I had borrowed from Ivan. He had recently moved into his dead grandmother's house and was in the process of rehabbing it, and thus he possessed the requisite hardware. I also borrowed a sledgehammer—which Ivan assured me I would not need—mostly for the purpose of making myself feel professional. I strolled to Maureen's house with the shop vac in one hand and the hammer slung over my shoulder, looking, I hoped, like a man who knew what it was he was doing.

Maureen was gone when I arrived, but I let myself in and set to work. I cleared the second floor of its furniture, which consisted of only a mattress, a box spring, and a Z-rack of clothes. I removed the bedroom doors from their hinges and carried them to the bathroom, where I leaned them like dominos against the shower tile. I ripped up the remaining carpet from the back bedroom and continued through the hallway into the front bedroom, cutting it into slices every few feet and rolling them into cylinders, which I cinched with duct tape and deposited in a construction dumpster I'd noticed squatting in front of a gutted house on Moyamensing Avenue. I pried out the tack strips and swept up the dust. I threw the windows open to coax in a breeze and exorcise the stale whiff of old carpet padding. It took all afternoon and was the most sustained labor I had done in several years that didn't involve stacking banquet tables or operating a commercial dishwasher. It was gratifying work, in the psychosomatic, muscle-straining sense. It made me feel as though I might be able to function in a world of tasks and transactions. I was exhausted by the end of it but spiritually renewed. When Maureen came home around six o'clock to find me uprooting the last of the carpet staples with her newly purchased floor scraper, she was so delighted by my efforts that she crossed the bare space of her bedroom and kissed me on the mouth.

I kissed her back, catching her arm in my palm. After a moment, she pulled away. I stepped away, too, toward the window, unsure of what to do.

"Sorry," she said. "I was going to wait to do that."

"Wait for what?"

"Until you finished with everything. I have trouble waiting. It's a thing with me. But I hope I haven't taken away your incentive."

"Incentive?" What had been my incentive? I'd thought about kissing Maureen at some point, of course. I'd been excited by the possibility of it. But I'd also wanted to do something useful with my hands, something that might last for a while. Maybe the hardwood I exposed that day would still be exposed in a hundred years' time. As someone who mostly participated in minor actions of temporary consequence, such a legacy appealed to me. I had never made a house more beautiful.

"Not incentive. That wasn't the right word." Maureen was blushing now. The room was hot, the air smoggy with dispersed specks. I reeked from the day's grime and exertion, and I'd marked Maureen's arm with a gray streak of carpet dust. "There is no incentive," she said. "I'm not going to sleep with you, I mean."

"Okay."

"Sorry, I sound insane. I would sleep with you. Or I would have, before. I'm trying not to jump into bed with people. I move too quickly. Or I have. In the past."

"It's alright," I said.

"But I like you. I'm attracted to you. Fuck, I really blew this moment, huh?"

"I'm attracted to you, too." I stood holding the floor scraper, which, rather than lending me a purposeful carriage, felt like a useless, over-sized utensil. "Always have been," I added, though I wasn't sure if it was true.

I was attracted to her now, in any case. I'd attempted, during my hours of yanking and slicing, to remember if Maureen had been serious with any of my friends. She'd been unserious with a number of them, but the ones who came to mind were no longer in my social circle, and I was in no position to hold anyone's past against them. There were a dozen good reasons not to get involved with any particular person.

"It's mostly just vacuuming up at this point," I said to fill the silence. Maureen was standing there, expectantly, though I was not sure what action I was meant to take. "There's still some staples scattered around here."

"Yeah, you did great," said Maureen. "Do you want to take a shower? I mean, use the shower? Just you?"

I did. I moved the doors back into the hallway, then tried to make as little a mess as possible as I shed my dust-stained clothes. After I'd rinsed the muck from my limbs, I lingered naked beneath the faucet. I half-suspected that Maureen might join me—my imagination was crowded with possibilities not previously considered—and I tried to make the soft, pale planes of my body presentable as I listened for the creak of the door. She did not appear. When I stepped cleanly into the kitchen, she was ordering chicken tikka masala. After dinner and post-dinner coffee, when it was surely time for me to go, she convinced me that I urgently needed to see the 1988 movie *Clean and Sober* starring Michael Keaton and Kathy Baker. We fell asleep on her couch during the third act, pretending it was far too late for me to walk all the way back to Ivan's for the night.

From then on, though nothing was articulated, I was a full-time resident. I gradually relocated my clothes from the spare room at Ivan's grandmother's place. Maureen would go to work in the morning, and I would spend my day doing small jobs around her house. I moved the upstairs furniture back into position and rehung the doors. I finished painting the wall on the first story—it had been white, and I completed its metamorphosis to blue. I painted the rest of the first story's non-brick walls, then did the second story too. Maureen would come home in the evening, usually with takeout, and compliment my work. She called me a godsend, and, in truth, I felt like one. Not in the sense that Maureen needed me so desperately in her life—nothing I did was anything that she couldn't eventually have done herself—but in the sense that the universe had brought me to a place where I might have some value. A place where the normal economy of pay stubs and taxes and rent and bills mostly disappeared and was replaced with labor for room and board and companionship. The way things used to be, maybe, in earlier periods of history.

And though I was sleeping nightly in her bed and our legs were often tangled up together when we woke in the mornings, Maureen continued to not have sex with me. We made out frequently, ran our hands up and down each other's bodies like curfewed teenagers in the back of a borrowed car, but it never progressed far enough to meet even a puritan's definition of intercourse. I never saw her naked. She would chastely direct me out of the room while either of us was getting dressed. I didn't press the issue, though I thought it odd, since her desire to take things slowly seemed undercut by the fact that I was already living in her house. But what did I know about anything? I admired that she was working on herself.

Which isn't to say that sex with Maureen didn't occupy a substantial swath of my thoughts.

After two weeks, I was running out of projects. Once I'd tamed her feral backyard and mulched her flower beds—which she hadn't even asked me to do—Maureen told me that she'd been thinking about turning the rear bedroom into a home office and wondered if I might build her a custom desk. She assumed that I had the ability to do so, which I appreciated. For the sake of transparency, I told her that I'd never built a desk before, but that I was confident that I could.

"You know, I've always thought about becoming a furniture maker," I said, which wasn't even a little bit true. And yet it seemed the most desirable of occupations. I could see myself selling my wares out of the shops in the neighborhood, or even from my own studio in a renovated warehouse or factory. I could stroll around Pennsport and be known for my trade, putting to shame all the cool kids in their vegan boots and thrifted jackets, for I would possess the practical skills that their ironic, post-industrial pretensions merely aspired to. I would grow a beard and smell always of sawdust and smoke a pipe and learn to play the mandolin. I would build cribs and beds for the brood of children that I would conceive with Maureen, and we would be one of those quietly blissful couples whose lives suggest effortless fecundity and sturdiness and the wisdom of simpler eras.

I set about searching the Internet for pictures of desks. IKEA. Wayfair. Office Depot. I figured that I could simply replicate a proven design, augmented with a few minor personal flourishes. I read a blog in which the author built a desk from found filing cabinets and a butcher block. Reclaimed materials seemed to be the way to go if I wanted to achieve the kind of unique visual style that would impress people. There was an abandoned hospital at 4th and Reed where I thought I might go spelunking for a filing cabinet. I called up Ivan to ask if I could borrow his car to haul the thing once I found one, but when I explained to him my plan, he told me he had an old filing cabinet in his basement that I could use. I had him drop that one off instead.

I led Maureen to believe that I had spelunked it from the hospital anyway. She was less impressed than I'd hoped.

"What if it's, like, haunted by the ghosts of sick children?" she asked.

"It was in an office," I lied. "So it was away from the sick people. Hospital ghosts would probably only haunt the objects they interacted with, like wheelchairs or those mobile IV stands."

"It's just that I don't really need to file anything." The cabinet's rollers let out a rusty squeal as she pulled open one of the drawers. "I think I'd actually prefer several shallow drawers over these two really deep ones. If that's not too much trouble?"

"You'll have plenty of drawers," I said. "This is going to be a massive desk. So let's not assume we can't find space for this vintage, reclaimed filing cabinet." I smacked the aluminum with my palm. It rumbled like a kettledrum.

"My inflexible artiste," said Maureen, pinching my shoulder. "I should know better than to question your vision."

For the desktop, I planned to use the shelf of an old entertainment center that I scavenged from a sidewalk on Wilder Street. I'd wrenched it free and left the remaining components in a heap on the curb. It was a thick, solid piece of something or other—maybe pine. I also found a coffee table with a nice top, though there were a few rings of hardened yellow goo that I had to scrape away. I planned on joining these to two tops to make an L-shaped corner desk, supported by the filing cabinet on one end and a still-to-be-scavenged chest of shallow drawers on the other. The coffee table was a darker wood than the pine, streaked with knots and swirls like a loaf of marble rye, but I figured I could stain one or both of them if necessary. The whole thing was coming together with remarkable ease. I could imagine Maureen so elated at seeing the finished project that she dispensed with her caution and begged me to take her there on the freshly exposed floorboards. My path as a craftsman unfurled before my eyes like a roll of torn-up carpet, leading me into a radiant future that smelled of varnish and turpentine.

Then Neal arrived.

\\\\\\

It was nearing six o'clock one Friday evening. I was lounging on the living room couch, reading about bracings and waiting for Maureen to bring home some dak bulgogi, when a man walked into the house through the front door. I sat up and watched him ease himself into Maureen's lone armchair. He was a tall man—six inches taller than me—and the top third of his head was wrapped in a medical bandage. He was about my age, maybe slightly younger. He sat staring at me in a way that I found difficult not to interpret as hostile, his mouth sagging and his eyelids half-shut. My initial emotional response, I'll admit, was fear.

"You hit your head?" I asked him. I tried to recall where I'd stored Ivan's sledgehammer.

The man's hand rose to the ribbon of gauze. "Feels like it," he said. "Don't remember, though."

"Hate it when that happens," I said. "You a friend of Maureen's?"

He sneered. I was beginning to suspect that a lunatic had wandered in from the street, and that he was about to force me into a mortal struggle from which I was unlikely to emerge alive, when Maureen came through the door, flustered and empty-handed. "Sorry, I had to park all the way up the block. Have you guys met? Dennis, this is my brother, Neal."

The relationship now revealed, the resemblance became obvious. I had let the head wound distract me from the fact that Maureen and Neal had the same face: the same round cheeks, the same jutting nose, the same earlobes dangling like pea pods. It was unsettling, seeing Maureen stare back at me from the masculine visage of her sibling.

I extended my hand. "How you doing?"

"Not good," said Neal. His hands remained gripped around the chair's armrests.

Maureen slumped onto the couch next to me, a smaller, female Neal. Her hand found mine and she clasped it tightly, as though she required reassurance in the things that were to come. "Okay," she said to Neal. "Tell me again what happened."

It was, I learned, the third time Maureen was hearing her brother's story. Neal's account was confused for a number of reasons, not least of which was the fact that he had been drunk or unconscious during most of the events he described. The key incidents were as follows: Neal had been found, early that morning, in a roadside ditch in Bucks County. A concerned motorist had spotted him and called the authorities. When the EMTs arrived and attempted to rouse him, the insensible Neal had responded with a bout of somnambulant tussling, necessitating that he be strapped to a gurney. At the hospital in Bristol, Neal attempted a wordless, semiconscious escape, during which he tired himself out sufficiently for the doctors to confirm that his head was concussed and to treat the severe gash along his hairline. Neal fell asleep. When he woke to full consciousness and realized where he was, he launched a second escape attempt. ("I hate hospitals," he explained.) Again, he was foiled. He had no identification—Neal was in possession of neither his wallet nor his phone—and it was only then in the chronology that the harried nurses could ascertain his name and the number of an emergency contact. Because Mr. and Mrs. Muehl were at their shore house in Brigantine for the week, Neal had requested they call Maureen, who was forced to leave work early and drive to Bristol to collect her ill-tempered brother, much to the relief of the hospital staff.

"God, those poor nurses," said Maureen.

Neal rolled his eyes. "They get worse than me in Bristol."

I considered Neal's story impartially. "Where was the ditch?"

"Out in the boonies of Falls Township," said Neal. "By the river. They dropped me out there like a fucking corpse."

"Who's they?" I asked.

Maureen sighed next to my ear. She had heard this part before as well.

"Gord Sinnamon and Cousin Roy," said Neal.

Gord Sinnamon, I soon learned, was a salesman at the company where Neal worked. They had been paired together on a big deal that had gone well, after which Gord Sinnamon had invited Neal out to dinner at a steakhouse on 15th Street. They were picked up from the office by Gord Sinnamon's cousin Roy in a rented limousine, and after dinner the trio had proceeded to one of the strip clubs along Columbus Boulevard. The details following the first hour at the club were hazy to Neal, though he could remember being back in the limousine with Gord Sinnamon. There had been an offer to drive him home to Morrisville. After that, blackness.

"Maybe you gave them the wrong address," said Maureen. "Maybe they thought they were dropping you near home?"

"Do they think that I live in an abandoned steel mill?" said Neal. "Because that's what they fucking dropped me near, Maureen. These guys left me for dead."

"They wouldn't leave you for dead, Neal," said Maureen, her voice flecked with frustration. "They were in a hired limo with a hired fucking limo driver."

"And how'd I get this gash on my head, Maureen? A fucking lap dance? You think they give lap dances this good on Columbus Boulevard?"

"I don't know, Neal, maybe you got it from wandering around the fucking countryside in the middle of the night whacked out of your mind? You're lucky you're not dead. I've told you you need to lay off the drinking and the drugs. They react poorly with your medication."

Neal sat forward in his seat, his hands in the air as if he hoped to zap his sister with lightning from his fingertips. "I didn't take any drugs, Maureen, first of all, and second of all, I haven't been on medication for like two years, so thanks for even being aware of that. And third of all, I didn't even drink that much. I had two whiskey gingers, three tops, and I had a twenty-ounce porterhouse in my stomach. I probably got dosed."

"Dosed?" asked Maureen.

Neal nodded violently. "These strippers see a successful-looking guy come in, they think he's got a lot of cash on him, so they dose him with GHB in his whiskey ginger and steal his wallet while he's zonked out. That's probably what happened. Either that or Gord Sinnamon and Cousin Roy dosed me themselves because they wanted to fuck me, which I wouldn't rule out either, 'cause they were getting pretty grabby with me when we were drinking vodka in the limousine."

"Well have you talked to Gord Sinnamon?"

"Maureen, I don't have a phone. They stole my phone."

"Have you called your phone?"

"How would I do that, Maureen, when—and sorry if I'm repeating myself—I do not have a fucking phone?"

"I'll fucking call it, then." Maureen held her own phone to her ear. "It's going straight to voicemail."

"Gord Sinnamon probably threw it out the limousine's window. He probably threw it out right after me. It was probably in the ditch next to me when those idiot EMTs captured me. Or a stripper has it." Neal's fingers flitted over the armrest. "Or, you know, I might have actually left it in my car."

"I can't fucking deal with you if you're going to be this fucking crazy." Maureen stood and stomped off to the kitchen.

"Oh, am I crazy, Maureen?" Neal called after her. "Sorry I'm not responsible like you. Sorry I didn't go to college and fuck all my professors." He turned his gaze toward me. "She got one of her professors ousted, you know that? By fucking him."

That was true. I had known, and forgotten, about that. "Yeah," I said.

"You live here?" asked Neal.

"I'm sort of crashing here. For the time being."

Neal raised his hand to his bandage and rubbed it like a crystal ball. "You know, I don't remember Cousin Roy in the limo at the end of the night. Which means maybe he was up front, driving. Which begs the question—what happened to the limo driver? Maybe they killed the limo driver."

I could hear Maureen behind me, in the kitchen, ordering a pizza. She came back with a glass of seltzer and handed it to Neal. "What do you think, Dennis?"

"About the limo driver?" I asked.

"About the whole thing."

I wasn't sure how much of Neal's story I was supposed to believe. "Well, you still have to go to work on Monday, right? Won't this Gord Sinnamon guy be there? You can talk to him about it. Figure out what happened."

"Yeah." Neal nodded as though the idea hadn't yet occurred to him. "Yeah, that's smart. I'll see how he reacts. Whether he's relieved to see me, or nervous, like he's seen a ghost."

"You can stay here this weekend." As Maureen spoke to her brother, she seemed to look past him, as if she were planning not only the days ahead, but the months and years as well. "I don't want you by yourself with that head injury. I'll drive you home Sunday."

Later, in bed, Maureen asked me, "Has something like this ever happened to you? Like this thing with Neal?"

"Sort of." I'd blacked out a hundred times, woken up in odd places with odd injuries. Though I'd never, to my knowledge, been thrown out of a car. "Maybe he vomited in the limo, so they ditched him. A cabbie will kick you out if you throw up in his taxi."

"Or maybe he blacked out and got violent," said Maureen softly. She was turned away from me toward the darkened bedroom wall.

"Maybe. Does that sound like something Neal would do?"

"This happens a lot. Not this thing exactly, but stuff like this, you know? Crazy stuff like this."

"Huh." In the quiet of the house, I could hear Neal's snores rising up from the living room.

"And he always comes to me to bail him out," said Maureen. "It's always been like that. He'd always come to me to help him so he didn't have to go to our parents."

"Huh," I said again.

"It's just, with Neal, I'm always going to have to be there for him, you know? Like a caretaker. Our whole lives. I've always known that."

"You're a good sister." It felt like the right thing to say. "It's important to be able to turn to someone, when you have problems. To have somebody on your team."

"Team Muehl," said Maureen bitterly. She turned around and lay her head against my chest, as though I, too, was a part of Team Muehl. An essential part.

\\\\\\

The next morning, I returned to the back bedroom to work on Maureen's desk. I'd found a three-drawer nightstand, which I planned to attach to my coffee table top after heightening it with a set of cabinet feet. I would then fasten the pine top to the filing cabinet. The two tops would meet in the middle, supported by some ornate table legs I'd found and planned to brace along the back for stability. I'd elected to sand the thing for the time being and let Maureen decide for herself how she wanted the desk stained.

I had just laid the two halves upside down and was positioning the brackets for the table legs when Neal wandered into the room. I nodded at him, and he nodded back. He stood there for a moment, watching me work on my hands and knees in a way I found discomfiting.

"I've seen this desk," said Neal. "IKEA, right?"

I glanced at him, then at my salvaged materials. Even a man with a head injury should have been able to discern they were not from IKEA. "This is a custom desk," I said.

"No, look." Neal held up his phone to show me a picture of the desk he was referencing. It was the desk on which I had modeled my own. "I just typed 'desk' into Google and this is like the third thing that comes up," he said.

"I *designed* this desk to fit the contours of this space." I could hear the defensiveness in my voice. "It's made of *found* materials. This is a *one-of-a-kind* desk."

"Well, you should keep the halves separate, anyway," said Neal, watching as I placed a bracket over the seam between my two desk-tops. "If you screw it all together, it'll be too big to fit out this door. If you keep it as two pieces, Maureen can just carry them out one at a time if she finds a better desk." He must have sensed my irritation. "Or if she moves. Whatever."

"I would need more legs for that," I said.

"No you wouldn't." Neal walked over and rearranged my brackets. "See? You're basically building two tables. This is more structurally sound, anyway. It'll hold more weight."

I saw what he meant. It made a lot of sense. "Do you know about furniture?" I asked.

He leaned against the windowsill. "I mean, I took shop in high school. I made a folding stool. Like, a folding chair, but without the back. Honestly, it works better as a little side table to set drinks on."

I nodded. I didn't take shop. In high school, as in college, I loaded up as many literature classes as were available to me. I'd been misinformed regarding the centrality of F. Scott Fitzgerald to the American job market. "What do you do now, Neal?"

"I sell computers to old people. They're special computers, with bigger screens and simpler keyboards. They're easier for old people to use."

"That's very altruistic."

"Not really," he said, fiddling with the window lock. "They're super expensive. Like, criminally overpriced. We basically need to find old people without children, so there's no one around to warn them what a scam it is."

"Well. All jobs have their drawbacks."

"I guess." Neal strolled to the opposite wall and back. "Have you known Maureen long?"

"We were friends back in college," I said. We hadn't been friends, really, but we had moved in the same social orbits. I was starting to think that maybe we hadn't liked each other at all, but that seemed a needless subject to broach. "We recently reconnected."

"In college she used to date that guy John O. Did you know John O.?"

"Yeah," I said. John O. was an ecstasy dealer and a general scumbag. "I actually lived with him one year."

"And a guy named Craig? And another guy named Brian?"

"Yeah." I knew them as well. They weren't scumbags so much as harmless fuckheads. I hoped that Neal wouldn't bring up the professor again.

"But you and Maureen are alright?" I got the sense, from the way Neal was watching me, that my response mattered very much to him.

"Yeah," I said. "Things are pretty good with us."

Neal touched his hand to his bandage. The mummy gauze was gone, replaced with a cotton ball taped across his hairline. "Are you and me alright? After that stuff you heard yesterday?"

I shrugged. "Sure. It wasn't that weird, all in all."

"I'm not crazy." Neal said it like it was important that I believe it.

"Hey, I get it." I got to my feet and wiped my hands on my jeans. I figured I needed to offer Neal something of myself, to make him feel less exposed. "I've had issues with substance abuse. Waking up in strange places, with strange cuts and bruises. Not remembering what happened the night before, who I might have fucked things up with. I'm not saying that you have those problems, too. I'm just saying life is confusing sometimes. You're lucky to have a friend in your sister to fall back on when you need her."

Neal stared out of the window. He struck me as the sort of person for whom admissions of weakness were especially difficult. The sort of person on whom the world had heaped humiliation after humiliation, leaving him to scrounge for dignity wherever he could.

"Yeah, I am lucky," he said after a moment. "I hope you and me can be friends, too."

He extended the hand that he had refused me the day before.

"Of course," I said, accepting it. "I'll be your friend, Neal."

\\\\\\

After the melodrama of his arrival, the rest of Neal's visit was mercifully uneventful. Maureen spent the day cooking a rather flavorless stew in a crock pot, some family recipe that seemed to please her brother. The following morning, she drove him home to Morrisville. When she returned, I was ready to unveil her finished desk. I had taken Neal's suggestion and built it in two pieces. They fit together so neatly you'd swear it was all one. It was a motley composition—a jumble of colors and textures, wood and steel—but done in a way that suggested it was by design, rather than ignorance or bad taste.

"It's amazing." Maureen opened the shallow drawers of the former nightstand. She sounded genuinely pleased. "I can't wait to sit at it."

"Ah, fuck, I forgot to get a chair." I had come across several chairs perched on several curbs during my salvaging expeditions. It would have been so easy to grab one.

"Don't worry about it." Maureen ran her hand against the newly sanded surface of the pine top. "It's so smooth. How much weight do you think this thing can hold?"

She hopped up onto the desk and parted her thighs, beckoning me over with a coy expression. Her fingers cantered up and down my spine, though after a minute of enthusiastic kissing she slid out from under me and suggested we go out to dinner.

"Let me get my phone," she said, leaving me alone in the back bedroom lying prostrate on her desktop, my weight held aloft by the strength of two discrete tables.

She wanted to take me to a cocktail bar in Queen Village called the Southwark. It was a walkable distance from the house beneath a leisurely descending summer sun. The bar's name was an artifact. That whole area of the city was called Southwark for a couple of centuries until some real estate agent decided to split the district right along Washington Avenue. The blocks to the north became Queen Village. The blocks to the south became Pennsport. The agent tossed out Southwark and with it two hundred years of associations: immigrant slums and Bible riots and murdered Scarfo associates. I wondered if that would be the ultimate fate for all South Philadelphia, to be divested of its mummers and mobsters and cheesesteaks, until only a collection of interchangeable overpriced zip codes remained.

The Southwark was all polished wood and dim light pulsing from baroque sconces. Its aesthetic seemed to reference Prohibition. We sat at a table by the window and Maureen ordered a boulevardier on the rocks. It arrived with a toothpick-speared olive balanced across the rim of the glass like a pig on a spit.

"You don't mind if I drink, do you?" asked Maureen. In the few weeks we'd been cohabitating, I hadn't seen her consume any alcohol. She didn't keep it in the house.

"It's fine," I said. I'd ordered water.

Maureen pulled the olive off the toothpick with her teeth. "It's so weird," she said, chewing. "That was the way I always thought about you in school. That you drank a lot."

I shrugged. "It was college. Everybody drank a lot. You drank a lot."

"Yeah, but with you it was like . . ." She paused and studied my face. "I don't know. A defining characteristic, you know? I hope that doesn't sound . . ."

I nodded slowly. "I know what you're saying."

"But it is still a part of you, isn't it?" She looked at me conspiratorially, as though she understood me in a way that no one else could. "Like, it's still in there, isn't it? Something that never goes away."

"I don't know." If her question was whether or not I would have liked to drink her boulevardier, then the answer was yes. I would have liked to drink it. I would have liked to drink all the liquor in the Southwark until I passed out. Then I would have liked to wake up in the morning and drink it all again. But it was equally and simultaneously true that I did not want it at all, not any of it. That I was happy not to want it, and proud of myself for being able to sit there and drink water and have no part of it.

"People change," I said. It was an oversimplification, but oversimplifications are sometimes necessary, particularly in restaurants.

"People change," repeated Maureen. "I'm sure you thought of me as, like, a slut, or something, right?"

I had, yes. But not from a position of moral superiority or even honest consideration. Only because it was an easy thing to think about a person. "No. Just a girl."

"I think you're lying. But that's okay. It was college, like you said." She finished her drink. She smiled a smile that initiated a new topic of conversation. "I love my desk."

"I still have to stain it. Whatever color you want. Give it a more uniform look."

"I like it how it is."

"It's unfinished," I said.

"It's sort of folksy. It's perfect. It's done."

I wouldn't push her on it if that was what she thought. "Well, I know you said you wanted more drawers. I was thinking I could probably hang some shelves in there. Up on the wall. It would give you more storage space."

Maureen smiled again. "You don't have to do all these jobs, you know?"

"What do you mean?"

"I think that you think that you have to earn the right to live in my house. But you don't. I like having you there. You can just live there with me."

"I want to be helpful," I said. "I don't want to feel like a sponge."

"You are helpful. Just by being with me, you're helpful."

Yes, I wondered, but how long would that be true?

"So you like the desk?" I asked.

"I love the desk." She cupped her palm over my hand where it lay on the table. "It's a perfect desk."

Maureen had another cocktail with dinner and paid the bill. We walked home holding hands like romantic people. When we reached her door, Maureen leaned in to kiss me. I stopped her and asked her if she could brush her teeth.

"Because of the booze," I said.

"Oh. Right. Of course. I wouldn't want to tempt you."

I sat on her bed, listening to the gurgle of water in the bathroom sink. Maureen came into the room. She wasn't wearing pants, just a thin pair of underwear that hid barely anything at all. We had reached a new phase. We were moving fast again. She slunk into my lap, clutching the back of my head and bringing my face to hers. We kissed, and I felt myself searching for it. I didn't want to, but I couldn't shut off my senses. There, I thought, I could taste it, there behind the spearmint and the sorbitol, behind the farro and the foraged ramps, there it was. Rye whiskey. As if my tongue were plugged right in the bottle. Even if the taste wasn't really there, I could imagine it, hiding behind her lips, behind her molars, at the base of her gums. In her spit and, a second later, in my blood, seeping into my marrow, where it would linger forever and never disappear. I tasted the rest of my life, and it was the same as what had come before.

Her fingers grabbed the fly of my jeans, and I found myself brushing them away. "Are you tired?" I asked the confusion on her face. "I'm so tired."

Much later, Maureen shook me from my sleep, her phone to her ear. "Neal is at Methodist Hospital. He's having some kind of episode." I looked at the clock. It was past three in the morning. I clambered from under the sheets and searched the floor for my pants. "Can you drive?" Maureen was asking. "We'll take my car. How the fuck did he get back to South Philadelphia?"

I dropped Maureen off on Broad Street in front of the hospital's entrance and watched her scramble toward the doors. I circled the block to park the car, turning down an alley with arrows directing me toward a garage. My way was soon blocked by a commotion in the thoroughfare. A group of orderlies was spread out in a triangle near the hospital's back entrance, attempting to apprehend a tall, shirtless man whose arms were flailing like severed telephone wires. Terror contorted Neal's face. I could tell he needed to escape those men. The world was trying to imprison him, and he had no recourse but to match its mania with his own.

I stopped the car in the middle of the asphalt and stepped out. I walked slowly into the beams of the headlights with one hand raised to show I meant no harm. Neal spotted me and his entire disposition changed. The fear melted into gratitude. He knew he would be saved. The orderlies registered the change in his posture. They allowed Neal to dash past them, toward me, where he prostrated himself at my feet.

"My friend," he said, with a warble of relief in his throat. "My friend. My friend." He reached one clump of fingers up my leg, searching for my hand, grasping to find an affirmation in my grip. "My friend. My friend." The word sounded strangely false. Not on Neal's lips—there was nothing false about Neal, in his grotesquely earnest pose—but in my ears. *Friend*. Friend?

No, Neal. Not me. We are strangers, you and I. There's no one else in the cab, in the ditch, in the bedroom. To love me, you would have to know me, and you can never know me. The chasm between us is the width of two lifetimes: yours and mine.

Neal's one arm was coiled around my calves, and his other floundered blindly for my palm, but I held my own hands high in the air, high enough that he couldn't touch them. High enough to make clear to anyone who might be watching that I was my own man, of whom nothing and no one else might form an essential part.

NEW POETS

The Dogman snuck back from the bar with two kölsches and stuck one in front of me. An old gesture. Old for us, old for history.

"I quit drinking," I said to him.

"You did? I keep forgetting."

I was in a dark mood. The Dogman had been forgetting all week long, ordering two drinks and planting one before me, expressing mock astonishment at my refusal of it before downing both himself as though it were an imposition. He thought it was funny. The Dogman had a mean sense of humor. It had been two months since an Amtrak train derailment in Port Richmond killed eight people, and the Dogman was still making jokes about seeing the ghosts of dead commuters.

"I guess I'll drink it for you." He extradited my kölsch to his side of the table. "Don't worry about paying me. I make good money."

He said this every time. Every single time.

The Dogman was an accountant in the Philadelphia office of one of the country's largest banks. It was by any measure a boring job with a modest salary, but the Dogman presented himself like a Wall Street bond trader in 1987—a figure of surplus and insouciance. Maybe he was, but only in comparison to me. I'd recently taken a job as a delivery driver for a catering company and was therefore a man to be pitied. My life was not as I'd imagined it would be.

"You know, Monk," said the Dogman. "I heard that alcoholism isn't even a real thing. Like, you can only even get it if it runs in your family."

"That isn't true," I said patiently. "And it does run in my family."

"Oh. Well." When outmaneuvered, the Dogman retreated to his fallback position, which was grinning like an idiot. "What does it matter if you're a drunk, though, with your job?"

"I have to drive a van, for one."

The Dogman grinned wider. "Didn't stop that Amtrak engineer."

Marc Dogana wasn't an idiot, per se. Some people possess an emotional intelligence, and that was perhaps the sort of intelligence that the Dogman lacked. That and common sense. He wasn't terribly book smart, either. He had a business major's disdain for objective truth. He offered a lot of opinions that sounded as though he had spent some time on their crafting, but which revealed themselves to be pretty asinine if you thought about them for more than a second. I'll say it like this: some people might call the Dogman an idiot. Not me, though. Me and the Dogman were friends.

And by friends, I don't mean that we liked each other. I mean that we had, for a period of our lives, spent a lot of time drinking together and had never formally become enemies. It would have required too much effort to be an enemy. I was staying in his apartment for the time being and mostly tried to be polite to him.

"If you're not drinking, that means I'm drinking by myself," said the Dogman. "Which is a warning sign of alcoholism. So think about the danger you're putting me in."

It was because of the drinking that my memories of college were hazy. The hows and whys of any one friendship eluded me. I believe I met the Dogman when a girl at a basement party threw a cup of vodka into both our faces. I never received an explanation, but if I had to guess I'd say she was trying to throw the vodka into the face of the Dogman alone, and that I was simply collateral damage, condemned by the spot on which fate had led me to stand. Our eyeballs burned, and it was in that burning that my friendship with the Dogman was cauterized. "We should sue the shit out of her," he had advised, perhaps as an activity to further bond us together. "I know all about that yak. Her family is finished in Montgomery County." These were the sort of things that the Dogman said.

"Why are we here?" I asked, watching the Dogman sip his kölsches, one then the other so that their volumes remained equal, while he peered around the room as though expecting a visitor. The Dogman had asked me to meet him in the Victory, a cavernous corporate sports bar that looked not unlike a pavilion at a Renaissance fair. We were seated at a standard four-top, but the massive refectory tables that ran the length of the hall could have accommodated fifty people each. There were not nearly that number present. There were barely any people at all. The Victory was housed within a larger complex of bars. A mall of bars. The complex was named for the local Internet provider, and it sat on the infinite plain of parking lots in deep South Philadelphia that ringed the city's sports stadiums. Only malefactors would drink in such a bar on a Tuesday night if they weren't waiting for a game to start. We were not waiting for a game to start.

"It's a surprise," said the Dogman. "A surprise guest."

I didn't care for the sound of that. There was no living person whose arrival would please me. If I knew them, I didn't want to see them. Reunions had lost their novelty. I had already reached my point of saturation with the Dogman.

I wondered if the bar served coffee. The decor—the tables, the Eagles banners, the bouquets of beer taps springing from every surface— suggested that the consumption of anything without booze in it was categorically discouraged.

"Okay, I'll tell you, because I'm a little nervous," said the Dogman. "We're meeting Sudimack. Steve Sudimack, from school. You goddamn lungfish."

I did not want to see Steve Sudimack. "Huh."

"Are you excited? He called me out of the blue. He's moving back to Philadelphia."

"Is he still unstable?"

"More unstable," said the Dogman. "Way less stable than before. That's why we're meeting him down here. I don't want him to know where I live."

"Why did you agree to meet him at all? Why did you answer the phone?"

The Dogman sat with his mouth ajar, as though the idea of refusing a call was anathema to his truest being. "Because it's Sudimack. From school." He grinned. "You gotta be there for your friends, Monk."

\\\\\\\

Steve Sudimack, as the Dogman reminded me, had dropped out of college senior year when the girl with whom he had been sleeping informed him that she was pregnant. The girl, Sonia, had herself dropped out the year before but was still loitering around North Philadelphia, going to parties and trying to "latch onto some dickhead like a remora" (to use the Dogman's phrase). Sudimack was that dickhead. He packed up Sonia and their collective possessions in his busted Mercury sedan and drove them back to his parents' house in Scranton, PA. The Dogman had a clear memory of the event because Sudimack had called him from a gas station outside Allentown to keen for the loss of his future. "I just laughed at him," remembered the Dogman. "I told him to wrap it up. Get it?" The kid, Jayden, was born that fall. For the last four years, Sudimack and Sonia had lived in a cramped basement apartment, him doing contract work with his father and her cashiering part-time at Gerrity's, raising their child in an environment that was surely characterized primarily by angst and hostility beneath the slate skies of Lackawanna County. Then, one abrupt Saturday in early July, when the sun was hot and the cocktails were strong, Sonia got hammered and revealed that young Jayden was not actually Sudimack's son. Sonia had been sleeping with another man at the time, and that man, when faced with the prospect of fatherhood, had summoned the cruel pragmatism necessary to tell Sonia to fuck off. She had gone to Sudimack next, and had Sudimack reacted in the same fashion there was a third man Sonia could have gone to, and even a fourth. Sudimack, predictably, lost his shit. Tables were flipped. Cops were called. When everyone's blood alcohol level fell back to normal, Sonia attempted to retract her admission, but Sudimack nevertheless demanded a paternity test. Three days later, after the results returned negative, Sudimack again called up the Dogman, this time to lament the needless sacrifice of four years of his youth and announce his desire to return immediately to Philadelphia. "I just laughed again," said the Dogman. "What an asshole."

"When was this?" I asked.

"This was today. This was like three o'clock."

"Wow. So this is pretty fresh for him."

"Four years fresh," said the Dogman, finishing the second kölsch. "I would have gotten the test done the first day that toad tried to swindle me with her little miracle. Here, I think this is him now."

The Dogman nodded toward the entrance where a compact figure had just stepped in from the night. Sudimack strode resolutely through the bar, his short legs chopping briskly in a pair of maroon sweatpants. Sudimack wore a white tank top, as though he had just come from the gym. Sudimack did not, by the look of it, give a single fuck.

My initial instinct was to go rigid and hope that Sudimack would fail to notice us, but the Dogman gave us away. "Look at this gullible Scranton-ass cuckold."

Sudimack raised his index finger, suggesting that we wait a moment. He beelined for the bar to place an order.

"Getting straight to business," the Dogman whispered, loosening his necktie. "Classic Sudimack."

I had witnessed a half-dozen of Sudimack's altercations back in college, usually from across a room, usually with no knowledge of what had caused them, not while they were happening and not afterward. I would hear a scream or something break, look up, and there would be Sudimack locked in with another guy, one or both of them bloody, a crowd of people shuffling back, forming a circle, ogling the spectacle. Sudimack wasn't particularly strong, nor was he particularly adept at landing a punch. What he had was a willingness to make use of the tools he found in his environment: keys, ashtrays, ping-pong paddles, fire extinguishers. Glassware was a go-to. It did so much more damage than you'd expect. Even an inconsiderate brawler knows not to fight that way—if only because it can easily land you in prison—but this near-pathological disregard for consequence was what set Sudimack apart.

"Sudimack, you remember Dennis Monk?" asked the Dogman as the guest of honor arrived at our table, a trio of whiskey tumblers nested in his hands.

"No talk till we do this," said Sudimack.

"I don't drink," I said, as one of the glasses slid in place before me.

"What?" Sudimack spat the word, like he'd never heard a statement that made less sense to him.

"Alcoholic," said the Dogman, nodding at me.

"What is this?" demanded Sudimack. "I thought we were unwinding." He pulled the three tumblers back before him and started downing them, one then another.

"It's just Monk who has the problem." The Dogman reached for his erstwhile whiskey. "I'm still drinking."

"Well why don't you fucking buy a round for fucking once, you cock?" demanded Sudimack, his voice rising to a shout. He poured the contents of the last glass down his throat.

Then he flipped the four-top.

\\\\\\

It turned out that on his way to Philadelphia, Sudimack had stopped in Bethlehem to buy a handful of dexedrine capsules, which were making him a bit fidgety. He now wanted some methamphetamine and was more than a little annoyed that the Dogman didn't have any on hand. I could tell that the Dogman was genuinely offended that Sudimack would think that he, an accountant at the Philadelphia branch of one of the nation's largest banks, would be in possession of a drug that everyone knew was for hayseeds, and yet the Dogman suffered from the tragic flaw of always wanting to please those whom he identified as greater bullies than himself. It was therefore decided that we should go acquire some meth, and that I should drive, since I was sober. It wasn't as though we were welcome in the Victory any longer.

"You really shouldn't have flipped that table," I said, peering at Sudimack in the rearview mirror. It was the Dogman's car, a leased Cadillac, and Sudimack struck a discordant image perched in its backseat with his sweatpants and dexy jitters. I wasn't annoyed that I now had a useful excuse for never returning to the Victory, but being forced to run out of an establishment at age twenty-six was an unflattering reminder of the ever-deteriorating quality of my social circle.

"I've been flipping a lot of tables lately," said Sudimack. With the stadium lights illuminating half his face, he appeared to be caught in a moment of genuine reflection.

"You know who flipped tables?" asked the Dogman, grinning. "Jesus. In the Temple."

Whatever the reaction the Dogman hoped to get for that observation, we offered only silence.

"And you know who got tricked into raising somebody else's kid?" The Dogman turned in his seat to face Sudimack. "Joseph. What a fucking idiot, right guys?"

Like a viper, Sudimack's arm shot forward and bashed the Dogman in his nose. The latter flopped back toward the dashboard. "Fuck," he cried. "It was a joke, you shithead." A runnel of blood dribbled from the Dogman's nostril.

I drove east on Pattison Avenue through the flat expanse of industrial lots, for no other reason than I had nothing else to do and nowhere else to go. I resented the Dogman for putting us in this position, driving through the night on a quest for methamphetamine with an emotionally unstable coal cracker glowering at us from the backseat. It was not Sudimack's self-destructive urges that bothered me—from my point of view, abetting in his acquisition of meth was not markedly different than abetting in the Dogman's acquisition of kölsches—but I would have preferred not to do anything that would put me on the wrong side of the law. Criminality was not sober behavior. I was wondering what the chances were that Sudimack could be convinced to go to a diner instead and fill his emptiness with black coffee and a corn beef special when he started tapping on his window. "This looks good. Pull over here."

We were stopped on the old trolley tracks a few dozen yards from the Delaware Expressway overpass. Through a hole in the fence, a group of figures was partially visible in the reflected glow of a Tastykake billboard. "When I get to the fence, flash the lights a few times so they know people are waiting for me," said Sudimack, opening his door. He slammed it with a bang and stalked off through the weeds.

"We should ditch him," said the Dogman. He was pinching his nose shut, attempting to staunch the blood with the fabric of his necktie. He sounded like a goose.

"This is the middle of nowhere." I flicked the headlights per Sudimack's instructions. "You're the one who called him your friend."

"That was before he broke my nose," honked the Dogman. "That bear is bad news. I wish he had taken the Amtrak here, if you know what I mean."

I thought back to my reunion with the Dogman the week prior. I'd had to deliver a crate of boxed lunches to one of the glass towers in Center City, and I knew he worked somewhere in the neighborhood, so I shot him a text. He met me in front of his building for a cigarette—he had an engraved holder, of course—and cackled with delight to hear of the many misfortunes, earned and unearned, that had stalked me since the end of college.

"Did your buddy Denhelder really die of pancreatitis?" he'd asked, his grin as wide as the Walt Whitman Bridge. "I heard that from Seamus, but I thought he might be fucking with me."

"Why would he fuck with you about that?" I asked, but the Dogman waved the question off into the breeze of Market Street.

When he discovered that I was without a permanent address, the Dogman offered to sublet me the spare room in his own apartment at a rate to be later determined. "It'll be just like college," he insisted. "I'll give you a break until I can get you a gig here, data entry or some shit, and you can stop bringing people lunches." Caught in a pink fugue of reconciliatory goodwill, I'd accepted the proposal, already inanely picturing an engraved cigarette holder of my own, even as I knew that such holders were markers of the exact sort of people with whom I could never get along.

Now the Dogman and I were sitting in an idling Cadillac, waiting for drugs, one of us bleeding from the head. Somewhere in the night, a train whistle droned like a banshee heralding our doom.

Sudimack reemerged into the light of the trolley tracks, cuts checkering his face and blood spouting from his lip. He hurried back into the car. "That didn't work," he said, securing the door behind him. "They beat the shit out of me. Drive. *Drive.*"

\\\\\\

One of the developments of my sobriety (which still felt, at eight months, quite new) was that I found myself traversing a landscape of undulating sentiment. Some days I walked the streets of Philadelphia humbled by the inimitable majesty of life, finding every joy and every sorrow experienced by any person that I might meet (or see, or learn of) innately and gloriously accessible to me. Other days Philadelphia was just Philadelphia, and I was a miser, discerning nothing pitiable in any human being besides his ignorance of my own tribulations. Thus I could, one day, be overcome with gratitude and optimism from something as meager as an offer to share an apartment with Marc Dogana, only to feel, less than a week later, apathetic as to whether he and Sudimack made it through the night with all their blood still inside their bodies. I was, day to day, recalibrating myself for a new world. The process was ongoing.

The Dogman knew a guy on Ritner Street who sold cocaine out of a row house basement. "How's that sound, Sudimack?" he asked the battered malcontent in the backseat. "Would coke be alright?"

"I guess so," came the response.

The dealer's block of Ritner Street was crowded and bright. Strands of Christmas lights crisscrossed the low sky between the houses: fat multicolored bulbs suspended like angels, offering their glow to the pedestrians who crept in twos and threes down the pavement. There seemed to be a party going on in one of the houses. A door shuddered open and shut. A yellow window fluttered with the movement of bodies. From the wrong side of the street I could hear the muffled babble of conversation, but no music. I thought the party might be our destination, but the Dogman stopped before another house across the way and banged his fist beneath the peephole.

The door opened a few inches. The chain of the lock hung taut across the gap. Above the chain, a face floated like a moon and frowned.

"Attilio." The Dogman spread his arms in the pantomime of embrace. "Remember me? The Dogman? I came by with Shishkin those two times?"

It was difficult to tell from Attilio's expression whether he remembered the Dogman or not. Perhaps the issue was that during his previous visits the Dogman had been without a streak of blood dabbed from his nose down to the end of his dangling necktie. "Why are you bloody?" asked Attilio through the gap. "Somebody fuck you up?"

"Nah, we were playing rugby." The Dogman grinned like a mule. "Why don't you let us in? It's warm out here."

Attilio considered us for a moment and unfastened the lock. We followed him through a living room of plastic-coated furniture and artificial blossoms, past a looming grandfather clock whose face told the wrong time by many hours, and down the steps to the finished basement out of which Attilio managed his business. There was a small refrigerator and a wall-mounted television and an aquarium with some sort of reptile curled in the corner. There were two parallel couches with a glass coffee table between them. Attilio ushered the three of us onto one of the couches: Sudimack, then the Dogman, then me. He sat on the other, lit a cigarette, and subjected the Dogman to a probing stare. The Dogman stared back.

"How's Shishkin?" asked Attilio.

"I actually haven't seen him in a while," said the Dogman. "Have you?"

"No."

"He's kind of an asshole. Like, he's . . ." The Dogman clicked his tongue sadly. "I don't know, he just says mean things sometimes—"

"You got meth?" asked Sudimack. Beneath the recessed white lighting of the basement, Sudimack's face was a crime scene. A deep gash disfigured one of his eyebrows, a swollen ridge already forming above the socket. A sooty scrape scored his cheek where it looked as though his head had been dragged against asphalt. His lip continued to bleed, and he continued to wipe at it with the collar of his tank top, which had accumulated a ghastly parody of a lipstick stain.

"What?" asked Attilio. "Do I have *meth*?"

"We know you don't have meth." The Dogman's voice was meant to be assuaging. "If we could get an eight ball, though, that'd be fantastic." He tapped his finger to the side of his own bruised and puffy nose.

Attilio turned to me. I was free from blood and cuts and thus may have looked like the most sensible member of the group. "What do you want?" he asked me.

"I don't want anything," I said. "I'm sober."

"That's true," said the Dogman. "Put a beer in front of him. He won't drink it."

"Sober?" asked Attilio. "Why would you come here if you're sober?"

"Don't worry about him," said the Dogman. "He's the designated driver."

"What the fuck is this, a DUI class?" asked Sudimack. "Bro. Drugs. We have money."

Attilio held a hand up to Sudimack, which I did not consider advisable, though it seemed to confuse Sudimack enough that he stopped speaking. Attilio looked at me. "Why are you here?"

In the metaphysical sense, I was there because the world had brought me there. My life had thus far consisted of the world bringing me to various places, sometimes for the best, more often for the worst. The most aggressive action I'd ever taken—the act by which I'd most attempted to buck the order of things—was to get sober. Though even that was not an act so much as the cessation of an act. And even sober, the ride continued, through landscapes hospitable and otherwise. When I heard people speak of their great plans, their ambitions, the ways they were going to change their lives, I was always dumbfounded. What could you do, really? What could any of us *really* do? I couldn't stop time, couldn't go back, couldn't divert the flow of the universe. No one could. If there was a key to being a person—a functional person, one who lived a long time in a relatively small amount of pain—it seemed to be to do as little as possible.

"I'm just seeing where the evening takes me," I said.

Attilio shook his head. "I can't help you," he said to the Dogman. "I don't have anything."

"Attilio, buddy," said the Dogman. "Come on. You know me. If you could just—"

"I don't have anything for you. I don't like him"—Attilio pointed to Sudimack—"and I don't like him"—Attilio pointed to me—"and I don't like you. Maybe you'll come back with Shishkin and I'll have something for you. But this is weird." He waved his hand across our triptych. "This makes me uncomfortable."

The Dogman frowned. I laughed.

Sudimack pointed at the aquarium. "What kind of lizard is that?"

\\\\\\

It was the Dogman who flipped the table that time.

He had been attempting, with greater and greater adamance, to convince Attilio to sell him an eight ball, but Attilio was too busy protesting the fact that Sudimack had risen and started toward the aquarium in the corner of the room. "Yo, don't go over there. What are you doing? What is he doing?"

"Attilio," said the Dogman, as though all the other words in the English language had fled from his vocabulary. "Attilio. *Attilio.*"

"Don't go near that tank," called Attilio. "Yo, Dogboy, you gotta get your friends the fuck out of here—"

"Attilio. Attilio. Attilio."

"—before this busted-face freak touches my lizard." Attilio was shouting now. "So help me God—"

When the table flipped, no one was more surprised than me. The Dogman had a temper, but it manifested verbally, never physically. When he shot to his feet, his palms lifting the edge of the glass tabletop, my expression must have been one of pure incredulity. The table hopped a foot into the air, tipped perpendicular, and met the floor with a crash and a hail of shards. Before the pane had shattered, Attilio leapt backward onto the seat of his couch. I looked up to see him wielding, as if from nowhere, an eighteen-inch wooden baseball bat. It was the kind they handed out at the ballpark on fan appreciation days. He must have kept it hidden in the couch cushions. I sank lower into my own seat, wondering if Attilio regarded me as an enemy combatant, and if he would be correct to regard me as such. The Dogman was on his feet and therefore posed a greater threat to him than I did. Standing on the couch, Attilio had a significant height advantage, and the Dogman, who seemed to have run out of ideas after flipping the table, looked very much in danger of having his temple beaten in by a miniature bat.

Then Attilio was pelted in the face by his own lizard.

The animal flew through the air with such swiftness and precision that it took me a moment to realize it had been hurled. The Dogman dove at the momentarily confused drug dealer's knees, knocking him to the glass-strewn floor. Sudimack leapt onto the pile, and I, surmising that my participation was unneeded, ran up the basement stairs and out of the house.

The world is, at times, confounding. I stood on Ritner Street beneath an artificial sky strewn with a thousand multicolored Christmas stars, even though it was the first week of July. Night is dark and sometimes we let it be dark, and sometimes we drown it in tinted light. Night is lonely and sometimes we let it be lonely, and sometimes we settle it with strangers. Half a dozen people stood across the street, smoking cigarettes before the party house. One of them was holding a steaming paper cup and I could almost smell the coffee. A woman came out of the house and stood on the stoop and said, "Come inside, everybody, we're starting again." She looked right at me and said, "Come inside, we're starting the second half." I walked across the street, under the lights, and I followed them as they filed through the doorway.

What I'd mistaken for a party was actually something more organized, with a collection of mismatched chairs arranged around the cozy, lamp-lit living room, all oriented toward one corner where an area had been cleared for a speaker. About thirty people were finding their seats or filing themselves into the spaces along the walls. I took an empty spot by the side window, next to a thin table with a spread of fruit, antipasto, wine, and a carafe. The wine precluded the possibility that I had wandered into an AA meeting. Perhaps it was a prayer group. A real estate seminar. I didn't care. I helped myself to a cup of black coffee and stood there with my nose in it, the pungent steam rising up and loosening all the muscles in my body. An older woman reached over for a napkin, flashing me a *beg-your-pardon* smile, and I knew I was in a place of benevolent humanism.

The woman from the stoop stepped into the speaker's corner with her palms clasped and her eyes gleaming. I inferred from her praise of the previous performers that I had entered some sort of storytelling event, one where people got up and told an unwritten anecdote from their lives. I did not find that premise immediately appealing, but no one in the room was covered in blood, and that had become an increasingly endearing quality for me over the course of the previous hour. I could withstand a story or two.

"Our next performer," said the host excitedly, "is a South Philadelphia native and a genuine treasure. We're so lucky to still have her here among us, and so very, very grateful. Please help me in welcoming to the stage our friend Tracey Basilotta."

There was an inordinate amount of clapping as Tracey moved to the speaker's corner. She must have been a scene favorite. I could sense the simmer of anticipation in the modest audience, the flicker of attentiveness throughout the room. She was a small woman, right on the cusp of middle age. Her hair and sweater both suggested the staticky lightness of feathers. She held an apple in one hand, gripped like a skull, her wrist bent beneath the weight of all its inherent symbolism. I could tell she was a woman who believed in her own purpose.

"This is a new story," she said. "I'm still figuring out the shape of it. Part of it only happened recently. And, actually, I suppose, it's still ongoing. Because I myself am ongoing, and life is ongoing, and we don't yet know what the end looks like."

Around me, people nodded. They appeared so vulnerable in their chairs, so hungry for a narrative that might supersede their own.

Tracey cleared her throat. "I was on a train that flew."

\\\\\\

The components of Tracey's story went like this. She was not a successful person. She was not an ambitious person. If she was an intelligent person, it was the kind of intelligence that had never led her to any money, which was therefore no kind of intelligence at all. She'd grown up not far from where we sat, on Iseminger Street near Marconi Plaza. She'd grown up with the vague notion of leaving the city, though where she would go was never a fixed location in her mind. She ended up in Chicago. It was a school that lured her there, though once that was done she had struggled to find a reason to remain. A vocation would have served, but she had none. A passion, perhaps, though an inventory of herself did not identify one. She was not a skilled person. She was not a talented person. If she was a funny person, it was the sort of funniness that appealed much more to those who understood her intimately than to those who didn't know her. She had few of those intimate people. She stayed in Chicago anyway. She married a man, though he quickly felt less like an anchor than a millstone. She loved him, yes, but it was relative. Their love was a small love. Greater love was reserved for greater, lovelier couples. She was not a beautiful person. She was not a person who people remembered once she walked out of a room. If she was notable in any way, it was that others assumed, with very little evidence, that she was dependable. She was forever being asked by acquaintances to water plants, to look after pets. She was forever being listed as a reference for job and apartment and adoption applications. Even though her bills were paid late. Even though she left her husband after an unremarkable weekend in Bayfield, Wisconsin. She was not a dependable person. She was not an organized person. If her life conformed to any recognizable shape, it was simply because she had not found a way to break that shape. A recognizable shape was a mark of smallness. She wanted bigness. She left Chicago. She lived in Seattle. She lived in Boston. She lived in Washington, DC. Her apartments were so similar to one another that she could not now remember which belonged to which city. She married another man. She left him, too. She took him back, two years later, out of resignation more than anything else. She was not a stubborn person. She was not a steadfast person. If she had any consistency of behavior, it was a tendency to waffle. Which was just a form of inconsistency, when it came down to it. And inconsistency was a state upon which others could graft whatever tendencies they wanted to behold. She left her second husband again. She got a tattoo. She entered a graduate program and dropped out after two semesters. She came home to Philadelphia, where an old friend gave her a stable job. She lived now, again, not far from where we sat, on Randolph Street near Whitman Plaza. And she supposed she was the sort of boring person who was always destined to end up back where she started. And she supposed she was a foolish person to have thought that any other life might lie before her.

Even so, she was a person with self-awareness. And she was a person conscious of the brevity of life. And if she kept on living in a way that left her less than satisfied, it was only because there was no other way that she knew how to live. She tried to cook different foods. She tried to date different men. She tried to go different places, to see different neighborhoods in different cities whenever the opportunity arose. Just that May, she had boarded an Amtrak train at 30th Street Station. She had meant to go to New York but ended up, via circumstances that were painfully confusing, no farther from home than a gravelly field in Port Richmond.

It was only later, when the events were explained to her, that she was struck by their significance. She had, at four decades and one hundred miles per hour, come to a place where the tracks curved one way and the train went another. It slipped the rails and sailed over air, into nothingness, untethered to the predetermined course of zones and maps and schedules, unconcerned with the laws that governed physics and nature, and it flew—for who is to say that a train cannot fly? Simply because, on all the days that preceded that one, trains had clung to the earth? But any day, any moment, is new and different than any moment that has ever come before it, because the order of occurrences has not yet solidified into unyielding history. It is still pliable and subject to influence. Subject to improvisation, to spontaneity. To whim. She inhabited a present—a present finite only if one insisted on measuring it in time—and in that present a train could do such unexpected things. It could drive across the empty air as though it were solid as any rail, as though the only thing keeping any of us from liberation was our insistence on hewing to the tracks before us.

"And I won't talk about the way it came down," said Tracey. "I'm not yet ready to talk about the way it came down, because it hit the earth in a way that I will never forget. But that is not the topic of this story. This is a story about flight."

The room was silent. I could hear the hum of the refrigerator in the kitchen, the rattle of the air conditioner in the backyard.

Tracey held the apple aloft. "We know that it's the nature of all objects to fall through space. I understand that. I accept it. But one day, in this universe of endless universes, I believe there's going to be something that doesn't fall. That doesn't have to fall. I have to believe that." She gripped her prop by its stem, and we all looked on, soundlessly, breathlessly, as she let it go. We half-expected, half-desired, half-required with half the fibers in our bodies that the apple would float there once she released it from her grasp. We watched like children, we idiots. It fell to the floor, made a soft crunch where its flesh compacted under the force of its plummet.

We laughed. Laughed at ourselves. The tension broke. The spell snapped like a soap bubble.

Tracey smiled, shrugged. "So not tonight. But one day. Thank you, everyone."

\\\\\\

I saw them after the applause began, when I cast an investigative glance around the room. They had snuck in during Tracey's story and were loitering quietly along the back wall. The Dogman's mouth was now as bloody as his nose, and his shirt was dotted with tiny stained holes where the glass shards of the coffee table had pricked through to his skin. Sudimack had blood on his knuckles. In his hands he held and absentmindedly stroked Attilio's pet lizard like a familiar spirit. The two of them were glassy-eyed from whatever substances they had found in the dealer's basement. They swayed, smiling like lunatics, mutely at the edge of the room.

The host returned to the speaking corner and requested another round of applause for Tracey. "These are difficult times," she said solemnly. "Death and injury seem to come sneaking up in ever more sudden and upsetting ways." There was a gentle murmur of agreement from the room. I may have murmured along with them. "I thought," the host continued, "that it might be alleviating in these times to go around and each speak a name of someone we've lost. It doesn't have to be from violence, necessarily, since a loss is always violent. Just someone who has passed from our lives. I'll begin." She said a name, a name that meant nothing to me, a name that might have meant nothing to anyone in the house other than herself.

Tracey, who still stood near the front of the room, said her name next. I didn't recognize that name either.

The remembrance continued through the audience, with strangers saying strange names, and I thought of what name I might say when it came to be my turn. I thought of the dead people I had known. That was the assignment, to name one of them. But, really, I had lost more than dead people. Most of the people I had ever known, most of the people I had ever cared for, had exited my life, and I would only ever know them again if I sought them out and reconciled. Friends and family and people I had loved, whose lives had diverged from mine in sharp and gradual ways. I could have said any of their names and meant them just as strongly as the names of my dead. I could have said my own name, and the people in that room would not have known. Except for the two who knew me.

I looked back at them, their bruised and broken faces. I hated them for knowing me. They were a check on me to remain myself and to never be any other person. How can you ever change if every mistake and humiliation of your life is folklore for those who witnessed it? An anecdote in the mouths of those whom fate sat on the stool next to you while you were young and brutal and gullible and scared? Dennis Monk was still those things. Why couldn't I say that he was dead? Why couldn't I be a new man tomorrow?

The remembrance was moving clockwise around the room, and I realized it would reach Sudimack and the Dogman before I had a chance to speak. I realized it before they did, even, lolling like sunflowers against the wall. I watched as the last anonymous audience members spoke their anonymous names, and it was Sudimack's turn. Sudimack, who fought dirty and indiscriminately. Sudimack, who looked so much like a battlefield ghost that I couldn't believe he'd been let into the house.

Sudimack, whose eyes were welling with tears.

"Jayden," he said to the assembled people. "My son. I lost my son today."

In the room there was an intake of breath. I felt it pass my own lips. Next to Sudimack, the Dogman—who had taken possession of Attilio's lizard and was squeezing it like a leathery doll—wailed with all the muscles in his throat. One of the men sitting nearby reached out and placed a hand on the Dogman's shoulder. I set my fingers down on the refreshment table to steady myself.

"I had a three-year-old son," said Sudimack, his breath fragmenting into syllable-length gasps, his knuckles clenched and raised to his temples. "And I lost him today. I lost him forever."

"My god," prayed the host at the front of the room.

"You poor man," sighed Tracey, her voice as soft as feathers.

The tracks pull the train out of the station, thread it through the woolen night. Feel its compelled glide along the curves, its fixed orbit, the spine of rails that dictates the arc of cars, the transit of passengers, the order of days, the epochs of a life. Could you stop it with your mind alone? With your shoulder braced against the window? Could you will the flanges to crumple, the wheels to hop the rail? *I think we'll go this way, now. This way over here.*

And with a swat I overturned the table, because there were new poets in town, and I knew that words alone would never sate them.

KID STUFF

Me and Cudahy were strictly anti-violence.

There was enough of it out there already. We read about it in Cudahy's Twitter feed, and on Facebook, and, a few days after the fact, in *Philadelphia Weekly* and *Philadelphia City Paper*, which we always remembered to pick up at the Pharmacy in Point Breeze. We sat in Cudahy's kitchen and read the papers with our coffee mugs in hand. When the weather permitted, we sat in her backyard. We drank coffee at all hours of the day and night. We were both on the wagon.

There was one story about an assault at our alma mater in North Philadelphia. A man got knocked down coming out of the Hillel center by a group of guys who had just been turned away from a frat party down the block. Slurs were deployed. The man's nose was broken. He was a Jewish guy. He was not a student at the university, just a caterer leaving after Shabbat dinner. His assailants were garden-variety gentile hoodlums. They *were* students at the university. It wasn't a terribly elite university. The frat that turned them away was the Jewish frat, so I could kind of see how the whole thing came about. Booze was involved, that spirit of discord. The papers called it a hate crime.

"You can't just go around hitting random Jews," I said to Cudahy. We were sitting in her backyard. She had a little garden table topped with blue and green tiles where we could set our mugs down, next to a pot with a basil plant. "If anybody, they should've just hit the frat guys. That's who they had the problem with."

"Nobody should have hit anybody," said Cudahy.

"Well, yeah," I said. "Obviously. But, I'm saying, if they had to hit somebody, hit the frat guys, you know?"

"What are you talking about?" said Cudahy. She had a sincerity about her—a way of sitting perfectly still, a way of holding eye contact— that made whatever she said seem like the most sensible thing in the world. "Nobody had to hit anybody. Nobody should ever hit anybody."

"Right," I said. "That's how I feel, too."

\\\\\\

We lived by a code. We lived in Grays Ferry because Grays Ferry was real as fuck. Cudahy used to live east of 25th Street in Point Breeze, but Point Breeze had gotten too gentrified. I'd decided that the Dogman's Bella Vista apartment was too stressful a spot for me, especially since Sudimack had taken up residence on the couch. It was all crushed pills and vodka Red Bulls over there. I didn't need to be around that type of goonery. Cudahy was the same as me. We were done with kid stuff like getting drunk and making bad decisions. We liked mature things like drinking coffee in the backyard and reading the alternative weeklies. Most days we brewed our own coffee, but sometimes we went out for it. The closest coffee shop was the Dunkin Donuts in Forgotten Bottom, but we didn't go to that one. We didn't patronize chains. That was part of the code. When we wanted to go for coffee, we walked the ten blocks to the Pharmacy. There, we could sit and sip and watch the Point Breeze hipsters in their Castro caps and candy-hued sneakers and laugh to ourselves about what gentrifying fucks they were.

Cudahy got sober about a year before I moved in. That's when she left Point Breeze for Grays Ferry. She got herself a sober roommate, but the roommate stopped being sober and had to move out. That was why Cudahy was so committed to the code. I didn't really have a code prior to living with Cudahy. I just lived where people would have me, even if it meant tolerating occasional antisocial behavior from the likes of Sudimack and the Dogman. I was eight months sober when Cudahy suggested I move in. She offered me the empty bedroom at a price even I could afford. Part of Grays Ferry being real as fuck was that it was cheap as fuck. I felt like I'd finally stumbled into having my shit together.

Cudahy worked at two places, a breakfast place and a sandwich place. The places were both in Point Breeze, where shiny new row houses were quickly rising up in the empty lots between the old ones. There were not a ton of employment opportunities in Grays Ferry. "Yet," said Cudahy, like she was afraid they were coming. I was working as a delivery driver when I moved in, but that, too, was an antisocial environment. People acted like they didn't have to tip me as long as they avoided looking at me directly. I told Cudahy how I hated it and she told me I should quit, like it was the simplest thing in the world. I told her I wanted to go back to freelancing, which filled me with a sense of self-determination, and she told me to follow my bliss. So that's what I was doing. There were plenty of gigs out there on the Internet. Sometimes I wrote ad copy. Sometimes I wrote listicles. I did a lot of things on spec and sometimes I didn't get paid for them. It was an inefficient way to make a small amount of money, but I didn't have much else going on, and Cudahy said it was good to keep busy.

Sometimes I picked up something fun. One day I wrote flavor profiles for various exotic teas. Fifteen bucks per profile. The company wouldn't send me the teas, so I had to imagine how each one might taste.

"What do you think chrysanthemum tastes like?" I asked Cudahy from the couch.

She looked up from the list she was making in the kitchen and guessed, "Floral?"

"Nice one, Cudahy," I said, even though I'd already used *floral* for the Bangalore rose chai. *Floral* was sort of an obvious one when the tea had a flower right there in its name, but I wanted Cudahy to know how much I valued her opinion.

\\\\\\

Me and Cudahy didn't do AA. We recognized that it had helped a lot of people, but it wasn't for us. We each had our own reasons. Cudahy rejected the idea of a power greater than herself, and I didn't want to make amends with all the people I'd wronged. It wasn't a pride thing, for me. I was being considerate. I was confident the people I'd have to apologize to were uninterested in receiving my apologies.

"I'm sure they would love to get an apology," said Cudahy.

"And I'm sure God would love for you to believe in him," I said.

We didn't need AA because we had the code. The code wasn't a literal code. Specific rules were articulated on occasion, but it was more of an ethos. Do good things, don't do bad things. Drink coffee, not booze. We were both raised Irish Catholic, which is why Cudahy didn't believe in God and why I didn't like making amends. It was why we understood one another so well, even if we sometimes got competitive about our respective upbringings. Cudahy insisted she was more fucked up than me because she went to Catholic schools. But Cudahy grew up with money, so that balanced things out in my opinion. Not that I ever said that to her. She worked two jobs, and I was a guest in her house. I wasn't even on the lease or anything. If I had to play shrink, I'd have said that Cudahy carried a lot of guilt around with her, just because her dad owned a Mercedes dealership out on the Main Line and her family had a beach house in Avalon. I didn't understand why she would feel guilty about those things. The only guilt I felt was for the things I had done personally. In that respect, I was pretty well-adjusted.

Cudahy was Cudahy's last name. Her first name was Tara. Tara wasn't a great name, sure, but it worked perfectly fine. I didn't know why she felt the need to go by Cudahy. It had been that way since college, where we lived in the same freshman dorm. It struck me as a bit masculine, her going by Cudahy, but I knew enough not to say so. People called me by my last name, too, since Dennis was a terrible first name. But I didn't really care what people called me.

"Then why do you care what people call me?" asked Cudahy.

"I'm just curious," I told her.

\\\\\\

We didn't smoke. That was part of the code. I used to smoke. I had only just quit. Right when I moved in with Cudahy. If I wanted to, I could still have smoked away from the house, and even if Cudahy had smelled the cigarette fumes on my clothes, she probably wouldn't have said anything about it. Respecting personal boundaries was also part of the code, unless it directly pertained to falling off the wagon. But I didn't smoke anywhere, out of respect for her home, which was not my home, even if I paid a portion of the rent. It was a small portion, less than half, and I hadn't actually paid it yet. We both chewed a lot of gum.

Ivan laughed when I told him I'd be living in Grays Ferry. I told him it was cheap and he said, "I bet it is." Honestly, there was not much else to recommend the place. It was a neighborhood of tiny row houses and railroad tracks and overgrown lots, hugged by a muddy bend in the Schuylkill and shackled with highways. The old whites of the neighborhood resented the blacks—so much so that Louis Farrakhan once got involved—and the blacks seemed to resent us new whites. Though there weren't very many of us new whites. If some innate charm was a prerequisite for gentrification, the Pharmacy set would be a while in following Cudahy to Grays Ferry. That was probably why she liked it. There weren't many bars or stores. There were a fair number of heroin addicts. A few had set up shop in the vacant house at the end of the block, and they shuffled up and down the street at all hours. Sometimes we could hear them rustling in the weeds beyond our fence. I had lived around heroin addicts in other neighborhoods—we'd called them fiends—but I'd never given much thought to their inner lives. Now I couldn't help but stare at them, fascinated by the decisions they had to make and could not make, blown around like phantoms in a phantom city.

"There but for the grace of God, right Cudahy?" I said.

Cudahy shook her head.

Grays Ferry was rough, but Cudahy knew how to handle herself. She took self-defense classes at a Muay Thai place on Washington Avenue. You wouldn't have guessed it to look at her, but she probably could've snapped your wrist or broken your nose.

"Maybe I should take a class," I said. "I never really learned to throw a punch."

We agreed that when the shit went down, Cudahy would come to my rescue.

We read another story in the paper about a gay couple who were assaulted in Center City. There were three assailants, two male and one female, all violently drunk. The assault upset Cudahy. She said there was an epidemic of hate crimes in the City of Brotherly Love. Mildly acquainted with hate and drunkenness, I thought that the latter was at fault more than the former. "If they hadn't been drunk," I said, "it probably wouldn't have happened."

"If they hadn't been gay-bashing pieces of shit," said Cudahy, "it definitely wouldn't have happened."

Cudahy's sentiment lay unshakably with the gay couple. As did mine, of course. Of course.

And yet I couldn't help but briefly inhabit the perspective of the drunks, who happened to be from Bucks County, just like me. The female assailant was the daughter of the police chief of the town next to the one where I grew up. We'd been in neighboring parishes, attended neighboring high schools in quiet suburbs where people were supposed to behave themselves. I felt guilty, for some reason. Not that I had ever bashed a gay couple, or wanted to. But I couldn't shake the sense that something broken in that woman might also be broken in me.

\\\\\\

We didn't fool around. Not with each other. That was Cudahy's idea, though I wasn't sure if it was part of the code. Before she suggested it, it never would have occurred to me to fool around with Cudahy. Back when I met her, Cudahy was dating girls. As far as I knew, she'd never stopped. Not so. When I moved in with her, she was with a guy named Nate who had tattoos of nautical stars on each of his hands. I wanted to ask her what had changed, but I didn't want to sound parochial.

"You've lived with women before, haven't you?" she asked me.

"Of course," I said.

"Platonically?" she clarified.

"Of course," I lied.

"We don't want to risk falling in love," said Cudahy. She said it in a jokey voice, drawing out the words so they wouldn't sound so awkward. We shared a sense of humor.

Cudahy had changed a lot since college, which was the last time I had spent any time with her. It was mostly house parties then, where we were mostly pretty drunk, and Cudahy didn't speak or act all that differently than me and the guys I hung out with. I wasn't sure which of her changes had come with age and which had come with sobriety. Old Cudahy followed whatever thought fell out of her mouth. New Cudahy seemed to pick her words like she was choosing a perfect cantaloupe. Old Cudahy was impossible to offend, but I feared I was often in danger of offending new Cudahy. I tried not to, of course. I amended my behavior. I followed the code. But it seemed to go deeper than the things I did, like the problem was more in the things I said and thought, the ways I interpreted the world. I sensed that this new Cudahy sometimes wished that I was a different person. New Cudahy seemed to sometimes wish that even new Cudahy was a different person.

"Everybody changes," said Cudahy, when I mentioned how she seemed different. I did so with tact. I told her how she seemed to have matured since the days of house parties, back when she always had a blunt tucked under the rim of her beanie and a bag of gummy worms in her sweatshirt pocket.

"Not that you were immature before," I said. We were wandering back from the Pharmacy, alt-weeklies in hand. She knew what I meant.

"You live your life not appreciating what it is," she said as we passed under the railroad viaduct that squatted above 25th Street. "Then something shifts. Like if you moved a bookcase in your house and found a window behind it that you never knew was there. You'd have a whole new view of the world."

I thought I knew what she meant. "Sobriety is our window," I said.

"There are lots of windows," said Cudahy. "Everybody finds their own windows."

I definitely felt like I was seeing Cudahy through a new window. Old Cudahy was my friend. New Cudahy was also my friend, but a friend whose body I found myself sneaking glances at when she walked into the kitchen in her underwear. Cudahy wasn't bashful about flashing her skin. Not that she should have been. She was in her own house, after all, and the summer heat seeped in through every aperture. Cudahy had a large tattoo of a sunburst on her thigh, and my eyes often got caught up in its gravity, orbiting like inferior planets until I pried them away.

Me and Cudahy observed Dance Party Sundays. Her friend Smashley Smaniotto would come by and the three of us would go down to the basement, switch on the black light, and gyrate to synthwave. Smashley was Cudahy's best friend from college. The two of them were nearly identical back then, slim and small and spiky-haired, but Smashley had gained some weight and shaved her head, and if Cudahy hadn't told me who was coming over, I don't know that I would have recognized her. The first thing Smashley said when she saw me was "Is that really Dennis Monk?" She didn't say it like she was pleased, more like she was puzzled or slightly disgusted. Smashley and I had never really clicked for whatever reason.

"Stop calling me Smashley," she said as we clomped down the basement stairs. "Like you're one to talk."

No one got smashed at Dance Party Sundays. The three of us didn't even dance together. Instead, we each took a corner of the basement,

Cudahy by the furnace, Smashley by the water heater, and me by the laundry machines. At first I didn't really know what to do with myself, but when I realized the others weren't looking at me, that they just kept their eyes closed and swayed with the synthy ripples, I was able to let go a bit, to let my arms and legs work out whatever it was they needed to work out. It felt more like exercise than dancing, cathartic and detoxifying, and at the end of an hour or so the three of us would emerge steaming into the backyard to dry our sweat in the afternoon sun. I let them take the chairs on either side of the little table, and I sat on the back steps, reclined on my elbows. By the end of that first Sunday, I think Smashley had warmed up to me. I started to call her Ash the way Cudahy did, and I told her all about the code.

"I like to believe people can change," said Ash, and I remember thinking, yeah, of course people can change. The old Monk was never much of a dancer.

\\\\\

Nate came by once a week or so. I didn't usually hang out when he was around. I was not a huge fan of Nate. He didn't drink, but he smoked a lot of weed. Not in the house, but sometimes in the backyard. I mentioned this to Cudahy.

"Weed's non-addictive," said Cudahy, though we both knew it was a gray area.

Nate lived in Fishtown. If I were to get pedantic about it, he lived in a part of Kensington that the real estate agents had started calling Fishtown. I told Nate how I used to live in that neighborhood, a few years back. I told him how a lot of formative shit had happened to me in that neighborhood. Nate wasn't particularly interested in my formation. He just nodded his graying head at me, gauges wiggling in his earlobes. Nate didn't seem to like me very much. But I guess there was bound to be tension between two men who occupied our positions vis-à-vis Cudahy.

She and I spent a lot of time together. There was the coffee, the newspapers, the kitchen, the backyard. We walked to the corner grocery on Tasker, and sometimes to the Pathmark by the Schuylkill, which was a chain supermarket, yes, but which carried things like lentils and kalamata olives that the corner grocery did not. We listened to records on Cudahy's record player. We watched Netflix on Cudahy's laptop. Documentaries, sitcoms, shows where people renovated houses and restaurants and bars. Cudahy had a big, lumpy couch where we lounged as we watched. Sometimes we'd be lounging there and Cudahy would fall asleep with her head on my shoulder. It was comforting to spend time with a person who understood my particular incongruity with the world. I'd never spent time with a person like that before Cudahy.

Cudahy and Nate didn't seem to have much sex. I knew because I listened. Not like that. Not on purpose. It was a small house and our rooms were quite close to each other. Maybe they were doing it very softly, but I didn't think they were doing it at all. Maybe they abstained for my benefit. Maybe that was why Nate was antagonistic toward me. Mostly I just heard them speaking quietly to one another. They probably had sex at Nate's place, I imagined, but Cudahy didn't spend many nights away from home. I think that was also part of the code. Our house was a sober refuge in an impaired world.

We didn't eat meat. I did eat meat, before I moved in with Cudahy. Cudahy was a vegan. I drew the line at vegetarianism. I found eggs and dairy too pervasive to avoid. And I liked cheese. We could agree on no meat, though. Cudahy knew a ton of vegan recipes. She knew about vegetables I had never heard of before, jicama and kohlrabi and kabocha. When even the Pathmark did not have the vegetables she required, we rode our bikes across town to the Italian Market. Technically the bike I rode belonged to Nate.

It was at the Italian Market that I'd run into Cudahy in the first place, following several years of absence from each other's life. I'd been sitting under the umbrella of a sidewalk café, taking a breather from the intemperance of the Dogman's apartment and wallowing in the funk that characterized my general emotional state at the time. It was one of those mornings of early sobriety where I would just sit under the vacant sky and think, "Here I am, Most Benevolent God, so what comes next?" Then Cudahy walked up to me with a head of fennel in her hand and a backpack full of tubers weighing down her spine.

"Monk!" she said, like she was the happiest that any person had ever been to see me. When she heard about my living situation, she invited me to take her old roommate's room. Our hearts were both so big that day, at having found each other—old friends—and having encountered in one another the same deficiencies.

"Us addicts need to stick together," said Cudahy, cupping her hands over mine.

\\\\\\

In Grays Ferry, sometimes people shouted things at me when I was walking down the street. "The fuck you doing here, white boy?" Things like that. It was worse for Cudahy. She got catcalled, and it could get graphic. She was used to it, and she had her Muay Thai at the ready, but she didn't like to be alone on foot. She rode her bike everywhere. She used to have a car, but it was stolen from the spot in front of the house the month she moved in. I didn't know why she didn't just ask her father for a new one, since he owned a car dealership. Cudahy made it seem like she didn't talk to him too often. She didn't leave her bike outside. When she got home from work, I would try to meet her on the stoop and help her get the bike into the house, since the security door had a tendency to pinch shut like a fly trap if someone didn't hold it open.

I asked Ivan to get me one of those "Protected by Brinks" stickers. I stuck it in the front window one day and showed it to Cudahy when she got home. She didn't like it. She said it made us look like we were suspicious of the neighbors.

"What are you talking about?" I asked. "The neighbors all have them too."

"We don't need it," she said.

"There's a house full of heroin addicts at the end of the block," I said. "And somebody stole your car."

"Just take it down," she said.

We read about a college student who was murdered in Old City. He was a student of that same university that Cudahy and I had attended. He was stumbling home from a bar when three assailants emerged from a car and beat him to death. Or, they beat him to the ground, where he hit the back of his head on a step, which killed him. The dead man was white. Two of his assailants were brown and one was black.

"Are the streets of Philadelphia no longer safe for drunks?" I asked. We were in the kitchen because it was raining outside.

"We don't know what happened," said Cudahy, raking dairyless butter across sprouted toast. "He probably said some shit to them."

"What's that assumption based on?" I asked.

"Come on, Monk," said Cudahy. "You know how guys like that are. Especially when they're drunk."

"Guys like what?" I asked. "We don't know anything about this guy other than that he was drunk on a sidewalk."

"Well, if he hadn't been drunk," said Cudahy, "it probably wouldn't have happened."

"I think you've got a double standard for different kinds of people," I said.

Cudahy didn't have a response. Just the scrape, scrape, scrape of the butter knife.

"I think you're wrong on this one," I said.

Cudahy set down the knife. "Well, I think you've been smoking cigarettes."

"Have not," I said. "How would you know?"

"You reek of cigs," said Cudahy. "I can smell it right now."

\\\\\\

In truth, I had been smoking cigarettes, occasionally, while out on walks and such. It turned out my willpower still had some cracks in it. I figured that after quitting booze I could quit anything, and yet I kept finding myself before the counter at the corner grocery on Tasker, asking the kid who worked there for another pack of Camel Blues and paying for them with money I barely had. The writing gigs were not as plentiful as they initially appeared to be.

The Internet said that quitting nicotine was almost as hard as quitting heroin. I had never tried heroin, but I found that comparison difficult to believe. The stakes with cigarettes were much lower, at least. Relapse for a cigarette smoker was a bummer, but you could just try again. Even relapse for a drunk probably wouldn't kill you, at least not that first day. But an ex–heroin addict could take the wrong pill and end up OD'd in a house off Kensington Avenue twelve hours later. Those were sky-high stakes. I was grateful not to be a heroin addict. I couldn't have handled the stress of it.

But relapse made me feel like a failure, even if it was just a cigarette. And failure was bad for morale. Sometimes I wondered if Cudahy was setting up too many trip wires around herself, with the no smoking and no meat and no chain stores and no gentrified neighborhoods and no fooling around with roommates. If she accidentally stepped on one it might trigger an explosion of self-loathing, setting off all the others at the same time and blowing her right back to booze. A sober person needed rules, but too many rules could doom the whole project.

In my defense, I hadn't eaten any meat since I moved in with Cudahy. I told her that, but I didn't know if she believed me.

Cudahy had to serve animal products at work, at the breakfast place and the sandwich place. She had to serve alcohol. I knew she found it demoralizing. There was no greater poke in the eye for a sober Marxist vegan than the modern American iteration of brunch. When the breakfast place added bacon to its Bloody Mary, Cudahy told me she was thinking about moving to Saudi Arabia.

"I think they have a pretty troubling human rights record," I said.

"It was a joke," she said. "They don't drink alcohol or eat pork there. 'Cause of Islam."

"Oh, right. Good one, Cudahy."

\\\\\\

One night, while Cudahy was taking off her helmet on the sidewalk, a guy shouted something to her as he walked down the far side of the street. It was an appraisal of her white ass. I was holding open the security door for her.

"Hey, fuck you, dickhead," I called after him. I watched him stride away down the block. He wore a t-shirt with the name of the local high school stamped across the shoulders. He looked like he might have been a teenager.

"Monk, just go inside," said Cudahy, dragging the bike past me.

I shut the door. I felt slightly bad for calling him a dickhead, if he was just a teenager. Though, to be fair, a lot of teenagers were dickheads.

"Can you not shout things at the neighbors, please?" asked Cudahy. She lifted her bike up to the rack on the wall.

"They shout shit all the time," I said. "I'm just shouting back."

"Can you not shout at me, please?" she said. She was having trouble getting the bike up on the rack. Her hands weren't steady, and she couldn't slot the frame onto the hooks.

"I'm not shouting at you," I said. "I'm just speaking emphatically. Why are you always so sensitive about everything?" I walked up behind her to help lift the bike onto the rack, but when I tried to take the frame from her hands she let go of the whole contraption. The bike clattered to the floor as she dropped down low and knocked my legs out from under me with a swift sweep of her foot. I crumpled and smacked my head on the coffee table.

I lay there for a few dazed seconds, Cudahy standing by the wall, her breaths short and heavy, her hands out in front of her chest. I touched my head and felt the blood seeping out of it.

"What the fuck, man?" I asked.

"Jesus, I'm sorry," said Cudahy.

"I was just helping with your bike." I kept my voice as calm as I could. "Did I do something wrong?"

She didn't kneel down to assist me. She just stood there by the wall mumbling, "Sorry. Sorry. Sorry."

I stood up, winking idiotically from the blood in my eye. She offered to call an ambulance, but I said I didn't need one. Then I examined myself in the bathroom mirror and saw how much blood there was. I wadded up a handful of paper towels and held them to my head as I rode Nate's bike to the urgent care. Cudahy tried to go with me, but we were both pretty embarrassed, and I was happier riding alone through the darkened streets, navigating with only my left eye and left hand.

\\\\\\

Nate came to the house while Cudahy was at work. She'd picked up somebody's shift at the last minute and Nate didn't know about it. He expected to find her at home. I told him she was gone. I enjoyed the fact that he didn't know everything about Cudahy. Nate didn't seem too perturbed.

"What happened to your head?" he asked.

I had six stitches above my right eyebrow. Cudahy had offered to pay the bill, but I spent my rent money instead. I was pretty impressed by how magnanimous I was being about the whole thing. I suspected that magnanimity was a part of the code.

"Dance Party Sundays," I told him, tapping my stitches. "It can get pretty wild around here, Nate."

He asked me if he could smoke a bowl in our backyard before he left. I didn't really want him to, but since I'd borrowed Nate's bike a few times I felt like I needed to be hospitable. We sat out there together, on either side of the garden table, and I watched him exhale his hits into the leaves of Cudahy's basil plant. I moved the plant.

"Are you a pacifist, Nate?" I asked him.

"I work at a food truck," he said, his voice wet with smoke. "It's called Cabbage Boy?"

"How do you know Cudahy?" I asked.

"NA."

"NA?"

"Narcotics Anonymous," he said.

"I know what it is," I said. "Cudahy was in NA?"

"For a minute," he said. "We both were. It wasn't for us, though. They wanted me to stop smoking weed. And Tara, you know, she doesn't believe in God."

"Why was she in NA?" I asked.

Nate's tone suggested he thought I was some kind of substance abuse rookie. "Let's just say that, for Tara, heroin is the one that got away."

After Nate left, I smoked two cigarettes in the backyard. I'd never smoked out there before. Then I washed all my clothes to make sure they didn't smell like anything other than our scentless plant-based laundry detergent. It started me on a cleaning kick. I opened the windows to let the fresh air fill the house. I vacuumed and swept and scoured the countertops. I washed all the dishes. I washed all the mugs. Some of the mugs had coffee stains that wouldn't come out no matter how hard I scrubbed. There were cracks in the glaze where the coffee had seeped underneath, and there was simply no getting it out.

\\\\\\

One time, back in college, I went to a party with Cathy Tomlinson somewhere on Diamond Street. The party was in one of those grand old three-story brownstones that seemed to lurch up away from the sidewalk, like the whole building would have toppled over backward if too many people stood in the kitchen at once. It was during a period when I was trying not to drink too much, especially in front of Cathy, who I had embarrassed the previous New Year's Eve by getting shit-faced in front of all her high school friends. She was so angry afterward that she didn't talk to me for a week. At the party on Diamond Street, I drank a bit too much anyway, and Cathy got pissed and went home, and I figured what the hell and let myself go. My memory of the evening was spotty, but at one point I was standing in the backyard with this couple, not with them but near them, all of us in our winter coats because it was February, the trees naked and shivering against the houses, the moon leering in the starless sky. The guy of the couple started talking shit to me, saying he didn't like the way I was looking at him or his girlfriend, and I was calmly trying to explain to him that I didn't know any other way to look at them, and that if he knew so much about how to look at someone maybe he could demonstrate it for me and not be such a whiny little bitch about it, especially in front of his little bitch girlfriend, and all of a sudden the guy was beating the shit out of me. I was on the ground, my hands caked in spilled drinks and dead leaves, the guy's sneaker drilling me in the rib cage, darting at me again and again, shiny and persistent as the snout of a bull terrier. It didn't hurt too much. I was insulated by my coat and the cups of beer and Banker's Club, which muffled the worst of it, but also made it difficult for me to do anything to extract myself from my indefensible position. After some amount of time—several seconds, several minutes—other people intervened. The guy and his girlfriend were ejected from the party, and I was left to mutter self-righteously until a furious Cathy, summoned back from her apartment, came to collect me.

It wasn't a completely out-of-the-ordinary situation. It certainly wasn't the first time my drunken provocations had persuaded someone to hit me. The more disturbing thing was that, when I woke up the next day, Cathy told me how several of our friends at the party, including Smashley Smaniotto, agreed that I had thrown the first punch. I had no memory of it, of course, and denied that I would ever do such a thing—it didn't square at all with the impression that I had of myself. Nevertheless, something buzzed inside my skull, suggesting it might be true. An extra, unplaceable pang of guilt that hit me with the morning's hangover, mixed in with the headache and the nausea, the dehydration and the bruised ribs and the taste of metal in my mouth.

And that was a night I almost remembered. There were so many more, later ones, worse ones, that I didn't remember at all. Blank hours, redacted weekends, years that skipped discordantly like warped vinyl records. A drunk on autopilot through the streets and houses of Philadelphia.

I'd never discussed it with her, but I had a feeling that Cudahy was also at the party that night on Diamond Street.

\\\\\

Cudahy was making herself scarce. She snuck home late at night and slipped out early in the morning. I didn't know if she was embarrassed about knocking me down, or if she'd learned that Nate told me about NA, or if she was simply tired of all the quality time we'd been sharing. I wasn't sure if I should call her for a wellness check, or if that would make it seem like I didn't trust her to keep to the code on her own. I acted like everything was cool, even when she wasn't around for the next Dance Party Sunday. Ash didn't show up either. I danced in the basement by myself for a little while, but I couldn't quite lose myself in the music.

There weren't many writing gigs to fill my time. I started going on long walks around the neighborhood, smoking cigarettes and taking in the scenery. The broken sidewalks, the run-down houses, the rusting industrial campuses. The vacant lots, the boarded storefronts, the expressway snaking by the river. I ended up one afternoon at the Pathmark, so I stopped in and bought two packs of Camel Blues and a Turkey Hill iced tea. I had a buy-one-get-one-half-off coupon from my last pack of Camels, but the woman at the counter refused to accept it.

"What do you mean you won't accept it?" I asked her.

"It's our system," she said, her tone flat and unfriendly. "The system won't accept it."

"But what does that mean, the system won't accept it?" I asked. "Can't you make it accept it? Just accept it."

We ended up in a slightly heated exchange—*Accept it*, I kept repeating, like a madman, *just accept it*—until the manager stepped over and sorted it out. Anyway, there were some foam earplugs on a rotating stand by the customer service counter, the orange kind that construction workers wear, so I bought a pack of those as well. When I got back to the house, I left them out on the coffee table.

"What are these for?" asked Cudahy when she came home. It had been a few days since I'd seen her.

"Oh, I figure I'll wear them whenever I'm in my room," I said. "You know, to block out the noise."

"What noise?" she asked.

"You know, the noise," I said. I meant the noise from her room, the talking or whatever else she wanted to do with Nate, but I didn't say that. "The street noise, you know, when I'm working. Or meditating."

"You meditate?" she asked.

"Yeah, I meditate," I lied. "I've been thinking about getting into it, at least."

I told her about the writing gigs, how little money I'd made. I told her I'd probably go back to delivering lunches, but that I might not make the rent that month. I didn't mention the bill from urgent care.

"I can move out, if you want," I said. "I'm fine with that, too, if you want to find somebody more reliable."

"Huh," she said. But that was all she said about it. She went into the kitchen and put on a pot of coffee. She made a salad with arugula and fennel. We ate it standing up at the counter.

"This is really good," I said. "I like the fennel."

"Me too," she said. "It's like celery but with an extra kick."

"Life's kinda hard, huh?" I said. "Like, it's good, but it's hard, too."

"Yeah," she said.

"We're not always ourselves," I said.

"No, I think we're always ourselves," she said.

"We're not always in control of ourselves, I mean," I said.

"I agree with that," she said.

"And that's the hard part," I said. "The part when we're not in control of ourselves. And so is the part afterward, when we're back in control, but we don't understand why we lost control. Or where we went, or why we went there. It's like, why can't we just always be ourselves?"

"We are always ourselves," said Cudahy. "I think *that's* the hard part."

〰〰

A man was kicked to death outside of Citizens Bank Park in South Philadelphia. The fight started in one of the bars attached to the stadium and ended in Lot K. The cause of the dispute was a spilled beer. The Phils beat the Cardinals 14 to 6. I read the story to Cudahy from her laptop while we sat on her couch.

"I don't get baseball," said Cudahy.

"I get it, but I know what you mean," I said.

"Of all the reasons to kill someone," says Cudahy.

"You know, America actually has relatively low levels of sports violence compared to the rest of the world," I said. "Because of soccer."

"I hate soccer," said Cudahy.

"Me too," I said.

Cudahy leaned her head against my shoulder. "Put on something with animals," she said, and I searched the Netflix offerings. Cudahy was balled up next to me, her arms and knees pulled close to her chest for warmth. She was wearing a t-shirt and pajama shorts, and though the day had been hot, the evening was beginning to cool. Goose bumps rose across the sunburst tattoo on her thigh. Her head rested in the crook of my neck as she leaned in to see the screen. Her hair smelled like all the exotic teas I'd never tasted.

"Are we okay like this?" she asked, about the way our bodies were huddled against one another.

I intended to say of course we were, but instead I started to tell her about something that had happened on my walk home from the Pathmark the previous day, after I bought the earplugs. After I raised my voice to the woman at the customer service counter when she wouldn't accept my coupon for the Camels. I felt bad about that as soon as it was over. The woman hailed her manager and disappeared, and the manager sold me the cigarettes and the earplugs and the Turkey Hill iced tea, and I hung out in the parking lot for a while, drinking the tea and talking on the phone with Ivan, who called to ask me how the Brinks sticker had worked out. Beyond the Pathmark's roof loomed the nine or ten smokestacks of the old brick power station in Devil's Pocket, and I ticked them off one by one without actually counting them as Ivan complained about the home security business.

After I got off with Ivan, I tossed the tea bottle in a garbage can and headed to the intersection of 30th and Grays Ferry Avenue. There weren't many people around, just me and a short woman in a Pathmark smock with her bag slung over her shoulder. She must have just gotten off her shift. I slid a cigarette from one of my new packs while we stood waiting for the traffic signal to change, but as I went to light it, I realized that I'd left my Bic back at the house. I patted my pockets, muttering curses to myself. There I was with two packs of cigarettes, one of which I had caused a small scene in order to purchase at half-price, and I didn't even have a way to light them. If I'd noticed sooner, I could have asked the manager for matches, but it seemed slightly pathetic to go back in now. "Fuck," I whispered. "Fuck, fuck, fuck." I turned to the Pathmark woman to ask if she had a lighter. Only then did I realize it was the same woman who had refused to take my coupon, the woman to whom I had raised my voice in order to save four bucks. Standing there on the corner of Grays Ferry Avenue, beneath a bleary summer sunset intensified by industrial pollutants, she didn't look as old as she had looked in the grocery store. She was probably a few years younger than me. Her Pathmark smock was big on her, her cheeks bumpy with acne. She might have still been in high school. Instead of asking her for a light, which would have been too ridiculous at that point, I just kind of smiled at her with what I meant to be an apologetic grin. She stared back at me, straight-lipped, like she couldn't believe I had come up to her after what happened at the counter. Neither of us said anything. When the signal changed, she hurried across the intersection.

I was headed in the same direction, so I kept walking behind her down 30th Street, not even thinking about it, or about how I had an alarming gash on my forehead, still concerned only with my desire for a cigarette. I was annoyed that I had to wait to smoke until I got back to the house, but I was also annoyed that I was annoyed at all, since it was such a small thing in the grand scheme of things. Waiting ten minutes for a cigarette should have been easy for someone who'd quit drinking, who should have been able to quit anything. I noticed that every twenty yards or so, this woman—or girl, maybe, this high school or college-aged girl—would look back at me over her shoulder with a startled expression in her eyes. Maybe she thought I was following her instead of just walking in the same direction, even though pretty much all of Grays Ferry was in that direction. The sun was dropping out of the tinfoil sky, and the empty lots on either side of the street yawned between us and the distant houses.

I told all this to Cudahy as she lay there with her head on my shoulder, the laptop screen bare before us, the windows slack-jawed in the walls.

The girl walked faster and faster until she was a block ahead of me, almost jogging down the sidewalk. I looked around, wondering what she was so afraid of. I expected to see a gang of ruffians behind me, some cracked-out lunatic or a fiend with a knife, but there was no one. There was only me. I was baffled. Imagine being afraid of me? Me, who'd never won a fight in my life. What was I going to do to her? I was just a guy trying to smoke a cigarette, just a guy trying to live in the world. My confusion turned to anger, an unforeseen fury that seemed to boil up out of nowhere, and I had to stop myself from shouting after her, "Yo, Pathmark girl, what are you afraid of?"

I waited for Cudahy to laugh it off, the girl and the cigarettes and the whole thing. Instead, she repeated my question back to me.

"What are you afraid of?" She said it like she didn't quite understand the words, like she was struck only by the whooshing sound they made as they parted the heavy summer air. *"What—are—you—afraid—of?"*

MOYAMENSING

On my second morning in the house, I climbed up from my basement cot to hear a Pheasant record playing on Yana's turntable. It was all mawkish whines and guitar string squeaks, real sad-kid nonsense. I'd never liked Pheasant's music, despite the fact that he and I shared a hometown, and that he was only a few years ahead of me in school, and that I had met him once at the wedding of a friend when we'd both sat in the pew farthest from the altar. I wanted to appreciate somebody like that, somebody from the same place as me, but at the end of the day I was just too punk rock.

Yana was in the kitchen making a big show of cooking something. I understood her new culinary interest as a declaration of her independence from Hector, who used to do the cooking. The choice of the sad-kid music, though, was a mystery to me.

"Did somebody die?" I asked.

"Yeah, Pheasant did," said Yana, scraping eggs across a pan.

"Wait, really?" I asked. "Did Pheasant really die?"

"Heroin," said Yana. "In a house on Snyder."

"I thought he lived in Brooklyn?" I asked.

"Couldn't hack it," said Hector. Hector was seated at the dinette, fingering a thimble of espresso. I sat down next to him. I wanted an espresso, but I didn't know how to use the espresso machine. I had to wait for someone to offer to brew one for me. I knew how to brew drip coffee, but Yana and Hector did not own a drip coffee machine. Theirs was a cultivated lifestyle. They drove a tiny, pre-owned Fiat. They wore brimmed hats. Their appliances, wall art, and condiments conspired to make me feel like a bumpkin.

The record warbling on Yana's turntable was the old one. The first one, the one that people liked. "Was he still playing shows?"

"I think he was just doing heroin," said Hector.

"And burglary," said Yana.

"What a waste," said Hector.

"At least he did something beautiful with his life." Yana gave her spatula an elegiac twirl. "Some people just get loaded and beat the shit out of strangers on the bus."

Hector performed a seven-eight-four breathing exercise. He had recently found himself in an inebriated altercation with a man on a city bus that ended with Hector striking the man several times in the face. Hector was wearing a cast on his hand and had come home with the man's blood caked into the fiberglass. He decided to quit drinking over it. A few days later, Yana decided to quit Hector. Then Hector started drinking again, and then, a few days later, quit again, and then, two weeks after that, I'd showed up looking for a place to crash.

It had taken me a while to suss out the fact of their breakup. Not because they weren't acting lovingly toward one another in front of me, but because they had never acted lovingly toward one another in the seven years of their relationship. The rest of us—their friends—had held them up as proof that just because something looked precarious from the outside didn't mean it wasn't stable on the inside. But nothing is stable, it turns out.

As we sat around that morning listening to Pheasant, Hector was still sober and Yana still planned to leave, but they had agreed to cohabitate until the lease expired. Hector's lone demand was that she quit her job at the restaurant where they both waited tables, where he couldn't do anything but stew if she started flirting with the customers. Yana took a new job with their old manager, a Belgian guy named Roel, at a bar that was about to reopen on 10th Street. Hector told me he was pretty sure that Yana was fucking Roel, but his suspicion seemed based more in fear than in evidence.

Suffice it to say, it was a tense arrangement into which I had stumbled. I would have left—I planned to leave soon—but I didn't have alternate lodgings. Or cash. I was more or less unemployed. I considered sobriety my sole interest, occupation, and residence. Everything else was fluid. Yana and Hector let me stay because they saw me as a potential boon to their situation. Yana thought I might prove a helpful model for Hector's behavior, and Hector was glad to have someone with whom to commiserate in locations other than bars. I was happy to fill those roles and grateful for the cot they set up for me in the basement by the washing machine.

"How exactly is burglary beautiful?" asked Hector as he scratched at an itch beneath his cast with a letter opener.

"It can be," said Yana, "if it serves a higher ideal."

"Like what, buying heroin?"

"Like chasing the sublime," said Yana, "in whatever form it's available to us." I was always impressed by these turns of phrase Yana spun out of the air. English was her second language.

I thought I could hear Hector grind his teeth over the chirruping of Pheasant's posthumous croon. Before he could formulate a retort, he noticed my empty hands. "Can I get you an espresso, Monk?"

"Tow truck!" shouted Yana, stabbing with her spatula toward the front of the house. "Hector, tow truck!"

Hector dropped the letter opener and leaped to his feet. By the time I had swiveled in my chair, he'd left the front door ajar. Through the living room window, I saw a man with a long, limp strap in his hand standing beside the bumper of Hector and Yana's Fiat, which was parked along the curb in front of the house. A tow truck idled in the street behind him. Hector sped into view and launched himself across the Fiat's shallow hood with a hollow thunk. He lay there, spread-eagle, and commenced a heated discussion with the man. Profanities fluttered softly into the room.

"The asshole next door is trying to bully us out of our spot," said Yana. "He must know somebody at the Parking Authority. They put up signs with these ridiculous hours—no parking on weekdays nine to ten, two to three, six to seven, blah blah blah."

"Huh," I said.

"We filed a complaint with the city but it probably won't get settled before we move."

On the other side of the window, Hector squirmed into a sitting position. He kicked at the tow truck driver with one leg.

"I can't believe Pheasant is dead," I said. "You know I met him once? At Nick Assogna's wedding."

"I made out with him," said Yana, smiling beneath the regal gaze of the Beefeater gin handle that she liked to keep perched atop the refrigerator. "I was like fifteen, and he was like nineteen, which is kind of skeevy now that I think about it, but also I'm pretty sure I gave him mono. Here, eat these eggs."

\\\\\

Hector and Yana worked most nights, leaving me the run of the house. It was a little 1920s brick box on 11th Street in Lower Moyamensing, hardly the sort of place you'd want to spend your whole life. Yana kept the front bedroom in the split. Hector had moved to the back one, which served as the guest room whenever Yana's mother was in from Ukraine. The third bedroom—not offered to me—was the middle one, the tiny one. All Philadelphia row houses had more or less the same layout, and I'd occupied that room's equivalent half a dozen times in half a dozen neighborhoods. Denhelder used to call it the Monk Suite, since I would always take that room in exchange for a smaller slice of the rent. The 11th Street version was bedless and crammed with junk: hand weights, yoga mats, disassembled furniture. A desk was stacked with Scandinavian crime novels, LSAT study guides, and aviation manuals from when Hector was trying to get a pilot's license. One slim window was set in the corner that overlooked the backyard, which wasn't a yard so much as a patch of concrete and a chain-link fence. The late-afternoon sunlight bounced off the walls of the other houses and angled through the cloudy windowpane in a way that turned the room a lonesome shade of gray, almost purple, almost orange.

I went up there the first time they left me alone, thinking I could clear a space for the cot and not have to sleep in the basement, but there was simply too much shit. I could barely pull the chair far enough from the desk to sit down. I rested my laptop on the aviation manuals. I thought I might try to write something about Pheasant. The information was out there on the Internet, but I could collate it, make it pretty. Insert myself into the narrative, maybe publish it somewhere. Sobriety was, among other things, self-aggrandizing. I was incapable of conceiving a project without placing myself at the center of it.

Pheasant's real name was Derek DiTraglia. He made demos in his childhood bedroom, got famous on Myspace. It was early in the century, when earnest guitar music for emotional teenagers was briefly cool again. Pheasant was one of a thousand swoop-haired muppets trying to be Elliott Smith. He wowed an indie-flavored imprint of a major label enough that they put out his debut. It got some buzz on the cool music sites and in the alt-weeklies. One of his songs was used on an MTV show about rich kids who lived at the beach. That impressed us, back home, even though we all hated the show. The record netted Pheasant a tiny bit of fame and a tiny bit of money, but mostly it spoke to his *potential.* When the follow-up failed to deliver on that potential, people lost interest in a third. I met him a few years after that at Nick Assogna's wedding. The open bar ran out of booze by nine o'clock, and I was pretending not to be bothered, sweating with my cigarettes in the parking lot of the banquet hall. Pheasant smoked too. Or Derek, as he introduced himself. I didn't even realize who he was, which was lucky for him, since it saved him from having to listen to my diagnosis of the missteps in his career, like how an Elliott Smith knockoff was bound to fail because Elliott Smith was trash and people only pretended he wasn't trash because he died young. Instead, we talked about Brooklyn. I didn't know anything about Brooklyn, but Pheasant had just moved there and had a lot to say about it.

A drunk and a junkie, watching the sky swoon and darken over the roofs of a nearby subdivision. That's how I'd need to frame the article. I'd need to claim that I recognized him as an addict right away—his skin crawling, his eyes glassy as he plotted his escape from the reception. But I didn't actually know whether he was using at the time. He left early, but he might have just been bored, or tired, or navigating his own yearslong existential predicament. A person in the midst of a serious opiate addiction might not have shown up at all. Pheasant may still have had it together at that point, more together than me, who ended up leaving the reception to hike half a mile down the highway to a pool hall just to get a drink. I nearly got nailed by two different drivers, tramping down the narrow shoulder in my black suit after dark. There were a growing number of people whose premature deaths, when held up against my own continued existence, just bewildered the fuck out of me.

\\\\\\

Hector and I walked to the ACME on Passyunk Avenue to buy a birthday cake. It was nobody's birthday as far as we knew, but Hector had a sweet tooth since he stopped drinking, and he'd read on the Internet that it was okay to indulge in some of his less destructive impulses, and there was an ACME circular in his mailbox with a coupon for ten percent off any sheet cake. Hector said he wanted a big one. He wanted to feast until his hunger for cake was permanently appeased.

Hector Villona was a different sort of alcoholic than me. I wasn't certain that he was an alcoholic at all. I didn't say that to him, of course. I expressed solidarity. My alcoholism was a lot of craving and scheming, sneaking and self-deluding. It was psychological. Spiritual. What some people found in the Church, or the natural world, or the accumulation of wealth and prestige, I found in booze. Its absence from my life was louder than the absence of God. But Hector was not called to strong drink in the same way as me. He liked it, sure. Everybody liked it. But most of the time, in his daily life, he was able to cut himself off when it came time to do so. A drink or two at lunch or dinner could be held at just that, without duplication, the way a person can eat two apples and not throw away the rest of his afternoon in order to eat thirteen more. Hector's problem was that sometimes, when he was drinking, something would try his patience and, exasperated, he would lash out with his fist. Normally it was against inanimate objects—brick walls, telephone poles, public art. There were only a small number of instances where he'd hit another person, and we, his friends, could normally summon some justification as to why that person deserved it. Everybody liked Hector. He was gregarious and knew a lot about wine. Whatever he had, he would gladly share it with you, from a six-pack to a dime bag to a twelve-by-sixteen-inch sheet cake. Plus, Yana had been with him forever, and Yana wasn't the sort of woman to stick around with some violent drunk. These things insulated Hector and kept him safe from the sort of accusations that got leveled at less popular substance abusers.

We picked chocolate on chocolate. Icing and cake both.

"I'm almost worried it will be too much chocolate," I said.

"I'm not fucking around," said Hector.

The day was warm and the walk home was long and it seemed sensible to eat at least some of the cake in the parking lot. We wandered the store's aisles in search of plastic forks and paper plates. The ACME was built on the former site of Moyamensing Prison, a medieval-looking fortress that once hosted a suicidal Edgar Allan Poe for a night. I liked to imagine that his spirit infested the property. There, by the bin of pomegranates, I pictured him on a cot just like mine, sleeping off a drunk after they fished him from the Schuylkill. There, by the display of coconut oil, he vomited whiskey and river water onto the floor of his cell. Around us, shoppers shopped, refusing to be haunted.

"We should get some almond milk for this jawn," said Hector.

We set up on a bench outside. It was a messy production. We'd bought forks but no knives. We speared hunks from the cake's perimeter. It was dense and flavorful, much better than I expected for a supermarket cake. So much of life was actually pretty good. I said that to Hector, how it was important to appreciate the day-to-day stuff, but he wasn't listening to me. He was just eating his cake and staring across the street at the Triangle, the bar where Yana worked with Roel. It was an old neighborhood spot, shut down for years by a late-night fire and slated to reopen in a few weeks under Roel's management. Yana was helping him get things going. I wondered if our errand to get cake was just about putting Hector within view of the place.

"You talked to Bors recently?" I asked him. "He moved back to Idaho."

"Yeah, he sent me a picture of him sitting in the bed of a pickup truck like it was a hot tub," said Hector. "He filled the truck bed with water somehow."

"Maybe you should visit him," I said. "Change of scenery. I moved home for a while when I first got sober. Just to get my head straight."

"Yeah, maybe," said Hector. A crumble of cake slipped from his fork and landed on his lap. He brushed it off with too much force and smeared it into the denim of his jeans. "Fuck," he said.

"This Pheasant thing is messing with me a bit," I said. "You know I met him at Nick Assogna's wedding?"

"Yeah, me too," said Hector. "I was at that wedding."

"Oh yeah," I said. "I'm starting to think maybe I never properly mourned certain people. People who died while I was drinking."

"Like who?" asked Hector.

"Like Denhelder, for one," I said.

"Oh yeah," said Hector. "That was sad."

"Do you think you fully felt everything, with Denhelder? All the things you needed to feel?"

Hector scratched at the stain on his lap. "Yeah, I think so. It was pancreatitis, right?"

"Yeah," I said.

"It's weird to die of pancreatitis so young, isn't it?"

"I think so," I said.

"Same thing happened to Dion Tilelli," said Hector. "Or maybe Dion had epilepsy."

"Dion Tilelli isn't dead," I said.

"Yeah he is. Of epilepsy. Or pancreatitis. One or the other."

"I don't think so," I said. "I think I would have heard about that. His brother is best friends with my brother."

"I'm pretty sure he's dead, dude. Or, like, pretty fucked up. Like, permanently hospitalized." A pigeon wobbled along the curb and Hector tossed a piece of cake at it.

"I had no idea," I said.

"Yep," said Hector. "Sad shit."

"I started to have all these feelings," I said. "For the first six months after I quit drinking, it was like I was made of feelings. I would cry over anything. Everything was so beautiful and devastating."

Hector thought for a moment. "I was thinking about my cousin Gwen the other day, you know. How she died."

"Your cousin Gwen died?" I asked. "When did that happen?"

"That was like a year and a half ago," said Hector. A second pigeon ambled up and he threw more cake. "She was with this guy for a long time, one of these psychos who doesn't believe in medicine. Anyway, she got pregnant, and then she got some kind of infection, and he wouldn't let her go to the hospital, and then she died. The baby too. We didn't know how he was treating her, of course, until afterward. I was gonna beat the shit out of him, but he got arrested, first, for something else."

"Christ," I said. "How did I miss that?"

"I called you," said Hector. "I don't remember if you picked up."

"Really?" I said. "I can't believe I missed that. Did you leave me a message?"

"Don't worry about it," said Hector. "It just would have been nice to beat the shit out of him before he got arrested. It was some drug thing."

"I can't believe I missed that," I said again. "Jesus."

"Yeah, it was sad," said Hector.

"Yeah," I said. "Do you want to talk about it?"

"We just did. I said it was sad as shit." Hector took a swig from the carton of almond milk. "We could go get drunk right now, huh?" He nodded to the Triangle. "Just for today. Start over tomorrow."

"I can't do that," I said. I was proud of how quickly I said it.

"Yeah, you've got nine months," said Hector. "I've only got sixteen days. That's barely anything."

"Time accrues slowly," I said.

"I feel like it used to move faster." Hector kept his eyes on the door of the Triangle. "That was the best thing about time."

"Relapse is always out there," I said. "No matter how long it's been. There's always a liquor store down the street. There's always a bar open till two in the morning. Most days you won't be tempted, as long as you've got your head on straight. Like just now. You suggested we drink, and I wasn't tempted."

Hector grunted.

"The problem," I said, "is when something goes wrong, some unrelated thing. Your girlfriend leaves you, for example. Somebody dies. That's when you really have to be vigilant."

"I shouldn't be drinking anyway," said Hector. "They've got me on oxy for this broken hand, and I think mixing it with the booze might have been the problem. The Internet said one of the side effects is heightened disinhibition." He took the pills from his pocket and gave them a shake. "Also respiratory arrest, changes in blood pressure, and dehydration. You want one?"

"You should take it easy with those," I said. "Don't take more than the doctor says."

Hector shook the pills at the pigeons. They didn't like the sound and flew away.

\\\\\\\

I decided I would call Pheasant's parents. It seemed like the journalistic thing to do. There were aspects of the story I could not glean from the Internet. The intangibles of it. The emotional architecture. I was sitting on top of the Fiat at Hector and Yana's request. The tow truck materialized unpredictably during the hours listed on the sign, and it was easier to sit there than to have to keep running in and out of the house. My shift was six to seven in the evening. I laid a cushion from a patio chaise lounge over the hood and windshield. It wasn't that bad, really. Six to seven was the prettiest time of the day, the sky electrified, the shadows crumbling off the buildings like cigarette ash. You could hear people, if not always see them, echoing from backyards or adjacent blocks. The thump of car stereos. The skirl of the Mister Softee truck.

The Internet provided facts. Two years after the wedding, Pheasant surfaced in the police blotter of the Southampton Press. Someone had lent him the use of a guest house in Wainscott for the summer. Long Island. I'd never been there. It was easy to imagine a songwriter secluding himself in a walled-off property by the sea to work on his art, but addicts did not generally go on retreats. My guess was that Pheasant reached a point where he could no longer pay rent, and that he was attempting to escape some deteriorating relationships in Brooklyn, and that he hoped a new location would help to sever whatever restrictive social bonds were keeping him from living the addict life he needed to live. Bouncing from place to place without the stress of obligations liberated a certain type of post-ambitious person. Even sober, I found existence simplified by sleeping on a cot next to a washing machine.

But Pheasant had expenditures. Here were the Hamptoms, affluent hamlets, resort towns, places where people tended not to lock their doors, where properties stood empty for weeks at a time. A strange face was not uncommon, and a young, thin, white man in a nice shirt was hardly a cause for alarm. The Southampton Press referred to it as "a four-day burglary spree" across Bridgehampton, Water Mill, and Sagaponack. When police searched the Wainscott guest house, they discovered that "Mr. DiTraglia of Pennsylvania" had stolen over $100,000 in jewelry, electronics, cash, and prescription pills. Pheasant robbed the properties in broad daylight, carrying his loot to his car in pilfered pillowcases. He only got caught because one of the houses proved not to be empty. The woman heard him rifling through the drawers in her daughter's bedroom. "I'm so sorry," he said when she confronted him. He dropped the pillowcase and walked slowly out the front door, apologizing the whole time. She got a look at the plates on his Subaru and that was that. Eight counts of breaking and entering. Six counts of larceny. One count of criminal possession of a controlled substance. The judge gave him eighteen months, a $3,000 fine, and an order to attend an inpatient drug treatment program following his release from prison. Plus he had to write letters of apology to the homeowners he'd robbed. Pretty lenient, all things considered.

I found a number for the DiTraglias in an online directory. I figured they would let it ring, I'd leave a message, they wouldn't call me back, and I wouldn't blame them. It had only been a few days since their son died. They would still be insensible with grief. I planned to express my condolences, then slip in something about the article right at the end. *I'm working on a celebration of Derek's career.* That sounded okay. *It will be a celebration of Derek's life and work.*

"Hello?" said a voice in my ear.

It was a woman's voice. I wasn't prepared for a person to answer. The words evaporated from my mouth.

"Hello?" she said again. Her voice was bassy, middle-aged, but she didn't sound as though she had been crying. She sounded like my mother did when I was young and someone called while we were eating dinner.

"Is this Mrs. DiTraglia?" I asked. I sat up straighter, lifting my back up off the cushioned windshield.

"Speaking," she said. "Who is this?"

"Yeah, sorry, this is Hector Villona." It seemed safer, somehow, not to be myself. "I'm a friend of Derek's? I just wanted to call and offer my condolences."

"Oh yes," said the woman. "Thank you."

"It's all very sad," I said. "I've been very sad about it."

"It's a nightmare," said the woman. "How did you know Derek?"

"From school. And we actually live quite close to each other, or did, these past few . . . how long did he live down here? In South Philadelphia, I mean?"

"Just a few weeks," she said. "He was here with us, before that."

"So not long," I said. "I didn't see him down here. That's why I asked. I didn't know he was down here."

"He may not have known you were there," she said. "He wasn't great at keeping in touch with people."

"Same," I said. I knew I should say something else, but my mind had gone blank as soon as she picked up the phone. I thought about hanging up.

"We bought him a guitar and a mixer when he got out of the treatment center," she said, filling the silence. "I don't know if he used them.

He was running a lot, around the lake in the park. Drinking a lot of juice. He would run for miles every day."

"Wow," I said. "To keep busy, you mean?"

"I think so. When he was a teenager he would work on his music in his room for hours and hours. When he moved back home, we got him a guitar and a mixer and thought, maybe he can throw himself into that again. But he chose running. Whatever works, we thought."

"Whatever works," I agreed.

"He must have gone through a bag of oranges a day," she said. I heard a car in the background, as though she had stepped outside. "I thought it would be good for him to move out. His father didn't want him to leave, but I thought it would be good for him to be back on his feet, out in the world. And Derek wanted that too."

"I can understand that."

"We cosigned the lease," she said. "We paid his rent. But maybe it was too early."

"Maybe," I said.

"Or too late," she said. "I don't know."

"Mrs. DiTraglia," I said. "I'm sort of a writer in addition to being Derek's friend. And I, um . . ." I thought about telling her about my alcoholism, but I didn't want it to sound like I was asking her for anything. At least not from that part of me. "I was thinking about writing an article about him. For a magazine. Or maybe a website." I tried to name one, but I wasn't up on my music websites. I didn't read music journalism.

"Oh really?" she asked. I couldn't tell how she felt about it.

"Really," I said. "So anything you could tell me about Derek, about these last few years, that would be really helpful."

"Do you have specific questions?" she asked.

I didn't. Whatever questions I'd had, I couldn't remember them. "I do, of course, but I can ask them later. This was just a call to offer my condolences. And to mention the article. To see if you'd be interested in participating."

"I'll have to think about it," she said.

"Of course," I said. "It will be a celebration. Of Derek's work. And his life."

"Right," she said. "I should probably go now. But I appreciate you calling. Your name is Hector?"

"It is, yeah."

"It's very hard to lose a child," she said. "They tell you it's hard, of course. Still, it happens all the time and people figure it out, don't they?"

"I guess they do," I said. I grasped for something more to say, but she hung up.

I lay on the Fiat's hood as the sunlight faded and shadows anonymized the houses. I marveled at how well Mrs. DiTraglia was handling things. I thought that my mother would probably manage my death pretty well. But, then, I had a brother. That would probably make it easier. I had not yet established, in my research, whether or not Pheasant was an only child.

At five minutes to seven the tow truck crept past, Hall & Oates blaring from his open windows.

\\\\\

Yana and I went to the record store on Reed Street to see if they stocked the second Pheasant album, the one Yana didn't have in her collection. She assured me it wasn't any good, but I needed to hear it for myself. The burglaries had recast Pheasant's music in a savage new light. Here was a man familiar with life's delinquent urgency.

Yana Bondar was born in either Kiev or Odessa—I could never remember which, only that she loved one and hated the other. She'd come to the United States at the age of twelve, just as her accent was solidifying, ensuring that she would forever sound like a foreigner in both countries. Her parents and sister had since returned to Europe, leaving Yana the lone practicing American in the family. She sent a portion of every paycheck she earned from her waitressing job to her sister, who was studying archeology in Berlin, with the understanding that the sister would one day return the favor when Yana started law school in the States. I told Yana I would never enter into that sort of arrangement with any member of my family. Yana said the arrangement was with herself.

It wasn't hard to discern in Yana's biography certain expectations that Hector might not entirely satisfy. He had dropped out of college and, at twenty-six, exhibited no signs of reenrolling to finish his degree. He was a good waiter, but that was hardly a career. Yana could scrimp and remit for a time, but not if such sacrifices were unlikely to be reciprocated.

The record store specialized in metal and hardcore punk, with only limitted offerings in other genres. Pheasant was unrepresented in their section for local musicians. I asked the clerk if there'd been a run on his albums since his death. She asked me who I was talking about.

"Pheasant," I repeated. "The seminal Bucks County singer-songwriter? Recently of Snyder Street? He died last week of a heroin overdose?"

"Oh, somebody mentioned him earlier," said the clerk. Dreadlocks dangled from the back of her head, while the tightly cropped hair at the top and sides was dyed yellow and teal. "I don't know his shit."

Yana took out her phone and played the single from the first album, the one with the music video of Pheasant running around in slow motion dressed as a bird. We stood, the three of us, listening to it. I felt for the briefest second like I was in danger of tearing up.

"Is this *not* Elliott Smith?" asked the clerk.

Yana bought the new Hop Along record. We got back to the house just in time for her two o'clock shift at the Fiat. She put the record on in the living room so we could listen through the open window, our backs warm against the car's sunbaked hood.

Yana had fixed herself a gin and tonic with the Beefeater she kept on top of the refrigerator. She fixed me a tonic with a slim, limp wedge of lime. She stuck some corkboard coasters up by the windshield wipers so the glasses wouldn't make rings on the paint. In the face of Hector's sobriety, Yana made no effort to curtail her own drinking. Not that she should have. I didn't see the point of sacrifice as a gesture to accommodate other people. Everyone ended up doing whatever they wanted anyway.

"My bus stop in middle school, when I lived on Briar Road?" said Yana, counting her fanned fingers. "There were only four of us. Me, Dusty Pio, Jake Heffenhoffer, and Scottie Straub. All three of them ODed before they were twenty-five. Fentanyl, my friend. Do not fuck with her."

I disliked tonic. It made me want gin. Not enough to drink gin, but to imagine how it would be to drink it. The day was hot, but the air felt kinetic. The record played in the invisible living room. The singer sounded throaty and exasperated, the kind of voice you might hear shouted after you down the street, asking just what it was you thought you were doing with your life.

"There's a lot I don't remember," I said. "You black out, something sets you off, and who knows? I could see how it happened, with Hector and the man on the bus."

"What's your point?"

"Just thinking out loud," I said. "I'm always afraid to go to parties. I'll see somebody looking at me, or maybe I just think they're looking at me, and I wonder if I've met them before. Did we talk, and what did I say if we did? And what do they want from me now? I never quite know where I stand with people."

"What parties?" asked Yana. "Who's inviting you to parties?"

"I mean, nobody," I said. "Not in a while."

"Well, tell me if you get invited somewhere," said Yana. "Because I would like to go to some parties."

Side A ended. The turntable's arm clicked back to its resting position.

"How are things going, breakup-wise?" I asked.

Yana took a loud sip of her cocktail. Gin would flow differently than tonic by itself, feel different in the mouth. Cleaner, somehow. "It's been fun sleeping with other people," she said. "I've been with Hector since I was nineteen. I kept wondering, am I going to give all of my twenties to this guy? This one guy? Forget the rest of my life. Giving your twenties to a person, that's the sacrifice. Hector's great, but is he all-of-my-twenties great?"

"Is that why you broke up?" The taste of quinine was like a film on my tongue. "I thought it was because he beat up that guy on the bus."

"That's just what he thinks it's about," said Yana. "And don't get me wrong, it's fucked up. But I mostly give him shit about it because he's been such a moody dick lately."

"So it's not really about his drinking," I said.

"Some people have to make themselves the guilty party. They can't deal with a universe governed by something other than their own bullshit." Yana collected our glasses and disappeared into the house. I heard the tonic fizz in the kitchen. What if she mixed up the glasses, I wondered? I would smell mine before taking a sip. But would I take a sip anyway, just to be sure? The record flipped to side B. Yana came out and sat back on the hood.

I sniffed the glass she handed me. Tasted it. Just tonic.

"I love Hector," she said. "Like I love my sister. I love my parents. But I have my own life to live, you know? I'm twenty-five years old. Like, when is it my turn to beat up a man on a bus?"

\\\\\\

I went to see Pheasant's house on Snyder Street. I figured I could pop over and get back before my six o'clock shift at the Fiat. It was only a few blocks from Hector and Yana's place, the same neighborhood, served by the same mini-mart, the same Mexican restaurant. Had I come to crash with Hector a few days sooner, I might have passed Pheasant on the sidewalk. We could have hurried by one another unacknowledged, our eyes on our shoes, our minds occupied with setting our respective ghosts in order.

There was nothing to mark the house. A smooth face of tan brick, three windows and a front door, plain as a sun-bleached skull. The blinds were drawn, veiling the front room from view. I didn't know what I expected. Some sort of sidewalk shrine, maybe. Votive candles and a floral wreath. Maybe a guitar pick Pheasant dropped on the stoop, wedged into a crack between the bricks. But what kind of house could have impressed me? A house was just a house, after all. A row house even more so. They were built to smooth away the irregularity of their inhabitants.

I sat on the stoop, thinking that Pheasant probably sat on the stoop a couple of times during the month he'd lived there. He'd been approaching two years of sobriety, two years since his Hamptons burglary spree. Two years was no joke. Most people who tried it didn't make it that long. He would have anticipated the anniversary, ticked down the days. He would have taken stock of his surroundings, that little house, that quiet street. South Philadelphia was strangely empty in the late summer. Neighbors disappeared down the shore for the weekend, shops shuttered earlier than expected. And yet there was always music playing somewhere, drifting in at the edge of hearing where he couldn't quite make out the tune, though he was sure that he'd heard one like it before. Maybe the air was warm and pliable and reassuring, like a hand on the small of his back. Maybe the scent of coffee crept from his kitchen as he smoked cigarettes in his open doorway, pondering whether it was indeed too early to go to bed.

Most days that would be enough. Most days, that would be more than enough for anyone. But there was always that rare day, that last day, when the thing that could not happen somehow did. On a long enough timeline, every addict found his relapse.

"Hector," said Mrs. DiTraglia after a couple of rings.

"How's it going over there?" I asked. "I just walked by Derek's old house, and I thought I'd give you a call." I was still sitting on the stoop, but that seemed like a creepy thing to admit.

"I haven't decided anything yet about the article," she said. "If I'm being honest, I haven't really started to think about it."

"That's alright," I said. "I'm sure you've got a lot going on."

"It's mostly just sorting through things at this point," she said. "His stuff is still in the South Philly house. I'll need to hire movers to clean it out."

"I thought I should mention," I started to say, then paused. I had no plan, and when I started again, the words came quickly. "I meant to mention it before. I'm an alcoholic. A recovering one. I'm nine months sober. I know that's different than what Pheasant—than what Derek was, but—"

"Congratulations," she said. "On your sobriety."

"I don't know what he went through, of course."

"Of course," she said. "Neither do I."

"But that's my point, I guess," I said. "Drinking was the loneliest time of my life."

"I'm sure it was," she said.

"And so I figured not drinking wouldn't be like that," I said. "You know, with so many people going through the same thing. But it's been the second loneliest time."

"And you think Derek was lonely, too," she said.

"Maybe he was," I said. "But I don't know."

"It's a shame he didn't know you were living so close by," she said. "Maybe," she started to say. "I don't know. It's hard to say."

For a few blank seconds, I could hear her moving around, walking down a hallway. "My husband just pulled in the driveway," she said. "He went out to get us some sandwiches."

After we hung up, I sat on the stoop for a little longer, replaying the conversation in my head. It went okay, I thought. Not perfectly, perhaps, but what had I wanted it to be?

I got back to Hector's at quarter after six. The Fiat was towed.

\\\\\\

The neighbor had squeezed his hulking Buick into the empty spot by the time Hector got home from work. I worried Hector might respond destructively. I waited at the dinette in case he wanted to yell at me a bit, but he only nodded and went upstairs. Yana was already in bed. They bickered for a while, then shouted, and then went quiet. I slunk off to my basement. When I woke in the morning, they were gone.

I spent my day in the little bedroom, typing out my ideas about Pheasant. Assembled on the page, they didn't amount to much more than some decontextualized quotes from online sources, plus my own half-formed thoughts. I found his second album on YouTube, hoping it would prove revelatory. I took my laptop out to the backyard and listened to the songs beneath the oil-slick sky. They disappointed.

Hector showed up around nine o'clock in the Fiat, freshly bailed from the impound lot. He banged around the house for a while, trudging up and down the stairs like he kept forgetting something, then asked if I wanted to go for a ride to the ACME. "I want a Klondike bar," said Hector. "Doesn't that sound good right now? A Klondike bar?"

When we got to 10th and Reed, Hector failed to turn into the ACME lot. Instead, he parked illegally in front of the Triangle. "There's an old mirror in there Yana wanted for the house," he said as he slipped from the driver's seat. "She asked me to grab it for her a couple weeks ago."

"Do you want help?"

"I got it," he said. "You sit with the car."

I reached across the dashboard and flipped on the hazard lights, then watched the shoppers in the ACME lot tuck their groceries gently into their trunks. There was something soporific about it—the swing of laden bags, the thunk of doors—until it was interrupted by the profane vibration of my phone in my pocket. I didn't recognize the number on the screen.

"Hector?" said the voice when I answered it. It was a man's voice.

"Excuse me?" I asked.

"Is this Hector, who's writing the article?"

"Um, yeah," I said. "Who am I speaking to?"

"This is Derek's father," said the man. He spoke softly, his words slightly slurred. "My wife said you are writing an article about Derek for a magazine."

"I am," I said. "Or, you know, maybe a website. Either or."

"Can I ask you a question?" The man's voice was quiet and disarmingly sincere. "What is it that you like about Derek's music?"

"What do I like about it?" I repeated. "The point of the article isn't so much what I like about it, necessarily."

"But you do like the music?"

"It isn't really my preferred genre."

"I never liked it," said the man after a pause. "I wanted to, after he was killed. Other people seemed to like it. I guess I was hoping you could explain it to me."

"I think he could have written good music, given more time," I said. "I'm sorry, did you say 'killed?'"

"Killed, yes," said the man. "What would you call it?"

"I'm not sure," I said. "I heard it was a heroin overdose."

"The murder weapon," said the man. For several seconds he filled the line with heavy breathing. When I said nothing, he continued. "The perfect murder weapon, isn't it? Who's going to think twice about a young guy with a history of heroin use turning up dead?"

"What are you saying, exactly?" I asked.

"He was *clean*," said Mr. DiTraglia. "He was done with that shit."

I shook my head, glad he couldn't see the look on my face. "It's very tragic when people relapse, sir."

"His mother," the man murmured, as though afraid of being overheard. "His mother seems *relieved*."

"You know, Mr. DiTraglia," I started to say, "I'm actually a recovering—"

I was interrupted then by the real Hector, who rammed his shoulder into the driver's-side window. "We gotta go," Hector panted, his words muffled through the glass. He was carrying a cardboard box. He balanced it on the roof of the car as he slid the door open. "Hang up the phone."

"Where's the mirror?" The box looked like a liquor box. "Hector, what's with the box?"

"Hector?" repeated Mr. DiTraglia.

"Yes, sorry, my friend just got here."

"I thought I was already speaking to Hector," he said.

"Get off the phone," repeated Hector. "Off the phone, off the phone."

"I am Hector," I said. "I'm also Hector. We're both named Hector."

"Who is this?" Mr. DiTraglia's voice rose and sharpened. "Who put you up to this?"

I hung up. Hector shoved the box onto my lap, turned the ignition, and pulled into the street. I peered into the box. Six glass bottles were nestled in paper straw. I lifted one to read the Hendrick's label.

"Is this gin?"

Hector stepped hard on the gas. He hooked right on Wharton without pausing at the stop sign. "Yeah," he said, "he was holding it."

"Who?"

"Roel," said Hector. "I think I killed him."

"What?"

"I went around back and he was unloading his truck. I hit him in the back of the head and he just crumpled. Like, hit the ground hard. Lots of blood. I didn't know what to do, so I took the gin and ran."

"And you think he's dead?"

"I don't know, man. He just dropped, and he didn't get back up."

My phone rang again. It was the same number as before. I let it ring.

"Why did you do that?" I asked. "Why would you do that?"

"Because that Belgian fuck stole my girlfriend."

"He can't be dead," I said. "Do you really think he's dead?"

"I hit him in the back of the head. He fell over. I took the gin." Hector repeated it as though it didn't make any more sense to him than it did to me. "I think maybe I just double-broke my hand." He held up the cast. "Is there blood on this?"

"We should go back and make sure he's not dead," I said.

"Are you shitting me? I just committed assault. With a deadly weapon, potentially. I gotta get rid of this fucking thing."

He reached over the box on my lap to smack the door of the glove compartment. It spilled out onto my knees and he grabbed his letter opener from the tangle of tickets and receipts. Without taking his foot from the gas pedal, he slid the narrow instrument under the cast and cracked it from within like a lobster claw, steering the car with his elbow.

"What the fuck are you doing?" I yelled. "Stop driving! Jesus Christ, stop the car!"

Hector refused to slow down until we were out of the city. He pulled off I-76 at the Conshohocken exit and turned into an empty Wawa parking lot. The only souls in the fluorescent-soaked store were the straggly kid manning the register and a brusque, scowling woman making sandwiches at the deli. They stared at us like we had barged in on something private and emotionally fraught.

We bought cigarettes. Hector bought a meatball hoagie. We sat in the Fiat, smoking and figuring out the next move. Hector thought he should drive to Idaho. He could stay with Bors, he said. Find a job at a restaurant. I wondered if I should go, too, but I decided that if Roel were truly dead, then leaving with Hector would probably make me some sort of accomplice. I'd be better off going back to 11th Street and pretending I'd never been anywhere near the Triangle.

"You don't think those two inside will remember us, do you?" I asked, casing the Wawa in the rearview mirror.

Hector stared vacantly through the windshield. Across the road, a bright, unattended gas station hummed in the night. Beyond it dozed a clump of tidy apartment towers.

"You should go to a hospital and get a new cast," I told him.

"I'll do it in Idaho," he said. "I can drive with my other hand."

"I don't think you should take the gin."

"Of course I'm going to take the gin," he said. "Hendrick's is a premium gin."

"You're not going to make it past Harrisburg if you're sipping gin the whole way."

"I didn't say I was going to sip it. I'll pick up a fucking cappuccino." He pulled one of the bottles from the box. "Just put this on the table when you get back to the house. For Yana."

I was alarmed to see the bottle there in my hand. "I don't think you should be handing me booze right now."

"You're making this about shit that this isn't about. Just leave it on the table. This too." He fished an envelope out of the glove compartment. "And there's one piece of cake left in the fridge. Put that out, with the rest."

He nodded toward the passenger-side door like he wanted me to get out of the car.

"What?" I asked. "That's it?"

"I gotta split. The cops might already be looking for me."

"Hector, how am I going to get home? We're in fucking Conshohocken."

"I'm on the lam, goddamnit," he said, raising his voice for the first time. "I can't solve all your problems for you, Monk. All you do is mope around and listen to sad-kid music like we're still in high school. Move on already. Get a hobby."

I slid out of the car and slammed the door. The thud echoed across the asphalt of the parking lot, reverberating over the lip of freshly sprinkled grass to the empty road. Hector rolled down the passenger window.

"Yo, thanks for talking to me about that thing with my cousin," he said.

"What thing?"

"My cousin, Gwen," he said. "Thanks for listening to me about that."

He rolled up the window, the glass reflecting the night back at me, obscuring him from view. Then his tires rumbled across the parking lot, and the Fiat was gone.

I stood there with the bottle of Hendrick's in my hand, pissed that I hadn't simply left it in the car. It felt different than the handle of gin that Yana kept on top of the refrigerator, a clear crystal jug whose surface line I tracked each day like a man checking the weather. The Hendrick's bottle was heavy and smooth, the glass so dark that you couldn't see how much was in it. I hadn't sought it out, hadn't bought it, hadn't stolen it. Someone had handed it to me.

I looked at the map on my phone. The black Schuylkill flowed a hundred yards to my right. A SEPTA station waited on the far bank. I tucked the bottle under my arm and began my hike down the street. A narrow walkway for pedestrians led up the ramp to the bridge. Cars sped infrequently within a foot of my left shoulder, their lights flashing as though startled to find me there in the dark. I kept the bottle under my right arm, tucked away from the light where no one could see it.

When I left the Wawa parking lot, I was one hundred percent certain that I would not drink the Hendrick's. One hundred percent certain that I could carry it all the way to 11th Street and place it safely on the table with Hector's envelope and the final piece of cake before smoking a cigarette in the backyard and going to bed. Envelope, cake, cigarette, bed. Easy. Sane. By the time I got to the bridge, however, with the invisible river sloshing beneath me, my certainty had slipped to eighty-five percent. A loss of fifteen percent in just a few hundred feet, with a long train ride still ahead of me.

I tossed the unopened bottle off the side of the bridge, slightly shy of the halfway mark. It dropped straight down, like Poe must have dropped when he threw himself into the Schuylkill years and years ago. I never heard the splash, just hurried the rest of the way to the far bank, and as I waited on the inbound platform, my confidence crept back up until I was once again one hundred percent certain that I would never have drunk the Hendrick's, no way in hell.

Forty minutes later, speeding along the nighttime rails in an otherwise empty train car, I broke out in a frantic sweat. It was smeared so thick across the vinyl cushions that I needed to change seats.

\\\\\\

When I climbed the basement stairs the next morning, Yana was seated at the dinette, eating the last piece of sheet cake in sullen silence. The envelope held a check for Hector's share of the remaining months' rent.

"This is terrible cake," she said. "I could bake a better cake than this."

Yana fixed me an espresso. As she did, she told me about the hysterical call she'd fielded from Roel, during which she'd claimed Hector couldn't have been his attacker, as he'd been out of town for several days.

"Roel was being such a baby about it," said Yana. "He has a very low pain threshold."

I was extremely relieved to hear that Roel remained among the living. I covertly texted the good news to Hector. By that point, he must have been somewhere in Illinois.

"That Fiat was half mine." Yana slid me the tiny mug. "This thing with the rent makes him look responsible, but he stole half my car."

I nodded. I felt like a fool drinking espresso, like I was drinking from a doll's cup.

"I'm just going to sell his shit. We'll see how he likes that, when he gets back." She forked another morsel of cake. "Who just leaves without saying goodbye to someone they love? What kind of person does that?"

I had two more unanswered calls from the DiTraglias on my phone. I wasn't writing an article, I realized. I wasn't doing anything.

"Did you say that you made out with Pheasant once?" I asked Yana. I'd already finished the espresso. I'd slept poorly, and wondered if Yana would make me another. "Back in high school?"

Yana smiled around the fork tines clasped between her teeth. "He was playing at that record store that used to be on State Street. Me and Kara Egli went. We didn't think the music was that good but we talked to him afterward, and I made out with him for a couple of minutes while Kara was in the bathroom. Then the next day I found out I had mono, which I got from Scottie Straub, and then a week later I heard Pheasant had mono too and he was supposedly pissed at me about it. So like two years after that, his first record came out, and Kara texted me, 'You remember Derek DiTraglia who you gave mono to?' And the music was really good, much better than the shit he'd been playing at the record store. That was the summer my sister went to France for college. My dad was already living over there. My mom and I moved away from the Briar Road house and into this shitty little apartment near the hospital, and I was completely hating my life. Then that Pheasant album came out of the air and it was so *real*. It was, I don't know, the exact thing I needed. And this guy had made it, this random guy from town who wasn't that bright or good-looking, who tasted like cigarettes and wasn't even good at kissing, and I thought, oh, of course, Yana, beauty will find you wherever you are. I listened to it all that summer and a long time after, until one day I didn't need it anymore."

TWO MUMMERS

I woke to Ivan standing over me in a baggy, high-collared satin frock. It hung down to his knees, spangled here and there with clumps of dyed feathers. He wore matching harem pants and a dented top hat, and he had a banjo slung across his waist that he strummed with the breezy imprecision of a kid miming air guitar. I was once again in Ivan's dead grandmother's house on Fernon Street in Pennsport, where I'd slept the last few nights on the vinyl-covered sofa. I'd slept right up until the moment Ivan struck the banjo strings and jolted me awake. It was seven o'clock on a Sunday morning.

"Look what I found," he said proudly. He meant the costume. The banjo was a previous discovery. He'd been noodling with it since Friday. Ivan O'Reilly had decided to become a Mummer, and it was fucking up my plans.

We were supposed to drive to Pensacola two days earlier. I'd packed up my nine-month-old sobriety along with four t-shirts and two pairs of jeans, ready to hop into Ivan's Jetta and head eighteen hours south to the Florida Panhandle. I had never been to Pensacola or anywhere near it, but something in the musicality of its name and in the pictures I saw online—the mindless blue of the water, the insubstantiality of its sand spits—beckoned me gulfward. Ivan only planned to stay for a week, but I was going to find a dishwashing job at a seafood restaurant and an apartment on the bay. If Pensacola turned out to be the wrong place, I could move on to Mobile, or even New Orleans if I felt the urge, though I didn't know if I was quite ready for New Orleans. I'd heard they drank on the street there, to excess and at all hours.

But it didn't matter what I was ready for, as it turned out. Ivan's regression to Mummery had put the trip on hold.

"Did you even wash that?" I asked him. I could see little flecks of wood and paper caught in the feathers of his frock. Mice had likely nested in the costume's folds.

"Think I should've?" he asked, inspecting himself. "It was in a box at the back of the basement. It's gotta be from the eighties."

The stairs creaked. Ivan's aunt Peg descended, belting her felt bathrobe around her hips. Fortunately for me, she became the new target of Ivan's strumming. He followed her from the foot of the steps to the kitchen, his legs flung out and his hips rolling in an exaggerated Two Street strut.

"Get out of my face with that shit," croaked Peg. "I'm just trying to get my coffee."

Ivan's grandmother had died the previous fall of a liver tumor. She'd left the Fernon Street house to Ivan and Aunt Peg in equal share. Peg showed up not long after I'd moved into Maureen's and claimed the futon in the extra bedroom. Now that I was back, I had to make do with the living room and its ornately uncomfortable furniture.

No matter. The house was ready to sell, and as far as I could see, Ivan was freed up to drive us to Pensacola. Yet there he was, dressed like a clown, noodling with his dead father's banjo.

"I hate that banjo," said Peg as she ladled Folgers into the coffee maker. "I hated it when Johnny played it and I hate it now."

Ivan strummed discordantly. "This is roots music," he shouted over the din. "This is our heritage."

John O'Reilly played banjo for the Fralinger String Band in the mid-eighties. That was before he decamped for Bucks County, fathered Ivan, absconded from family life, and eventually died of hepatic failure in Erie, Pennsylvania. To hear Ivan tell it, when he unearthed John's banjo in his dead grandmother's basement, the Mummer dreams of his childhood—dreams I don't remember him ever mentioning before—awoke like cicada nymphs. He started learning the chords, the old songs. "When You're Smiling." "Oh Dem Golden Slippers." "Happy Days Are Here Again." He started spinning Tin Pan Alley records on his grandmother's hi-fi. He tuned his bedroom television to subchannel 17.4—Mummers TV, broadcasting old New Year's parades twenty-four hours a day, three hundred sixty-five days a year. He started talking about tryouts, how the string band auditions were coming up, how he didn't know if he could drive to Pensacola yet because he needed time to practice. It was disturbing. Before all that, he'd been thinking about going to business school.

"Monk, don't drink any of this coffee?" Peg called me from the kitchen. "I'm gonna drink the rest of it after my shower." Peg had a way of reminding everyone that, even if Ivan was a co-owner, the house truly belonged to her. She was fifty-five and divorced, and she survived on disability checks for something to do with her back. She had a house of her own a few blocks away that she shared with her weepy, unmarried daughter and the daughter's squealing infant. I had come to suspect that Peg had no desire to sell the Fernon Street house at all, but coveted it for herself as a refuge from the racket at home.

Ivan stopped strumming. "Aunt Peg, what are you talking about? We can make more coffee."

"I already made it how I like it," said Peg. "And some guys are coming by to look at the living room furniture tonight. So, you know, do with that information what you will."

"But that's where Monk sleeps," said Ivan.

"I'll sleep in Pensacola," I said. I had to believe that the Pensacola trip was still happening, or else I didn't know what I'd do. I burrowed into the seam of the dead grandmother's sofa, swaddled in a crocheted afghan.

"If you're sleeping in Pensacola, hon, you're doing it wrong," said Peg, cackling to herself on her way back upstairs.

\\\\\\

That afternoon, the stylish couple who lived next door invited Ivan over for drinks. I tagged along. They were renters. Our age. New to Pennsport, which was one of those South Philadelphia neighborhoods that had stayed white through the demographic upheavals of the preceding half-century. The locals were so busy keeping a weather eye open for blacks that they hadn't noticed the pasty millennials in thick-rimmed glasses sneaking south of Washington Avenue until it was too late. Kai and Becca were the latter category. I suppose Ivan and I were too.

Despite the nearly identical layouts, their house was the inversion of Ivan's grandmother's. Because of his renovations—Ivan had updated the kitchen and bathroom, torn out all the cat-stained carpets—his grandmother's house felt oddly new, even as its surfaces remained choked with an old woman's doilies and knickknacks. Kai and Becca's place was still encased in a layer of mid-century shag and linoleum, pea greens and mustard yellows, but populated with light, modular IKEA chairs and shelves of potted succulents.

Ivan presented them with a housewarming gift: a wireless motion sensor and alarm.

"Even the best blocks have break-ins," explained Ivan. "It's the world we live in."

I nodded in agreement.

"Wow," said Becca, exchanging a puzzled look with Kai. "Thank you so much."

"I'd be happy to set it up for you," said Ivan.

"Maybe after drinks?" said Becca.

She gave us a tour while Kai fiddled in the kitchen. Their small backyard was much nicer than Ivan's. Nicer, really, than any backyard I had seen in South Philadelphia, where the backyards were generally too small and concrete to achieve niceness. Becca's had a pergola wreathed in clematis that formed an airy ceiling above the patio. "It was actually here when we moved in," she said. "Isn't it bewitching?" She took us to the dining nook, where a sweating pitcher of sangria and a charcuterie board with a sliced loaf of bread were laid out on the glass table beneath a Charles Sheeler poster from the Museum of Fine Arts, Boston. The image on the poster looked like a large white silo and barn. The buildings were stylized and flat and overlapped impossibly in space.

"Kai made the bread," said Becca. "I made the drinks." Kai, bearded and top-knotted, had the floury affect of a baker, though apparently during the week he worked in pharmaceutical advertising. Becca wore a cheery rose-colored jumpsuit, like an astronaut from a softer, more empathetic future. Her flitting movements suggested an enthusiasm for glassware and small gatherings. Before Fernon Street, they had lived in University City. They'd met at Penn, each having originated in a different corner of the wide Midwest. I found everything about them slightly intolerable.

"I don't drink," I told them, so as not to seem rude by refusing the sangria. Something in my tone of voice made the words rude anyway. Becca's bright face sagged into a look of horror. She apologized like she'd accidentally chopped off my hand, and I regretted saying anything. She insisted on making me a virgin cocktail despite my protests that she sit down and not worry. A minute later, she brought me a glass of seltzer and some kind of juice garnished with slices of orange. I took a sip. It was fizzy and not too sweet. I couldn't believe how good it was.

As Ivan was still wearing his satin costume and top hat, the conversation turned inevitably toward the Mummers. "Who are they again?" asked Becca. "They do the New Year's parade, right? I've always meant to go."

"Oh, you gotta see it," said Ivan, popping an olive into his mouth. "Pennsport is the Mummers neighborhood. The clubhouses are right along Second Street. They practice all year for the parade on Broad, and the clubs compete against each other in different divisions—comics, wenches, fancies, string bands—and there's a giant party afterward on Second Street and everybody gets shit-faced. Sorry, is there a pit in this?"

"And you're in a club?" asked Kai, passing Ivan a small dish.

Ivan spat out the olive pit. "I'm preparing my audition for the Fralinger String Band. My dad played banjo with them in the eighties. Tryouts start this week."

"Banjo?" asked Becca. "Is it bluegrass music? I like bluegrass."

"It's more like Dixieland jazz," I said. "Imagine a hundred banjos, saxophones, and glockenspiels played by middle-aged white guys in Mardi Gras costumes." I didn't want Kai and Becca to mistake the

Mummers for something cool. People thought the Mummers were a Philadelphia thing, but really they were a South Philadelphia thing. Those of us from elsewhere in the region generally thought the Mummers were pretty stupid. My friend Shelby dated a guy for a while who turned out to be a Mummer. She was rightly horrified, but she liked the guy, so she hid that aspect of his identity from her friends and family. Then somebody saw his costume hanging in the backseat of his car, and the comments started—crude, tasteless jokes about Shelby finding sequins and feathers stuck to her skin in the morning—and she had to break up with him. She claimed it had nothing to do with his Mummery, but we knew the truth.

"Mardi Gras, huh?" Becca gave her glass a gentle shake. "I should have made hurricanes."

"Many Mardi Gras traditions in New Orleans were actually influenced by a Philadelphia Mummer named Michael Krafft," said Ivan. "It's true. I'm reading a book about it."

"But isn't the whole Mummers Parade rooted in minstrel shows?" asked Kai, thumbing his beard. "They just had something about it on Radio Times. Didn't the Mummers used to perform in blackface?"

Ivan sipped his sangria uncomfortably. "I mean, it's a very old parade. It goes back to before the Revolutionary War."

"That's an excellent point, Kai," I said. I wagged my finger at him, then at Ivan. "Don't you guys think Ivan should drop this Mummers stuff and go with me to Pensacola?"

"We'll go after the auditions," said Ivan.

"What's in Pensacola?" asked Kai.

"The beach," I said. "The sea."

"Monk's just looking for a ride," said Ivan.

I hadn't owned a car in five years. The only vehicle I'd ever had was the white '93 Dodge Dynasty that I inherited from my own grandmother after she got too shaky to drive it, which I drunkenly rammed into a light pole in the parking lot of the ACME in Roxborough while stopping to buy Nicorette lozenges. But to say I was just looking for a ride made it sound like I was using Ivan, which wasn't the case. Ivan was one of my oldest friends. He'd spent the better part of a year fixing up his dead grandmother's house, and I thought he could use a vacation. Plus, I knew him to be a hobbyist. A trail of abandoned skateboards, telescopes, and camping equipment stretched back to his childhood. If it was only a matter of time before he dropped his Mummers infatuation, like all previous infatuations, why not skip right to the end and go to Pensacola?

Becca was scrolling on her phone. The horns of "Oh Dem Golden Slippers" crackled through the countertop speakers. Ivan rose to his feet and strutted around the living room, popping his shoulders, spinning on his toes, speeding up as the song's tempo increased. Becca and Kai clapped with the beat. The banjos came in, and Ivan strummed along at his own invisible instrument. A string band didn't need virtuosos, just a dozen earnest goons to keep the rhythm. Ivan was an earnest goon. I was something else. I didn't clap. I sipped my drink, the fizzy citrus of it sparking down my throat.

\\\\\\

When we got back to Ivan's house, a pair of bald men were examining the furniture in the living room as Peg observed them from the bottom of the stairs. They looked at us as we entered, looked at each other, looked at Peg.

"Were there cats in this house?" the shorter man asked.

I left Ivan and Peg to negotiate with the men and stepped into the kitchen. There was still some cold coffee left from the pot I'd made earlier, after Peg had finished hers. I poured it into a mug and wandered out to the backyard. There wasn't much out there other than some trash cans and a fallow, three-foot-by-three-foot vegetable bed. I peered in vain over the warped wooden fence, thinking I might see Becca seated beneath her clematis-covered pergola. I couldn't hear any music playing in her house, only the rumble of I-95 a few blocks east. It was the violet hour. The evening was up to its alchemical tricks. I sat down on the back step and sipped my coffee, which tasted bitter after the fresh fruit in the mocktail, and I pictured how the sky must look over the Gulf of Mexico. Blue over blue. Pink over silver.

Something rustled beyond the fence, not in Becca's yard but on the opposite side. The neighbor there was an old guy named Franny, a union electrician with a gut and a limp. I saw him shuffling around between the slats in the fence and heard the rattle of bottles as they landed in his bin. He brought the boiled ham of his face up to the top of the pickets, flecked with clinging remnants of white paint, and blinked at me.

"You the one playing banjo?"

"No," I said.

"You Eileen's grandson?" he asked.

"No," I said.

"I know I've been hearing banjo over there," he said. He kept staring at me. I wasn't in the mood to chat, but it was clear that he wasn't going away until I explained the situation. It turned out he used to strut with Hog Island before they quit the fancy division. "Now the only club left in the fancies is Golden Sunrise," he said, "and damned if I'll strut with them."

However one felt about the Mummers, guys like Franny infused South Philadelphia with a hint of the carnivalesque. Any bulky white man on the street—plumber, roofer, carpenter, cop—might abruptly slide into a swoop or a twirl, buoyant and sleek as a synchronized swimmer. He might prance like a reindeer, lurch like a tyrannosaur, pulse like a rave girl in a festival crowd. He would strut one minute and complain about Mexicans the next.

"You know, strutting ain't for amateurs," continued Franny. "Takes a lifetime to make a Mummer. You don't skip in off the street."

"I think Ivan just wants to do what his dad did," I said, though that explanation hadn't occurred to me until I said it.

"Johnny, was it? Never liked that kid. Hopeless alky." Franny paused as though he might go back inside. "How's Peggy doing?"

"They're getting ready to sell the house," I said.

"Everybody's selling now," said Franny. "You know, this neighborhood wasn't doing so hot for a long time. But people looked out for each other. I used to shovel Eileen's sidewalk in the winter. I'd prune her trees, too, before my leg started acting up. Just the neighborly thing to do. Now property values are up and everybody's leaving. New people are coming in. But they're not friendly like the old people, you know?"

"Why don't you sell?" I asked.

"Nah, put too much work into this place." Franny gazed up at the back wall of his house. I didn't know what he was seeing. All I saw was weathered siding and frayed window screens. "The place across the street, the one they just fixed up? That was empty for years. These hoodlums used to tag it, write graffiti, you know? But I'd go out there with a can of paint and make it nice again. Neighborly thing to do."

"I wish I had a house to sell," I said. "You ever live anywhere else, Franny?"

"Nope," he said. "Well, Vietnam."

"I'm trying to go to Pensacola," I said. "Florida. Maybe Mobile. Maybe New Orleans."

"Mardi Gras," said Franny. "You know New Orleans got the whole idea for Mardi Gras from the Mummers? Guy named Michael Krafft. White guy. Look it up."

I nodded. I made a show of finishing my coffee, said good night to Franny, and headed back inside.

"Good news," said Ivan. He was seated on the vinyl-covered sofa in the middle of an otherwise empty living room. "They didn't want the couch."

\\\\\\

For the next few days, I tried to avoid Fernon Street as much as I could. Ivan's banjo was maddening, but even when Ivan went to work, Peg remained at the house, eyeing me like a slow-growing water stain on the ceiling. I would grab one of the dead grandmother's paperbacks— she had a nice selection of Highsmith and du Maurier—and sit on a bench in Dickinson Square Park or on the reclaimed pier the city had fixed up at the end of Washington Avenue. I would read for a few pages until I got distracted by something, the humidity or the brightness of the sun, and I would end up wandering for blocks and blocks. I would buy a coffee somewhere, read a few more pages at a sticky table, wander some more. I couldn't settle in anywhere. It was like the city kept tilting in different directions, a tilt perceptible only to me, and I was rolling like a marble toward its peripatetic low point.

At night I slept with the living room windows open, hoping to coax a breeze off the river, but it was only the sounds of Pennsport that slipped in over the sill and across the vacant carpet. In my dreams I was always accidentally drinking—I would look down at my hand and, finding that it held a can of beer, realize that it was my fourth—and I would wake unsure of where I was. One night I sat up on Ivan's dead grandmother's couch at some indeterminate early hour, electric light beaming into my eyes. The refrigerator door was open. A small older man with an off-center tuft of white hair stood before the appliance, illuminated in its glow. He wore only a striped, buttoned dress shirt that concealed all but the very bottom of his genitals from my view, and he took deep swigs from a carton of orange juice. I watched him drink until he noticed me, though even after he became aware of my presence he showed no sign of embarrassment.

"Morning," he said. "You're a friend of Ivan's?"

"From when we were kids," I said, as though that somehow justified why I should be sleeping on the sofa.

"So you're from Bucks County?" he asked. He took another sip, then capped the carton and stuck it back on the refrigerator shelf. "Lovely place."

"I guess." To me, Bucks County had always felt generic and remote, a nowhere suburb, but to city people of a certain age—my parents' age, my city-raised parents—the lawns and little patches of woods held a profound allure. The same allure, I suppose, that the city's blocks of row houses had held for suburban kids like Ivan and me. The spell had broken in my case, at least. I'd seen enough of them to know those blocks were just a different kind of nowhere.

"I'm gonna be buried in Bucks County," said the man, his naked legs glowing white in the pale phosphorescence of the refrigerator's bulb. "Cemetery up in Chalfont, St. John Neumann. You know it? I'll be right in there. Gorgeous place." He shut the appliance's door and started up the stairs. "Well. Good night."

"Good night," I said and lay back down. I woke up a few hours later unsure if I had dreamed the whole thing.

\\\\\

I took a walk to the Italian Market to buy some oranges. I thought I would try to re-create Becca's mocktail, though I had only a vague idea of what went in it. At the grocer's I found a dozen different varieties of orange piled in precarious mounds. I'd never realized there were so many kinds. There were another dozen piles of fruits that resembled oranges but weren't. I bought a bag of navels—they were cheap and familiar—and a two-liter bottle of seltzer. The Mexican woman at the checkout gave me a free carton of blueberries.

Entering the house on Fernon Street was always a pain, especially if I was carrying anything. Ivan had installed two different keypads on the door, each with its own code, and they needed to be unlocked in unison. You only got three attempts before a stooge at a computer screen somewhere decided you were a burglar and froze the lock. The pressure always caused me to flub the first try, but I usually made it through on the second one.

Peg was sitting at the kitchen table with a mug of coffee and an iPad. "So you met Ken?" she asked me.

The image of the man's refrigerator-lit genitals flickered in my mind. I began to peel the skin from one of my oranges, the juice seeping beneath my too-short fingernails and stinging the tender skin. "He told me about his grave plot."

"He's very proud of it," said Peg, flicking at something on her tablet screen. "He's a sweetheart."

I stuck a wedge of orange in my mouth. It wasn't sweet like I wanted it to be. It barely tasted like anything. I pulled a handheld juicer from a drawer and squeezed what I could from the rest of the fruit into a water glass. I pressed a second orange and topped it off with a splash of seltzer. I took a sip, the effervescence detonating at the end of my nose. The juice was too strong, too pulpy. It was nothing like what Becca had given me.

"What are you making, hon?" asked Peg. "Italian soda?"

"I had this drink next door, a non-alcoholic drink with seltzer and orange juice. Maybe some other stuff. This isn't it, anyway. Do you like blueberries, Peg?"

"Can't stand them," said the woman, turning in her chair. "I want to talk to you about you and Ivan going to Pensacola. Are you still doing that?"

I shrugged. "I'd like to. Ivan has his audition with Fralinger today. That's been the holdup, allegedly. But I don't think he's even talked to his boss yet about taking off."

"The Mummers." Peg said it with the gravity of someone discussing a serious medical diagnosis. "Where did that come from, I wonder?"

"He found that banjo in the basement," I said. "Ivan throws himself into things."

"He told me he was leaving soon," said Peg. "I thought I'd finally get some peace and quiet, but it's been two weeks and he's still here. And now I've got you sleeping on the sofa every night. It's like a frat house in here, all this banjo-playing and . . . mixology."

Peg's gaze was fixated on the fizzing glass in my hand. She must have been anxious to use the house as some kind of love nest for herself and Ken. I wondered, briefly, how they managed with Peg's back injury. I couldn't blame her, precisely, for wanting the place to herself, though I didn't think Ivan should be forced out of the house before he was ready to go.

"Peg, if I could leave for Pensacola, I'd go right now."

"I think you should go and take Ivan with you," she agreed, returning to her tablet. "It's unhealthy for him to be cooped up in this house. He's getting nutsy."

I took my drink into the backyard, hoping Franny wouldn't be out there puttering around. I lucked out—not only was the electrician nowhere in sight, but Becca was seated on her patio beneath the dappled shade of the pergola. "Oh hi neighbor," she called, waving her reading material at me. It looked like an old copy of *Life* magazine. "Vintage," she said, setting it on her chair and walking up to the fence. The sun brought out her freckles.

"You have a very nice yard," I told her. "You don't normally see yards this nice in South Philadelphia."

She looked around her yard as though she'd only just noticed it. "What I really want is a birdbath. There's this beautiful old stone birdbath at my parents' house in Nebraska City. It belonged to my grandmother. I think it would look great right there." She pointed a slim, golden arm toward the far back corner near the gate to the alley. "I'd have to drive out and get it, though. The thing weighs about a million pounds. Kai has zero interest."

"Hey, what was that drink you made me the other day?" I asked. "I just tried to make it with seltzer and orange juice."

"Oh, no," she said, shaking her head. "No, that was essentially a virgin paloma. Club soda, grapefruit, lime juice, orange slice for garnish. I can show you how to make it sometime if you ever want to come over. I know how to make a lot of mocktails."

She was about to run out, but suggested I come over Monday or Tuesday afternoon. She'd get all the ingredients, she said. "Come thirsty."

When I went back inside I found Ivan's banjo propped against the newel at the bottom of the staircase. I could hear the sound of string band music wafting down from the second floor. I climbed the steps, which I had lately traveled only to use the shower, and poked my head into Ivan's bedroom. He lay on his mattress, his eyes glazed over, staring at the fuzzy screen of his television. Subchannel 17.4, Mummers TV.

"How was the audition?" I asked.

"I didn't get it," he said flatly. "They told me I play like shit."

"Ah," I said. I didn't know what else to say. I didn't want to sound insensitive. "So. Pensacola?"

"Avalon String Band has their audition next week," he said. "I'm gonna try for them."

That meant another week on the vinyl for me. I didn't know if I could handle it.

"I'm really trying to go to Pensacola," I said. "Have you talked to your boss yet?"

"Of course I talked to him," said Ivan. He sounded deflated rather than angry. "He won't let me off until next week anyway. We're here another week regardless, so I might as well try out for Avalon."

I didn't say anything. I glanced at the television. A fancy division strutted across the screen dressed as peacocks or angels or some similarly fluttering creatures, parasols bobbing in their hands. They wore porkpie hats. Huge pinwheels of snowy feathers fanned out from their backs.

"This is the '97 parade," said Ivan. "I think I was at this one, but I don't really remember it. I remember '98 pretty well. That was the last one before my dad left. They were all wearing those jester hats with the floppy points. I was nine. I was feeling too old for it by then."

I was surprised that Ivan had such a strong desire to follow in his father's footsteps, considering that the man drank himself to death in Erie. My own father had done a decent job—he stuck around and kept me fed and clothed and gave me some advice from time to time—but I didn't particularly want to be like him.

"I haven't seen the '98 parade on here yet," said Ivan. "I wonder if they lost the tape."

"Do you actually want to go to Pensacola?" I asked.

"Of course," said Ivan, staring at the screen. "We'll go next week."

\\\\\\

On Monday, I went to Becca's to make mocktails. She'd laid out the ingredients like a still life across her kitchen counter. Grapefruits, limes, oranges, clumps of mint and rosemary. Cherry juice, pineapple juice, ginger beer, simple syrup. A shaker, a jigger, a peeler, a strainer. Two tumblers, two mason jars, two brass cups for Moscow mules.

"I may have overdone it," she said.

Like me, Becca was someone with days to kill. She'd been working at a kindergarten for a bit, then decided it wasn't for her. At the moment she was exploring her other options. Maybe she'd go to grad school. Maybe she'd start an online vintage shop. She hadn't yet had to decide, thanks to Kai, who was doing well enough for both of them. She told me all of this as we mixed and sipped our virgin drinks, speaking in the falsely embarrassed, slightly amused tone of someone used to sharing her feelings with people.

I told her how I mostly spent my time walking around the neighborhood.

"You're a flâneur," she said. "An urban wanderer. A connoisseur of the city and its streets."

"I don't know about that," I said. It sounded silly, though a part of me liked the idea. "I just don't have a car."

"I would love to not have a car," she said, her hand swooping lightly in emphasis. "I have a recurring nightmare about getting carjacked."

"Why? Have you been carjacked?"

She shook her head. "Never. I don't know what my subconscious is trying to tell me."

Becca struck me, by and large, as a stranger to misfortune. It was a prejudicial assessment that I couldn't help but make of people whose lives appeared neater than my own. Her cuteness was a function of the world's decision not to press her too hard about anything, and she appeared to know this, and to be wary of anything that might change the world's mind. She seemed to love Kai, which disappointed me. I always expected love to be a performance. When I encountered someone's earnest love, I felt like I'd been left out of some part of the story.

"Kai likes his job, but he doesn't like Pennsport too much," said Becca. "Honestly, I think he's ready to leave Philadelphia."

"What doesn't he like about Philadelphia?" I asked. "What's wrong with Philadelphia?"

"Oh, you know, you get sick of a place," she said. She rested her jaw in her palm, her hand disappearing behind the curtain of her hair. "I'm not sick of it yet. I could see myself staying. But it might be nice to live somewhere else too." She tipped her brass mug at me. "Like Pensacola."

"Like Pensacola," I repeated. I had accepted that I was never getting to Pensacola. "Hey, remember you were talking about that birdbath in Nebraska? What if we drove out to pick it up, you and me? Get out of town for a while, get out of our own heads." A long-shot plan had formed in my mind over the previous days. If I caught a ride with Becca to Nebraska, I could potentially take a Greyhound from there to Idaho and hook up with Bors and Hector. Or maybe some time away would help Becca realize Kai was kind of a drip and we could keep going west together, elope to California, never come back. If I was going to fantasize, I might as well fantasize all the way.

"Maybe," said Becca, which wasn't a no. "It would be great to have that birdbath. But would you really want to go all the way out to Nebraska City?"

"It's only nineteen hours," I said. "We drive nine and a half each, do it in one go." I looked past Becca to the Sheeler poster of the white silo and barn, wondering if that was what Nebraska looked like. A place of clean, sharp lines. Fields of flat color.

"It's not the most exciting place in the world, but it's a cute little town," she said. "Birthplace of Arbor Day, you know. We could go to the Arbor Lodge Arboretum." It seemed like she was talking herself into the idea. "We could make a cooler of mocktails for the drive."

She asked about Ivan and his Fralinger audition, nodding solemnly when I told her he'd been rejected. "It's for the best," I said. "The Mummers are very stupid."

"They seem so fun," said Becca. "Why don't you like them?"

"I'm uncomfortable with overt expressions of joy." I meant for it to be a joke, but the way I said it, it sounded sincere, even to me.

"Maybe I'll become a Mummer," she said.

Becca gave me a mint plant from her garden in a plastic cup. When I got back to Ivan's, I took it out to the back step where it would get some sun.

Franny raised his head above the fence to ambush me. There was something about him—his heavy, stooping frame, his blunt accent, his burnt pink face—that reminded me of my father, who used to walk around our backyard with a beer when he got home from a day of delivering mail. If it was the right time of year, he would leave his shoes and socks in the kitchen and step barefoot into the grass so he could feel the cool green blades against his naked soles.

"You never go to work, huh?" asked Franny.

"Nope. Do you?"

"I'm retired," he said. "And disabled."

"I'm a flâneur," I told him.

"The hell's that?"

"I walk around and look at things." I swept my hand across the yard. "I'm a connoisseur of street life."

"Ah," said Franny. "You're a moper."

"What's a moper?"

"A bum. A loiterer. Used to be you could get arrested for mopery, back before they hamstrung the cops. Peggy really doesn't care that you just live in her house with no job? Do you pay rent?"

I could have told him that I quit drinking that year, but I could already imagine what he'd say to that. *So what? People quit drinking all the time. They don't fuck off for months and months, imposing on others to house them and drive them around. They get up and go to work and keep their shit to themselves.* I got angry at him for those words, even if he hadn't said them.

"You know what I heard, Franny," I said, flâneuring my way over to the fence. "I heard the Mummers parade has its roots in minstrel shows."

Franny frowned. "Well, you have to understand, the parade is very old. Its roots go back before the Revolutionary War."

"It seems like a pretty backward tradition," I said, relishing his discomfort. "Kind of embarrassing for the city, I'd say."

Franny scowled. "You got a lot of nerve, you know that? I've been here my whole life. Plenty of people left, moved to the suburbs, moved to Jersey. Not me, boy. I stayed and paid my taxes and gave out candy on Halloween. It's people like me that kept this city from crumbling for years and years, back when nobody gave a shit." His hands gripped the fence posts so tightly I could see flecks of paint rubbing off on his fingers. "Now all of a sudden the city is hip and you kids are moving in to tell us how we're doing everything wrong, how what we need are bike lanes and soda taxes, how the Mummers Parade is prejudiced or whatever it is you're implying. What kind of people look at something as innocent as a New Year's Day parade and think, well how can we ruin this?"

Franny paused like he wanted an answer. I didn't give him one. I hadn't expected him to get so irate.

"You're a joyless generation," he said finally. "And it's not gonna get any better for you, I'll tell you that. If you think you're going to get any happier as you get older, buddy, I've got some bad news for you." He spun with surprising agility and limped back into his house. He slammed his screen door so hard that it smacked once, then twice more, each softer than the last.

\\\\\\

I'd run out of cash waiting around for Ivan, so I called my old boss at the banquet hall where I'd worked earlier in the summer to ask if he needed a dishwasher. Dante told me there was a hundred-person wedding that night, and the job was mine if I wanted it. "Now I can get rid of the crackhead we've been using the last few weeks," he said cheerfully. "He's a nice kid but he's been stealing all my scouring pads."

It felt good to be doing something with my hands. Good to be out of the house and around different people, even if it was just a bunch of maniacal line cooks and pill-swapping waiters. It felt like we were all putting on a show together, filling up plates with chicken or beef, scattering them out among the guests, gathering them back in. I hosed them off in the sink and ran them through the commercial Hobart, which whistled and droned like a pipe organ. On my dinner break I helped myself to a plate of potatoes and asparagus and ate in the stairwell, listening to snatches of the wedding speeches muffled through the door to the ballroom. "Now let's see if these two can live together," the maid of honor was saying. She said it three or four times. Every time she said it, she got a bigger laugh.

It was becoming harder and harder to stay on Fernon Street. For the last week, I hadn't seen much of Ivan, though I'd found his baggy satin costume in a heap on top of the washing machine in the basement. I only knew when he was home from the muffled banjo strumming that echoed down the staircase. The incessant practice meant that Peg was spending more and more of her time on the first floor, flopped on the sofa that was also my bed, her head resting in Ken's lap. Ken always gave me a polite nod, but Peg's glares encouraged me to find somewhere else to hang out. She had taken to offering me prolonged goodbyes whenever I stepped out of the house. "And if I don't see you again before you leave, hon, have a wonderful trip."

I didn't approve of what Peg was doing to Ivan, trying to force him out of a house that was one-half his. I figured that if I couldn't get him to drive me to Pensacola, he might as well stay on Fernon Street and become a Mummer. After he was rejected by the Avalon String Band, I started to wonder if maybe the problem was the banjo. He had never managed to make the instrument sound much better than the yowl of a street cat. I found a listing on Craigslist for a secondhand marching glockenspiel. Percussion seemed a natural fit for Ivan. I figured he could learn the basics on YouTube and audition for the Quaker City String Band the following weekend. The guy only wanted eighty bucks for it, so I asked Becca to give me a ride to East Lansdowne to pick it up.

As I waited on Becca's stoop, I could hear a discreet, Midwestern argument unfolding on the other side of the door. Becca appeared, keys in hand, sunglasses perched atop her slightly flushed face. "Let's go buy a glockenspiel," she said, her voice light with forced gaiety.

"This is fun, right?" she asked as we drove. She threaded a strand of hair hesitantly behind her ear. "Maybe we really should go to Nebraska City, huh? There's a bunch of stuff at my parents' I'd love to pick up, especially if I start this vintage shop."

"You mean it?" I asked. "I've got a paycheck coming Friday, but I can leave anytime after that."

As we cruised through Southwest Philadelphia, I told Becca how Peg was trying to force Ivan out of the house so she could shack up there with Ken. "It's half Ivan's house, so she either needs to let him live there or buy him out of it," I said. "And, between you and me, I don't think there's anything wrong with her back. I think she's been faking it for the disability check."

Becca considered the issue for a moment. "I have a friend who's a real estate agent. I could set up a meeting. If the house is fixed up—you said it's fixed up, right?"

"Oh yeah, it looks great. Ivan did the whole place. It looks brand-new."

"Maybe they should just sell it and part ways," agreed Becca. "Maybe they just need a push."

"They should definitely sell it," I said. Ivan didn't need that house. He could turn it into cash and find a new spot. I didn't need the house either. I would soon be on my way to Nebraska City, then on to Idaho or California or wherever else.

Half an hour later, I had bargained the guy down to fifty bucks for the glockenspiel. The three of us were standing on the porch of his ramshackle twin in East Lansdowne, haggling above the snarl of a lawn mower in the cemetery at the end of the street. A pet ferret wriggled in the guy's sinuous arms. Becca tried on the instrument, harnessing it to her waist and shoulders. She looked like a beer vendor at a baseball stadium. "It's better than the banjo, right?" She plinked out a tuneless aire on its bars. "It sounds like wind chimes."

\\\\\\

The meeting with the real estate agent was scheduled for Saturday. Ivan was reluctant to meet with the woman, but Peg was unexpectedly game.

"We'll just see what she has to say," said Peg. "No harm in that, right?"

"No harm," Ivan agreed. "Yeah, we can hear her out."

I was glad to have played a role in the deal, given that my relationship with Ivan had suffered a bit in the last week or so. I hoped the glockenspiel would get me back into his good graces. I took the earlier shift at the banquet hall on Saturday. At six o'clock, after I'd finished up, I went to the locker room and changed into Johnny O'Reilly's Mummer costume that Ivan had left on the washing machine. I even put on the dented top hat. My plan was to walk into the house festooned like an idiot and tittering away on the instrument, all to show Ivan that there were no hard feelings.

Dante had let me stash the glockenspiel in his office during my shift. He was on the phone with someone when I came to pick it up. When he saw the costume, he placed his hand over the receiver and asked, curiously, "Who are you strutting with?"

"Nobody," I said.

"Ferko String Band," he said, pointing to himself. He wiggled his fingers atop a phantom saxophone. "We'll talk," he said, and waved me out of the office.

I caught some wild looks walking home from the banquet hall in the satin frock and harem pants, the glockenspiel strapped to my shoulders. It was a heavy piece of equipment, and I had to keep my spine erect to counterbalance the weight. A few strangers strutted at me as I passed them on the sidewalk, and I attempted, ineptly, to strut back. Some kids with a soccer ball demanded that I play them something on the instrument, puzzled when I couldn't manage more than a few discordant notes. Even so, it felt good to be dressed like that. To be silly like that. I could almost see the appeal. I got back to Fernon Street just as the light was softening. From a block away, I spied Peg and Ken sitting side by side on the stoop, their gray hair puffed by the humidity into jaunty unruliness.

Peg held her phone to her ear. The meeting with the real estate agent had been a few hours earlier, there at the house. I lay a finger across my lips so they wouldn't shout anything at me, but I needn't have worried. They just stared at me, unsmiling, as I paused before them.

Peg dropped her phone to her side. "He locked us all out."

"Who?" I asked.

"My nephew. He changed the locks."

"On purpose?"

"They don't work," said Peg, flinging her hand toward the door. "Give it a try."

I stepped past them and typed the code into both of the locks at once. The buttons beeped a red refusal. I rang the bell.

"He's not here," said Peg. "I don't know where he went."

"We ought to take this seriously," said Ken. "He isn't ready to sell."

"I don't understand, why did he lock you out?" I asked.

Peg nodded toward Becca's house. "Your friend next door, the chipper one? Her and her boyfriend made an offer. We accepted."

"Becca made an offer on your house?" I asked, stepping past them off the stoop. I found it difficult to believe she would make an offer on the house without mentioning it to me beforehand. I took out my phone and I dialed Becca's number. I wondered what this meant for our trip to Nebraska.

The phone rang a few times. Becca didn't pick up.

"It was a good offer," said Peg. "Ivan seemed fine with it at the time. The three of us went out to dinner to celebrate, then Ivan just got up and left halfway through. Said he had something to do at work. Now we come home and find he changed the locks."

"He changed his mind, that's what he changed," said Ken, his arms folded.

"Well, we already accepted the offer," said Peg.

"You want to sell the house?" I asked. "I thought you wanted to keep the house?"

"Why would I want to keep this house?" asked Peg. "I have my own house. I want to get rid of this house yesterday, and those hipsters offered me a lot of money for it."

"You should have asked for more," said Ken. "In a year or two, it'll be worth twice that."

I dialed Ivan's number and paced along the sidewalk. He didn't pick up either.

"It's his grandmother's house," said Peg. "Maybe he has fond memories. Not me. I grew up here. I hate this fucking house."

"It just seems like it's all happening very fast," muttered Ken.

"Well, it was never gonna be your house, hon," said Peg. "If you want a house, you can quit living with your mother and buy one for yourself."

"That's it. I've had it with the remarks." Ken stood and shuffled over to me. "You, Ivan's friend. Are you still driving to Pensacola?"

"What?" The straps of the glockenspiel pressed painfully into the skin of my shoulders. "Maybe. I don't know. Why?"

"I'm coming with you," said Ken, smacking his chest dramatically. "Let's get the hell out of this slum."

The man had on the same striped shirt as when I'd seen him drinking his late-night orange juice. Lower down, he wore sweatpants and filthy blue slippers. He looked like he hadn't been planning to leave the house that day. I wondered what restaurant they'd gone to for dinner. "Do you have a car?" I asked him.

He frowned. "I assumed we'd take your car."

"I don't have a car," I said. "That's my whole problem."

"Well I don't have a car either," said Ken.

"He doesn't even have a driver's license," said Peg. "He's blind."

"Only legally." Ken held up his finger and his thumb with half a centimeter of air between them. "I'm just barely over the line."

"You're too old to drive to Pensacola, hon." Peg rose slowly from the stoop and draped her arms over Ken's shoulders. "I'll tell you what, Kenny? Once we get this house sold, you and me, we'll fly to Boca, huh? Two weeks. Now how does that sound?"

I called Becca again. Then Ivan. Then Becca. Neither answered.

\\\\\\

Peg and Ken left for Peg's other house. I sat there in the Mummer's costume, waiting for Ivan to show up, or to at least call me back. Beside me, the glockenspiel rested on the stoop like the molted husk of a giant insect. I had my work clothes in my backpack, but they were soaked with sweat and dishwater. Besides, I didn't want to have to get changed there in the street. I sat in the waning light, thinking about Ivan and his dead father. Eventually I thought about my own father, who was still alive.

He wasn't from South Philadelphia, my father. He was from North Philadelphia, where white people didn't hold on past the 1980s. The Monks were actually the last white family on his crowded little block in Olney. When it was mixed, he told me, the kids all got along, but after the Romanellis and the Scheckenbachs split and it was just my dad and his sisters, the black kids decided they didn't like him anymore. They started kicking his ass regularly, for reasons he never quite understood, until finally his parents sold the house at a loss and moved across Tacony Creek to the Great Northeast and a new crowded little block that stayed white for another twenty-five years. My father told me once that he wanted to raise his kids in Bucks County because it felt like the countryside to him, like a flock of pheasants could take flight from a cornfield at any moment, or a gentleman farmer could ride up on horseback and ask if you'd just seen a fox run by. In actuality, Bucks County was filled with the same white people that used to live in North and South Philadelphia, watching the same TV stations and nursing the same grievances. The main difference was that their houses were spaced farther apart, and their commutes were longer, and they were all on the same page about the Mummers being dumb as hell. As I got a bit older, I realized it wasn't just that my father wanted me to grow up around trees and lawns—though I do think that was part of it—but that he hoped I would only get my ass kicked by kids who looked like me. If a white kid kicked my ass, his thinking went, I wouldn't have to wonder if it was about some bigger, societal thing. I would just know that the kid didn't like me, or that his parents were getting a divorce. And if I didn't have to wonder why some kid was terrorizing me—or so my father hoped—my mind would be free to ponder life's other, thornier mysteries, of which there were many. More and more all the time.

The streetlights came on while I sat there, and as night fell I imagined I could hear a New Year's parade, the music faint and staticky, like one of the faded, grainy processions on subchannel 17.4. It was like the string bands had marched into my head, accentuating my thoughts with incidental music. But no, I wasn't imagining it. I could literally hear "Oh Dem Golden Slippers" seeping up from the ground. I noticed a glow in the egress window of the house next door, the one that led to Franny's basement. I got down on my hands and knees and peered through the grime-yellowed glass, into a cellar lit by three naked incandescent bulbs. There he was, the limping electrician, in his calf socks and boxers and undershirt, a parasol in his hand. Somewhere unseen, a record played. Banjos strummed, saxophones yawped. Franny strutted like a buffalo. Like an acrobat. Like the man at the end of a noose. He danced across the concrete floor from one end of the basement to the other. His shoulders hopped, his elbows flapped, his feet sidled around and around, carrying him not to new years but back, back, back to all the old ones.

OLD CITIES

I went to Tasker Street with the idea that Seamus still lived there, though it had been a long time since we last talked. I walked fifteen blocks across a whole swath of city, all my possessions packed up on my back like a man gone out to make his way in the world. A purple evening had slipped over Point Breeze, and the streets were empty in a way that led me to suspect that everyone was somewhere else—had all known where to go—and that I was showing up slightly too late to be a part of it. Philadelphia was like that. Maybe the whole world was like that. You'd think you could hear something convivial happening on the next block, but you'd turn the corner and find a few empty bottles left out on a curb.

I'd texted Seamus the night before and heard nothing back, but his bike was chained up out front, so I pounded on the door. He lived at the top of an old three-story row house with a facade of bricks stained dark as muddled cherries. The bell had never worked. The windows were open. It was summer, still. A head protruded over a sill on the top floor. I determined after a moment of squinting that it could not be Seamus's head, though there were vague similarities. The head recognized me. "Is that Dennis Monk?"

"Seamus here?"

"He moved. Hold on. I'll come down."

When the door opened, the man who emerged was Seamus's brother, Teddy Waldron, still gangly as an adolescent with long, ill-considered hair crowding around his neck. The last time I'd seen him, Teddy was a dazed high schooler crashing Seamus's parties. The only visible difference between that Teddy and the one before me was an overeager mustache. It made him look even younger somehow.

"How you doing, Monk?" Teddy clutched my hand and ensnared me in a half-embrace. "It's been a while."

"You said Seamus moved?" I asked. "Where is he now?"

Teddy smiled like he was suspicious of the question. "California."

"Wait, really?" I was too shocked to be embarrassed. "When did that happen?"

"End of February. We had a going-away party and everything."

I tried to recall precisely when it was that I had last talked to Seamus. Before February. Maybe well before. I'd stopped drinking in November and ignored his calls in those first few months. At some point he'd stopped calling.

"But his bike's still here." I pointed to the fixed gear bound like St. Sebastian to the stoop's railing, as though its presence must be proof of something.

"He gave me the bike," said Teddy. "Well, he sold it to me. And me and my buddy took the apartment. The rent's pretty good."

"He really moved to California?" Seamus had never lived more than twenty miles from his mom's house.

Teddy looked disappointed to learn I had let my friendship with his brother deteriorate to such an extent that I didn't know what coast he inhabited. Teddy was an earnest guy. He had an earnest face, like a kid or a dog.

"I was hoping to crash with him for a few days," I said.

"You can still crash." Teddy's enthusiasm returned. "Of course. We got plenty of room." He removed a loosened brick from the stoop's edge and produced a spare key, which he placed in my palm like a communion wafer.

The apartment looked the same as when Seamus lived there. It occupied the second and third floors of the house, dark and cramped and musty. It reeked of something. That was new. At first I thought it was weed, but the scent was sweeter, almost milky. "That's the wort," said Teddy. He opened the hall closet and tapped his toe against a five-gallon water jug of unfermented sludge. "We're brewing beer."

Already I knew it wouldn't pan out. But I had walked fifteen blocks and the sun was down. I could tolerate it for a day or two. The roommate was at work. Teddy assured me he was a good guy and we would all get along. Teddy had just begun his last semester of college and was working as a barback at a place on Christian Street and what was I doing with myself these days?

I gave him a cursory and nonspecific inventory of my state in life: how I was between places, working part-time some of the time but mostly endeavoring to not need money. I didn't say that I was a dishwasher since that was not how I liked to see myself. I did mention two or three times how I was sober. By that point, I was pretty sick of telling people about it. It had been cathartic at first, but it quickly became the opposite, the more I had to hear myself explain myself. Every aspect of my life seemed to require justification. Teddy's face lacked the disapproval that I often saw on those of my peers when I gave them the rundown, which is a difference between age twenty-two and twenty-six—a tolerance for that sort of itinerancy. I didn't have any specific place I was heading toward, and I was grateful to people who didn't force me to admit as much aloud.

Teddy went to take a shower. He had plans to go out, and I would go with him. I sat on the couch in the living room, my backpack and laptop case piled next to me. The couch was temporarily mine. My bed, my piece of the world. I had slept on that couch before. I had slept on it in a few different houses. I remembered when Seamus and Conn Driscoll moved to the Tasker Street apartment two years prior. I was supposed to help with the move, but I slept late into the afternoon and showed up hung over after they'd already returned the U-Haul to the lot. We all went out to the American Sardine Bar, and over the course of the evening Conn disappeared, and Seamus took the girl I was talking to back to the apartment, and I ended up crashing with some people I only kind of knew who lived nearby. By crashing with them, I mean I ended up passing out on their roof and sleeping all night under the damp summer sky, which Seamus thought was the funniest thing in the world when I told him about it the next day.

California. I wondered how I might get out to California. I took a photo of the apartment with my phone, one that included the couch and my bags and the kitchen and the stairs, and I sent it to Seamus so he'd know I was there. I figured it would elicit some kind of response, even just a laugh, but I got nothing in return. By then Teddy was pulling on his shoes and it was time to leave.

\\\\\\

The sun was down, but the brick houses along Tasker radiated us with the September heat they'd stored up throughout the day. I felt a wave of vestigial back-to-school gloom. Not that I was tethered to the academic calendar—or any calendar other than the one that accumulated my sober days—but September always affected me. It got into my chest like ragweed pollen. I breathed it in and held it in my lungs and found a warped pleasure in it. I'd known enough depressives to know that I wasn't one of them, not clinically, but I could get a bit sensitive at certain times of the year.

We arrived at a pop-up beer garden in a wide, vacant corner lot on Point Breeze Avenue. A tractor-trailer bedecked in Edison bulbs dispensed cups of beer from the counter cut into its hull. Across the street, run-down row houses glared at us through unsmiling windows. There were people around. Not many, but some. Before we'd left the apartment, Teddy had asked me, considerately, if I was okay to go to a beer garden. I told him of course I was, but once we were there, I immediately wanted to leave. As much as I had earlier craved a gathering, when the city seemed empty, I craved my solitude again.

Teddy spotted the friend he had come to meet. She sat at a picnic table by herself, hunched in the semi-embarrassed, semi-dispirited posture of a person waiting for a train. She was flanked on either side by two potted saplings. Teddy knew Georgina from school, he'd explained. They'd had a class together two years ago, before she'd graduated and moved to Los Angeles. Georgina Keegan was always moving away, always coming back from some other place. When Teddy met her, she had just returned from a year in Seattle. Before Seattle, she'd had a six-month internship in San Francisco. Most recently she'd lived in Bozeman or Boulder or someplace like that. The country called to Georgina, Teddy said, in a way that it did not call to people like us, who sat around in various houses in various neighborhoods of Philadelphia. Or so I took to be his implication.

Georgina stood when she saw Teddy and wrapped him in a possessive hug. She pressed her face between his neck and shoulder, the rest of her body obscured by his bent, reciprocating form, and because of the way we were all positioned I stood directly in her line of sight. I glanced down at the wood chips beneath my shoes so that we weren't staring awkwardly at one another.

After they untangled, I introduced myself. Georgina was tall, with an open, square face and fervid eyes. Her hair was tied up loosely at the back of her head. She was older than Teddy. Older than me, I thought. She had the gravity of someone who had lived some, and seen some, and whose opinions were rooted in experiences that she would not feel compelled to explain to people whom she had just met in beer gardens. I understood all this about her in only a minute or so. She was not at all what I expected from a friend of Teddy's.

Georgina asked me to watch her saplings as she and Teddy walked off to get drinks. They stood about five feet tall, with three skinny trunks each, anchored in the kind of plastic planters you'd find in the nursery section of a hardware store. Their bark was lustrous as brass, with little flecks of white, and their branches terminated in clouds of leaves. As I sat at the table, I imagined that Georgina lived so lightly that these two trees were all she carried with her from place to place. That she had traveled to that beer garden from the high lonesome prairie bearing nothing but these two saplings, having learned over the course of her migrations that they were all she needed.

The couple returned, laughing at something. I waited for them to explain. They did not.

"What's with the trees?" I asked as they sat down.

"Oh, they're giving them away," said Georgina, waving vaguely toward the other tables. "This is the last weekend for the beer garden, so they said I could take some trees. They're river birches. When they're older, the bark peels off in scrolls, like paper. It's pretty."

"It sounds pretty," said Teddy.

"Teddy said you don't drink?" Georgina asked me.

"I stopped," I said. "Ten months ago."

"Monk used to drink a lot," said Teddy.

"I would assume," said Georgina.

"Seamus told me you slept on a roof once?" asked Teddy. "Right around here?"

"Over on Ellsworth," I said, annoyed that Teddy had brought it up. It really wasn't too funny, the way that it happened. I had been talking to this charmingly evasive artsy girl in the Sardine Bar, and Seamus swooped in and stole her attention. Not that she would have had much to do with me, I'm sure. I was already too drunk. I started talking to these other two girls and their friend at the other end of the bar. The one girl, Monica, knew my buddy Denhelder, who had died the year before. I recognized her from the funeral. The lanky, emphatic guy they were with was going on and on about becoming a storm chaser. He kept referring to "severe weather phenomena," but it seemed like he just meant tornados. People chased them in vans, out in Kansas or Oklahoma. He'd just seen a documentary about it. By last call, Seamus had split with the artsy girl, and Conn was gone, and these three people, Monica and her friend and the aspiring storm chaser, invited me back to drink more at an apartment on Ellsworth Street where two of them lived. I think I may have had hopes of hooking up with Monica, which was even less likely than me hooking up with the artsy girl, but more booze and a couch to sleep on would have sufficed. I only vaguely remember the walk, and I only vaguely remember being on the roof—I'm not sure how I got on the roof, but I had the sense that I was trapped out there. I couldn't get the window open and I didn't have my phone. For some reason, I thought I had dropped the phone off the roof. I was convinced that I had stood at the edge and let the weight of it fall from my hand. I remember, too, that the roof of the next house, the one across the alley, had one of those decoy owls perched beside the satellite dish, an old plastic effigy on a stake to scare nesting birds away. I don't know how much I even slept out there. I think I mostly sat up shivering until, just as the sun came up, the window opened and the aspiring storm chaser let me back inside. It wasn't funny at all. The interaction was entirely humorless. He gave me my phone without explanation, and I left. I had no sense of what had happened, but I stayed away from that part of Ellsworth Street after that, embarrassed I might run into any of them again.

I told Teddy and Georgina the story, though I told it in the funny way that I had learned to tell it. We all had a good laugh at my expense.

"I live on Ellsworth Street," said Georgina excitedly. "I just moved in this morning. My stuff hasn't even arrived yet. I'm having it shipped. The place is completely empty. There's only two suitcases in the whole apartment."

"There's a cool venue at Broad and Ellsworth," said Teddy. "An old honky-tonk bar. We should go sometime."

"Are you still in a band?" asked Georgina.

\\\\\\

Georgina had some drinking stories of her own. She still drank, but not like she used to. For a while, she didn't drink at all. In Los Angeles, she smoked weed and went to therapy. That's how she figured out that she didn't actually need to quit drinking. And rooftops—she'd spent some nights on rooftops in Oakland, but she hadn't usually slept because of the molly. And she once tried to sleep on the deck of a houseboat in Tacoma after her friend "lost the keys," but really he never had the keys, because really it wasn't his boat. She once got turned around going to take a piss in Joshua Tree and couldn't find her way back to the tent, and she was convinced she would freeze to death in the desert night, but luckily the mushrooms she'd taken kept her from panicking. And the calmest she ever felt was wandering down the broad, main boulevard of Caspar, Wyoming, at dawn, and she hadn't been on anything at all that time, though she also couldn't remember when it was or how she had got there. As she talked, Teddy sat captivated, grinning like a baby, and spoke only to offer to replenish his and Georgina's beers.

"I can get this round," said Georgina. "You're so generous, Teddy. I forgot that about you."

We watched her walk away and I could feel Teddy pine after her. Speakers at the edges of the garden whispered pop music. I had to listen hard to figure out what the song was.

"So Seamus has really been gone for seven months?" I said to fill the air. "There was a while he and I hung out almost every day."

Teddy gave a solemn nod, as though losing touch with someone was something he had been warned about but never personally experienced.

"Where's he living now?" I asked. "Where in California?"

"Sebastopol. Half an hour from the redwoods. Forty-five minutes from the ocean. That's paradise, for him."

"Yeah," I said. Though I would never have guessed that Seamus cared much for either redwoods or the ocean, and I'd known him pretty well. Or thought I had. "So what's your deal with Georgina?"

"We're friends." He got shy all of a sudden. "I don't know. I haven't seen her in a year. She texted me because she just got back to town."

Georgina reappeared, cups in hand. I asked her if she planned to garden at her new place.

"I'm on the third floor, sadly." She brushed her hand through the leaves of one of her birches. "But maybe I could have a garden on the roof? Oh, I'll need help carrying these, Teddy. If I have to carry both of them all the way to my apartment, my arms will fall off. And then I'll never learn to play the harp."

"You could play with your feet," I suggested.

"We'll help you carry them," said Teddy, but Georgina was laughing and kicking her legs in the air.

"I'd need stronger thighs for that," she said. "I'll have to train. I'll get a recumbent tricycle."

Teddy attempted to elevate his own legs in a harping motion but managed only to knock over his beer. Georgina laughed harder. Teddy's face reddened like a plum. He gathered his empty cup and went to have it refilled.

"So you like trees," I said.

"Of course." She smiled like it was a dumb thing to say. "Everybody likes trees."

"Not me," I said. "Don't care for 'em."

"What does that mean?" she laughed. "What could that possibly mean?"

"They're just not for me," I said. "They're strange if you think about it."

She lifted one of the trees onto the bench and shook the branches at me as though it were a hand puppet. "Look at this tree," she said. "You're telling me you don't think this is an adorable tree?"

I shrugged.

"That's just offensive," she said. "I adopted these trees. I plan to have them for years. They are essentially children to me now. I'm responsible for raising and nourishing them."

She tipped the tree forward until its leaves brushed against my face. They were soft like the tags on a pillow.

I swatted them away. "So where are you from?" I asked her.

"Jersey." She set her tree down. "Mount Laurel. My parents sold their house last year. They moved to Tucson to be near my brother." She produced a cigarette from her purse and thumbed her lighter several times before it lit. "I figured I'd come back to Philadelphia. Maybe go back to school. This is my city, if any city is my city. But you know, I got off the plane today and realized I only know like four people here anymore? I texted them all tonight and Teddy was the only one who responded." She smiled wistfully. "I sound like an ingrate. Teddy's the best. How long have you known him?"

"A long time," I said. "But not well."

"That's the opposite of how I know people. I know people quick and deep. I bet I could know everything about you by the end of tonight. I'm serious. As good as anyone has ever known you. Best friends by morning."

"You really think so?" I didn't believe her, but I liked that she wanted to know me.

"I've known a ton of people," she continued. "That's what's weird. A ton of people, all over. And yet I come back here, where I'm from, basically, and I hardly know anyone. How can the world get so empty all of sudden?"

I had the odd sense that she did already know me, maybe. That we were two people who had been having the same conversation, each by ourselves. "Most of the people I know live in this city," I said. "But it feels empty to me too. Even sitting right here, with all these people around, it feels empty."

"Yeah," she said. "What is that?"

"I don't know," I said. "I got sober and it's like a whole different city."

"Well, it is a different city," said Georgina. "Addiction and sobriety are different cities. You might as well have moved across the country. You're the new kid in town. You haven't met your new friends yet."

But here she was, I thought. My first new friend.

\\\\\

Teddy reappeared at the table wagging his cell phone in his hand. Within its compact square of plastic, the wider world stirred. "So my roommate just called," he told me. "He lost his key. And the spare isn't on the stoop, since I gave it to you. So we've got to go back and let him in."

I didn't say anything. The evening sputtered in the air.

Teddy attempted to save it. "But we can come back. It should only take half an hour. Or you could come with us, Georgina. I have some beers back at the apartment. We could hang out awhile."

"You know, I think I should probably just head home." Georgina sighed and gathered her bag. "My stuff is supposed to get here in the morning, so I shouldn't be out too late."

I was furious at Teddy, furious at the roommate. Furious at Seamus's couch, where I would soon be lying in the dark.

"Oh. Okay," said Teddy, disappointed. He took Georgina awkwardly in his spindly arms. "It was great to see you again. We'll hang out soon."

"Your trees," I said. "You still need help with your trees."

Georgina's eyes moved to me. "Right. My birches. Monk, would you mind? We could handle it, I think, the two of us, while Teddy goes to help his friend?"

"Of course," I said, delighted. I stood and gripped one of the trees by the lip of its pot. I moved quickly before another plan could be suggested. I placed my free hand on Teddy's shoulder and spoke so that my words held nothing other than their semantic meaning. "I'll find my way back to your place after."

Comprehension troubled Teddy's eyes. His mustache went limp. I thought for a moment he might object, as he should have, and I wondered what I would say in response, but he only said, again, "Oh. Okay."

Georgina and I walked quickly away and left him standing there on the wood chips, too pitiable to contemplate.

The birch in my hand did feel almost like a child, heavy and light in unexpected ways. A torso with many shifting limbs. Dense at the potted end, airy at the branches. Weighted like a bomb to orient itself toward the earth. The soil sucked at my thumb. The leaves nipped at my ear. I could see how carrying both trees would be a great inconvenience. Georgina had been reasonable in requesting assistance, and assistance might truly be all she had requested.

"Is it heavy?" asked Georgina as we strode north on Point Breeze Avenue.

"Practically carries itself," I said.

"That's what I like to hear." Her voice was strained from amusement and exertion. The breathiness of it excited me, the warmth of it. It wasn't a crowd I needed, just another lonely person. That's why you wandered through the city, to bump into someone else wandering through the city. Even with the birches rustling between us, I could see the shimmer of Georgina's hair, which I had not touched but might soon touch, and the curve of her hip where my hand might go, and I had a vision of us rolled up in some fevered corner of her empty apartment, seeing if we didn't fit perfectly together. It was an easy scenario to entertain as we danced with our trees along Point Breeze Avenue.

\\\\\\

Ellsworth waited inconspicuously in the glow of the streetlights. We paused on a step as Georgina dug for her keys.

"If you like trees," she said, "you should move to Sacramento."

"I said I don't like trees."

Her keys chimed softly as she held them up. "I don't think you would have dragged that tree all this way if you didn't like trees."

I set my birch down on the stoop and pressed the leaves of hers away from her face. I kissed her mouth, and she kissed back, and the geographic immensity of her life seemed to shrink away.

She laughed. "I'm so glad you don't have a mustache."

I felt a knot somewhere below my navel. "Ah, don't say that."

"What?" she asked. "You feeling bad about Teddy?"

"No," I said. "I don't feel bad about anything."

"Of course not," she said, pulling me toward the door with her free hand. "Forget I said it. I wish you did have a mustache. I wish we both had mustaches."

We hauled our trees through the vestibule and up the shabby staircase, the plastic pots thumping like tom-toms against the balusters. I had successfully pushed Teddy from my thoughts during the walk over—how he had accommodated me, offered me a spare key and a couch—but he had jostled his way back to the front of my mind. Teddy was a nice guy. A nicer guy than Seamus. A nicer guy than me. I watched Georgina huffing through her mantle of leaves and wondered why she would choose me over him.

"Ever been to Sebastopol?" I asked her as we rounded the first landing. I wondered if I could even go back to Teddy's, after, or if my belongings were forfeited, new unwanted features of Seamus's old apartment.

"No," she said. "It's above San Francisco, right?"

"My buddy just moved out there," I said. "I've never been either."

"Are you going to go?" she asked.

"Probably not," I said. "Maybe. I don't know."

"Why wouldn't you go?" she asked.

I imagined carrying the tree all the way across the country, shifting it from one shoulder to another as I traversed mountains, rivers, deserts. "I just moved to a new city," I said. "Remember? This is my new city."

At the top of the stairs we paused again. The landing was so small that it accommodated only Georgina and her tree. I hung back on the stairs with mine, my feet unlevel and my back braced against the wall. I could hear the keys jangling as she searched for the correct one. "Sorry, can you take this?" She nudged her birch toward me. I grasped it in my free hand. Where my vision had formerly been half-clear and half-concealed, I could now see only leaves. The rest of the world retreated behind a thin but impenetrable forest.

The door opened and Georgina flipped on the light. I followed her into a narrow living room, with closed doors on either side and a tiny kitchen visible down the hall. The apartment was empty of furniture, just chipped wooden floors and naked plaster walls. Two suitcases and a sleeping bag lay heaped in a corner. That was all. There was no place to sit, much less to lie down.

"I told you it was empty," she said, walking her tree to the middle of the room, her footsteps creaking on the boards. I followed and stood mine next to hers, a tiny copse in the midst of a barren floor. The mood was different than it had been a moment ago. Maybe it was the austerity of the overhead light, the vacantness of the apartment. I knew the moment called for some gesture, but I did not make one, and neither did she.

"I'm going to use the bathroom real quick," she said.

She opened one of the doors and disappeared into the shadow behind it. The whir of a fan switched on, a bar of gold illuminating the gap above the floorboards. I stood there for a moment with the birches, swatting anxiously at the leaves. I pictured the apartment filled with furniture. Not my furniture, since I didn't own any furniture, but furniture I might like. Not bulky, heavy wooden furniture, but light, thin, modern stuff. A sofa too narrow for guests. Plants in the corners and paintings on the walls. I wandered toward the kitchen. I could see a window next to the refrigerator that led to the roof of the apartment below—the second story of the house extended back farther than the third—and I remembered what Georgina had said about keeping the trees out there.

I may have already begun to recognize the kitchen as I moved through it, the cheap cabinets and appliances, or the familiar act of opening the window and stepping onto the roof. But maybe not. I had moved through many kitchens and stepped onto many roofs, cradling glasses or armfuls of bottles so they wouldn't spill. It was easier with my hands empty, my palms gripping the grooves of the window frame as I swung one leg over, then the other, and stepped out onto the rectangle of tar tiles illuminated by the kitchen light. The landscape was otherwise blue-black: flat and pitched planes of brick and tar, low-lit chasms in between, the sky brighter than the houses despite the absence of stars. I discounted the sense of familiarity—in Philadelphia, every row house was every other row house, every roof was every other roof—and even when I spotted, on the house across the alley, the decoy owl goggling at me from its stake, looking just as it had two years before, my first thought was only, *oh, they have one of those owls, too.*

The comprehension arrived a moment later, like the panic that comes from realizing you'd forgotten to do something that you swore you would. Monica and her friends. The aspiring storm chaser who'd let me back in through that very window in the morning. The look of revulsion on his long face, which I had never tried to describe to anyone during my many recountings. Additional things came to me as I stood gazing back at the window through which I had just climbed. It was open now, the apartment empty beyond the glass, but on that earlier night it had been shut and locked, with three faces staring out at me like mannequins in a shop display, and me crouched, staring back at them, a steak knife in my fist. I must have grabbed it off their kitchen counter and backed my way onto the roof. I could hear them saying they would unlock the window if I set down the knife, if I promised to calm down and come back inside. I must have refused—I can't say why, or how I came to pick up the knife in the first place. No explanation suggested itself other than the rational one, the sober one of hindsight: that I had been very drunk and something had turned, as it sometimes did. I stayed out there all night, shivering beneath the gaze of the plastic owl, playing some chess game against myself, my inscrutable motivations, my stochastic demons, until at some point early in the morning I crawled to the edge of the roof and dropped the knife into the alley below.

I heard a toilet flush, the shushing of a sink. Georgina wandered back into view. I saw her glance around the apartment for me, her look of confusion scanning the empty rooms. She opened the door to the stairs to see if I had gone. She noticed the window ajar and walked toward it.

Yes, at some point they must all have gone to bed, or at least the kitchen light was turned off, and I stayed out all night, blackout drunk, which isn't sleeping and isn't awake, but a third state, the one I must have preferred on some subconscious level, though what I liked about it, what I did while I was there, was always a mystery to me the next day. The lanky storm chaser let me back in just before the sun came up, and he didn't say anything, no questions, no admonishments. He just handed me my phone, which I must have left inside, and escorted me to the door. I could hear his footfalls tailing me down the steps, one floor behind. A safe distance. I hurried out the front entrance and away from Ellsworth Street, trying to suss out what had happened even as I was already beginning to pack it up in the attic of my memory. If I ever knew why I picked up the knife, why I went out onto the roof, I had forgotten it by the time the sun was fully over the houses.

Georgina stood with her face in the open window. She seemed not to see me, though I was standing right in the center of the roof, just beyond the rectangle of light that encased her silhouette. She shifted from one end of the window frame to the other, peeking out like she was searching for a pet cat, her eyes straining for discernible shapes in the night, rolling blindly until they found me in the darkness.

PASSYUNK

News of my sobriety had spread throughout the land, at least among a certain subset of individuals for whom sobriety was a rare and ill-considered state. It was Oktoberfest at the Brauhaus, which, in the name of public merriment, had shut down a block of South Street in order to validate a lot of debased and antisocial behavior. Not that such conduct didn't occur nightly on South Street, but the Brauhaus had welcomed it into the reputable light of day—to the accompaniment of Schlager and Volksmusik no less—which surely represented, if not an act of outright delinquency, at least some form of civic negligence. I came for a soft pretzel and to reaffirm my own constructive life choices.

Philadelphia was a small town when you got down to it, particularly if you sifted out those people for whom the Brauhaus Oktoberfest held little appeal. I ran into a number of acquaintances. Katie Doran was working the pretzel stand, and I imagine she mentioned my presence to Lilah Noth in the beer tent, who likely tipped off Rob Gill and his troop of inebriates, who accosted me outside the vegan café from which I was contemplating the purchase of a bubble tea. Gill had Sean Culp with him, and Sean Porth, and between the two of them they carried Mildew Hannafey like the crucified Christ, buttressing his slack, skinny arms with their shoulders. They cast the drunk man at me, repeating my name as though they believed it held incantatory properties. "Dennis Monk! Dennis Monk! Dennis Monk!"

"What?" I said. The lax face of Hannafey was pressed against my shirt. His flaccid limbs draped themselves around my neck.

"He's overserved!" cried Gill. Gill, too, was overserved. The whole group of them was overserved. They continued to overserve themselves from the plastic beer steins germinating from their hands. "You're sober, Dennis Monk! You need to take him home!"

"Is that Dennis Monk?" muttered Hannafey. "I know Dennis Monk."

"I don't know where he lives," I said, turning my face away from the semiconscious reveler nuzzling at my sternum. He smelled strongly of beer and slightly of vomit. I knew very little about Hannafey. He was around twenty-two, on the shorter end of average height, with elfin features that suggested intoxication even when he was sober, which he rarely was. I'd only ever encountered him in low-lit bars, where the regulars evolved a sort of cave-blindness toward one another. I was alarmed to see him in daylight.

"He lives way down Passyunk!" Gill had sardine eyes, eyes terrified of ever missing a thing that happened in the world. "Down past Nineteenth!"

"I'm not going to take him there," I said. "I don't even have a car. Just put him on a bench for a while."

"He'll get sunstroke and die!" wailed Gill. "He'll putrefy like a jack-o'-lantern!"

"Jesus, just put him in the shade," I said, though already the old guilt was revving in my chest. I wanted nothing to do with the chemically impaired—they annoyed the fuck out of me, in a way that only those exhibiting my own inadequacies could—but for that same reason I felt an obligation toward them. They brought to mind all the people who had aided me when I had been in similar states of degeneration. All the people, too, who hadn't bothered. Part of what impelled a person to substance abuse in the first place was the hope that, if he forfeited his faculties and lay himself before the mercy of his fellow man, some reluctant Samaritan might come along and look after him for a little while. I had once wobbled so discomfitingly before a bar in Callowhill that a woman invited me into her car and dropped me off at a friend's place in Fairmount, asking nothing of me other than a promise that I would go straight to bed and take better care of myself in the future. Another time, a group of college students five years my junior—not one of whom I'd met before or since—bought me a late-night doughnut in Old City before sticking me in a cab bound for an address I knew in Northern Liberties. One time I stayed on the Blue Line long past my stop, all the way to Upper Darby, just to prove to a girlfriend that I was as proud as I was angry (as I was drunk, as I was baffled by my life) only to get mugged outside the 69th Street station and stumble back to her doorstep, thirty-five shameful blocks on foot, without receiving a single look of human recognition from a single person who crossed my path. For all of that—the people who'd helped and the ones who hadn't—I agreed to get Mildew Hannafey to his bed, even though I didn't want to. He'd become me, there in my arms, and I was someone else.

"Hooray!" cheered the inebriates, Gill and Culp and Porth and all of them, like I had solved something permanent in their lives. "Hooray for Dennis Monk!"

\\\\\\

I walked Hannafey down 8th Street to where it intersected Passyunk Avenue, a veering, surly smirk that bisected the lopsided jowls of South Philadelphia. The East Passyunk corridor was the sort of place that, only a few years earlier, would have filled me with contempt, block after block of high-end vintage shops, small-menu cucinas, and pet supply emporiums. In my new humility, though, I recognized it as one of those good places that I would never afford to live near. I'd failed to save a cent during the whole of my adulthood up to that day, and the area's gentrification needle had recently ticked from *up-and-coming* to *no vacancy*. The likes of Hannafey and I were no longer welcome, at least, if the scandalized stares we inspired on the faces of the strolling Saturday lunch crowd were any indication.

"Pick your feet up," I hissed in Hannafey's ear, but he only gurgled and continued to drag the toes of his sneakers against the rough scalp of the sidewalk. I was beginning to sweat from the exertion, which annoyed me even more, since sweating at an inappropriate hour on a mild day was a drunk's affliction, and I was no longer a drunk. Hannafey was slick as a bag of fasnachts. I could smell the ammonia seeping through his pores.

At the corner of Cross Street, he made a sudden lurch away from me around the exterior counter of a gastropub. One second he was heaving hot breath into my nose and the next he was gone, like he'd been planning his escape for blocks. He stumbled thirty feet before one of his ankles rolled over the curb and he collapsed in a heap in the middle of the road. I ambled up to Hannafey with the intention of laughing at him—I had to laugh at him after something like that, for his sake and for mine—just as another pedestrian from the opposite sidewalk stepped over to check whether Hannafey had hurt himself.

We were each just beginning to bend over the splayed drunk and nudge at him with our feet when the spark of mutual recognition caught between this other person and me. It was remarkable how quickly the stranger transfigured into someone I recognized. Who I in fact knew very well.

"Monk?"

"Mangan."

He sounded more incredulous than me, even though, as far as I knew, Kevin Mangan lived in Texas, and I continued to live in Philadelphia, and the fact that we were in Philadelphia meant that it was much more likely for me to be there than him. But people were always reappearing in life. We did not hug. We reverted to our full standing heights, the well-being of the earthbound Hannafey momentarily forgotten.

"You're here," I said.

"I moved back."

"Where at?"

"Right there." Mangan pointed at the building behind him on Cross Street, a modest two-story row house with a tan brick exterior. "Do you live around here?" he asked me.

"No." I was, at that point, crashing on my cousin's couch in deep South Philadelphia, but I didn't want to tell Mangan that. When Mangan and I had lived together, I'd technically been crashing on his couch, as well, and I didn't want it to seem as though I'd made no progress in the intervening years. I had made progress. Just not in that specific area. I tried to think of something else to say, but couldn't, and we stood there for a moment not saying anything. Beneath us, Hannafey recommenced his gurgling.

"So," said Mangan. "I see you're still getting after it. What is it, one o'clock?"

"I'm not drunk. He's drunk." I pointed to Hannafey. "I haven't had a drink in three hundred and twenty-two days."

Mangan nodded like that datum was immaterial. I might be drunk or sober or anything in between, but Mangan's old view of me was unmodified.

"We're coming from Oktoberfest," I explained, gesturing back in the direction of South Street. "Hannafey was overserved."

"I don't know Hannafey."

"He's friends with Gill. You know Rob Gill? His sister is Amanda Gill? She used to date Luke Rimkus?"

Mangan shook his head. "I don't know any of those people."

"I guess I met Rimkus after you left. You've been gone . . ." I stopped to compute.

"Three years and change," said Mangan.

"Since Denhelder's funeral. You really got out of here quick after that, huh?"

"I was leaving anyway. I had already signed a lease down there."

"And now you're back," I said. A further oddity of the situation was that Mangan had a mustache, and I had never seen him with a mustache before. I didn't even know he was capable of growing a mustache. I would have commented on it, but the really strange thing was that I also had a mustache that day—I'd only just grown it out over the previous week for the first time in my life—and I was feeling self-conscious about it. We stood there as if neither of us had one.

The door to Mangan's house opened a crack and a woman stepped half onto the stoop. She held a fist-sucking infant in her arms and cloaked her concern in a smile. "You okay, Kevin?"

"Nicole, this is Monk. Remember I told you about my old roommate Monk? He needs help with his drunk friend."

Nicole opened the door wider. "Well bring them inside. He shouldn't lie in the street like that. Mrs. Sirolli's gonna lose her shit if she can't get to her parking space."

\\\\\\\

When I lived with Mangan, he hadn't owned much in the way of decor. He was a pragmatic person, left-brained and unsentimental. Whatever he did have—I remembered a battered leather club chair, a framed but glassless poster of Veterans Stadium—he hadn't taken it with him to Texas. He likely foresaw that in Texas he would find new things. I attributed the design of the living room to Nicole. There was a skinny bookcase laden with popular nonfiction paperbacks. A minimalist console table bearing an 18-inch bronze statue of Don Quixote. A modish track arm sofa where we set the recovering Hannafey. The walls were painted a deep, bold red. The red reminded me of elementary school field trips to the Franklin Institute, which boasted a 5,000-square-foot replica of a human heart. We would race through its red chambers, my classmates and me, our dozens of sneakered soles beating out erratic palpitations.

Away from the sun and the street, Hannafey returned to something closer to sentience. He was recovered enough to accept Nicole's offer of a glass of water, and he sat up so that I could take the cushion beside him on the couch. Mangan rested catty-corner on a matching loveseat, holding the butternut-squash-sized infant—whose name was Olivia, we learned—tucked in the crook of his elbow. Olivia continued to store her fist in her mouth.

"You've got quite the little family here," I said.

"Nicole and I aren't married." Mangan held Olivia like she was an extension of his own arm. I had trouble picturing myself holding anything so effortlessly. "There wasn't a wedding, I mean. I would have invited you to a wedding. If there had been one."

"You pulled a Steve Sudimack," I said. "Surprise parenthood. Funny story, how that ended up not being his kid. Did you hear about that?"

"It wasn't a Steve Sudimack. We wanted a kid. We're happy to have her."

"Oh, of course. That's really great."

Nicole returned from the kitchen with glasses of water for Hannafey and me.

"Congratulations," said Hannafey.

I sipped my water. I could taste the sweat that had collected in my mustache. I felt as drunk as Hannafey, just as embarrassing and unwanted.

Nicole draped her arm around Mangan and gave us an appreciative look. "It's so nice to finally meet some of Kevin's friends. We've been here almost six months and this is the first time I've gotten to meet anybody from the Kensington days. He's told me so much about you guys."

"Not him." Mangan pointed to Hannafey. "I don't know that one."

"We all know each other," said Mildew Hannafey. A substantial portion of the water in his glass had made its way down the front of his shirt. "From outside. We're all friends here."

"What brings you back to Philadelphia?" I asked.

"Austin's expensive. And crowded." Mangan shifted Olivia from one arm to the other. "There's more work up here. You remember those guys I used to do stuff with? They've got a deal with Comcast now. I'm basically their house sound guy. So that's made it easier."

Mangan had worked in film and television production since before we'd graduated. Scouting locations, wrangling extras, getting people coffee. For a long time, he did it for no pay. That was how everything worked, in every industry, he said: if you interned long enough, even for free, eventually something would open up. You would get the life you wanted, the house and car and family. At the time, I thought it was crazy to work for free—a transparent scam the rich had invented to humiliate the rest of us—and that Mangan was a rube. But I was wrong, as I often was.

"This is a great place," I said. "This is a great neighborhood. All these restaurants and places along Passyunk. Really great."

"We got a good price," said Mangan. "More than we would have paid three years ago, but you know how it is. Nicole does graphic design for a startup on Catharine Street, so she can walk to work."

"I do love that," said Nicole. "I drove everywhere in Austin. Where do you live, Monk?"

"Oh, here and there," I said. When it was clear that wouldn't be a sufficient answer, I clarified. "I'm currently staying with my cousin down by the stadiums. Temporarily."

"Monk was supposed to stay with me and Denhelder temporarily," said Mangan. "That turned into, what? A year?"

But that had been different. I had been different then. "I'd like to get my own place. I just haven't landed on a career path yet. The jobs I've been working aren't really long-term. I'm washing dishes right now." I didn't know why I was admitting to all these things. Beside me, Hannafey had fallen back asleep, the tip of his tongue clamped between his front teeth like a wad of gum. I took the empty glass from his hand and set it on the coffee table.

"Maybe Kevin can help you out with something." Nicole rubbed Mangan's arm in just the way you'd want a girlfriend to rub your arm. "You've got a few projects coming up, right? With Comcast? I'm sure there's something Monk could do on set."

Mangan attempted—just barely—to conceal his distaste for that notion. "We could maybe find something. A PA job or something."

"Oh, don't put yourself out," I said.

"No." Mangan spoke as though the whole thing were his idea to begin with. "We'll find you something. There's always something that needs to get done."

"I'd do whatever," I said. Sure, I could be a PA. The thoughts budded rapidly, one after another. Maybe I could get into the film production business. With Mangan's help, maybe I could skip some of those initial, unpaid steps, and soon I might have a house of my own. Not this close to Passyunk, obviously, but somewhere not too far away. An imagined middle-class future sprouted up before me. "Really. Whatever you could get me. That would be highly appreciated."

"Just whatever you can swing, Kev," said Hannafey, awake again. "We'll do such a job you won't believe how proud you'll be."

"I did try to set Monk up with a gig back before I left," Mangan told Nicole. "Monk was supposed to write something for Sam and Vinny. But I guess nothing ever happened with that?"

Hardly a gig, I almost said. It hadn't been for money. They were filmmakers, but they weren't writers. "We can barely string a sentence together," the one guy had said. They wanted me to write them a script. Just a little script, for a short film they wanted to make, about a dentist in the suburbs who sold cocaine out of his dental office. It was based loosely on a true story. They gave me a book to read and a documentary to watch. If they liked my script, they'd shoot it and take it around to film festivals, and if that went well maybe we'd work together on something else. They couldn't pay me, they said. It was just about making something, a first thing, and later on maybe there would be something that earned money. I said yes, of course, even though I had never written a script, had barely written anything at all. But I'd been drunk at the initial meeting, and I had a lot of confidence when I was drunk. I wanted to write, and here was someone offering me an opportunity to write something, and that meant quite a bit to me.

I was living in Kensington, then, in a house by myself. Denhelder had died a few weeks before, out on the sidewalk, and Mangan had moved to Texas. The introduction to Sam and Vinny was his parting gift to me. The rent had already been paid through the end of the summer. I spent a strange couple of months there, the house half-filled by the objects Mangan had left behind and the furniture Denhelder's parents didn't want back. I got drunk every day, which I had already been doing for a few years, but the drunks were weirder, and the time passed in unpredictable ways. Denhelder was a good friend of mine, had been since high school, and we were good drunks together. I think I had assumed he and I would both get sober at some point. I had known, even back then, that I would eventually have to get sober. There were plenty of moments to quit, moments of shame and embarrassment, moments of fear, and I figured I just needed to come to the right moment, that Denhelder or I or both of us just needed to shame or embarrass or scare ourselves in the right way, and then we'd hang it up. It was just a matter of finding my moment. But then he died, just seized up and dropped down brain-dead on the sidewalk one night as we were walking home from the Lost Bar, he and Mangan and I, arm in arm in arm like a string of paper dolls. That was a moment, the worst of them all, but it wasn't my moment. I didn't quit. I didn't even really try to quit. I'd expected something inside of me would burst open, and the sober version of me would come slithering out, wailing into new life, but it was nothing like that.

I never wrote a word past my name at the top of the screen, and when Sam and Vinny called me, I ignored their calls, and they stopped calling me. Eventually I had an awkward run-in with them at a bar in

Fishtown. I could still picture the way they looked at me, these two sane, art-minded professionals who had thought at one point that I was also a sane, art-minded professional. I watched them as they realized that I was in fact a deteriorating, untrustworthy alcoholic incapable of slapping together a few pages of dialogue. They were embarrassed for me. Years later, their embarrassment still rattled around in my stomach. I supposed that was another potential moment, but I didn't quit then either.

"Yeah, that one didn't work out," I said. "It just didn't come together."

"Dennis Monk's a good man." Mildew Hannafey smacked my chest with his palm. I felt the flesh redden beneath my shirt. "We were at Oktoberfest and the bartenders overserved me. And Dennis Monk came up and said, 'This man has had enough!' And now he's taking me home. My other friends all ditched me, but Dennis Monk is the kind of guy who makes sure people get home safe."

"That's very responsible of you," said Nicole.

"I just don't know why people do that." Hannafey looked as though he might start to cry. I hoped very much that he would not. "Rob Gill. And Sean. Both Seans. They're supposed to be my friends but they ditched me. Like, what the fuck, you know?" Hannafey looked at Olivia. "I didn't eat breakfast."

"Would you like some food?" asked Nicole. "I think we have some leftover pizza?"

"That would be so magnificent," said Hannafey. He lay his head against the back of the sofa and shut his eyes.

I declined the offer of pizza. "Nicole seems really great," I said to Mangan once she had left the room. "Where did you meet her?"

"A bar," said Mangan. "Austin is the same as here. You go to bars. You stay out late. Everywhere's the same."

"Better people down there?"

"Tech bros. Hipsters. Dickheads in cowboy boots. There were definitely times I missed the old days at the Lost Bar. You ever miss any of that?" Mangan nodded at Hannafey. "I guess you're still in it."

"I'm not," I said. "I'm really not. I don't miss it."

Nicole returned with a slice of pizza on a plate. Hannafey did not open his eyes when I nudged him, so Nicole set it down on the coffee table. She took her daughter back from Mangan. "Would you like to hold this little demon?" she asked me.

"Oh, I don't know if I should," I said. The thought panicked me. "I'm not very experienced."

"Don't worry, it's easy," said Nicole. She demonstrated how to position my hands and she deposited Olivia into them. The baby looked at me with wide eyes, her fist still clamped into her mouth. She was heavier than I expected, like a watering can filled to the brim. Everything about her was soft and new.

"How old is she?"

"Eight months," said Nicole. "She used to be half that size."

Olivia pulled her tiny fist from her mouth. She bumped it against my chin, coating me in her spittle. Her expression betrayed nothing of what she thought about me, but behind her eyes, a galaxy spun.

"There's a real person in there," I said, trying to move my face out of her reach. She rubbed her spit against my shirt. "She's amazing. This is amazing."

"She's got a big personality," said Nicole. "Believe me."

"She keeps us busy," said Mangan. "I kept meaning to call you. I was gonna have you down to Austin, before. I was just . . . you know. I got busy."

"Don't worry about it," I said. "I didn't call you either."

"Right," said Mangan.

"We'll all have to do a better job keeping in touch," said Nicole.

"I felt like I couldn't call," I said. I kept staring at Olivia, and she was staring back at me. She brought her wet fist again to my jawline. "It's hard to explain."

"Well, you could have," said Mangan. "We're friends. We've always been friends."

"It didn't really feel that way." I surprised myself by saying it. It was all very surprising to be sitting with Mangan after all that time, in his house with his girlfriend and baby, and Mildew Hannafey half-sleeping next to me. Olivia's drool evaporated cold on my skin. "You know, Denhelder died, and you bailed, right away. I had trouble figuring out what to do after that. You guys were my best friends, and you were both gone in the space of a week, and I didn't know what to do. It took me years to figure it out."

Mangan's face remained placid. "I didn't bail, I moved. I had things I wanted to do with my life. Getting sloshed in Kensington every night wasn't good for me."

"It's okay, Kevin," said Nicole. "Nobody's accusing you of anything."

"I lost someone, too," continued Mangan. "It wasn't like I was in great shape. And you were a mess. You were drunk every day. You mooched off of everybody. I left you with a free place to stay and a writing gig. I couldn't have helped you more than that. Maybe you think I could have, but I couldn't. People don't work like that."

Beside me, Hannafey inhaled sharply. Whatever pickled dreams danced behind his eyelids, they must have frightened him. Olivia was startled by his loud intake of breath and burst into a wail. Nicole, glad for the opportunity, stepped over and took the squirming girl from my arms. She cooed at her daughter as she carried her away into the kitchen. Hannafey, awake again, discovered the pizza on the table before him and gnawed at the crust.

"I have that kid there," said Mangan, pointing after Nicole. "I care about her more than I've ever cared about anything. She relies on me not to starve to death. But I still can't make her do anything. I can coax her, I can bribe her, I can worry, I can hope her life turns out good, but she's already her own thing. And she's a tiny baby."

"I didn't need you to parent me," I said.

"Good. Because you were a twenty-three-year-old with a severe drinking problem," said Mangan. "Which is about a hundred times harder to control than a baby. Like, come on, man. Have some perspective. Denhelder was my friend, too, and I was supposed to drop everything to take care of you? Because you couldn't take a few days off and clear your head? Adults don't get coddled. They get tough love. They're lucky to get that."

"I have to use your bathroom," I said, standing up. Mangan stared at me, nonplussed, then pointed the way.

There was only one bathroom in the house, up on the second floor. From the look of it, it had not been updated in fifty years. The tile and fixtures were shades of green that didn't exist anymore. I did not actually need to use it. I just intended to splash some water on my face, to wash away some of the sweat and baby spittle. I swiveled the sink's hot water knob and filled my palm. The first handful was cold, the second warmer. I looked at myself in the mirror, looked specifically at my stupid mustache bristling out from my wet skin. I looked like I had glued it on, a comedically ineffective disguise.

Coddled. Tough love. I formed Mangan's phrase voicelessly with my tongue. *Tough* love. I could have laughed out loud. It was like something a little league coach would say. Poor stupid Kevin Mangan, with his functioning mind and his life that had worked out just fine, who sat there in his house right off Passyunk talking to me about tough love.

I looked around for a razor but couldn't find one. There was none in the cabinet behind the mirror or on the built-in shelves above the toilet. Finally I spied one in the shower, a pink safety razor with its wide, ovular face. Nicole's razor, I guessed. I held it under the water until the blades were hot and I raked it across my upper lip. The hairs were long and thick and didn't give easily. I hacked through the wiry strands, yanking painfully at my skin.

Love wasn't tough, I thought as I shaved. Everything else in the world was tough. Solitude was tough. Uncertainty was tough. Canvas cots. Futons that stunk like sweat and mold. The same four t-shirts, over and over, that was pretty tough. Resume holes, minimum wage. Degrees for jobs that didn't exist. Disappointed parents. Married exes. The wrong side of twenty-five was pretty tough. Wasted years. Mistakes that followed you your whole life long. Human frailty in its innumerable variations. That's why we couldn't stay soft little toothless infants. That's why we grew into these awful, scabbed-over maniacs. The world was tough as gristle. Tough as artichoke leaves. But love shouldn't be tough. Love for your fellow man. That love should be so smooth you could sleep in it. So tender that you could forget your ache.

I washed the hair and blood off my face, rinsed the razor and put it back in the shower. I walked back downstairs, where Hannafey was sitting by himself in silence with a vacant expression on his face. I could hear Mangan and Nicole speaking quietly in the kitchen. They came back into the living room when they heard my footsteps on the floorboards.

"Hardly a gig," I said to Mangan. It wasn't precisely what I meant to say, and I said it too loudly. I could hear Olivia cooing invisibly in the next room. I hoped she wouldn't remember this visit. I hoped I had made no impression on her at all.

Confusion spread across Mangan's face. "Did you just shave your mustache?"

"I have to get going," I said. "I'm actually right in the middle of something."

I grabbed Hannafey by his arm and attempted to lift him up with my shoulder, though by that point he was fully conscious and capable of standing on his own. We half-marched, half-stumbled out Mangan's door and onto the pavement, fastened together like a fissioning starfish. Words followed us down the stoop. Nicole sounded upset, and Mangan sounded angry, but I didn't quite pick out what either of them was saying. Over his shoulder, Hannafey thanked them gratuitously for the pizza.

\\\\\\

Passyunk cut west and became less cute, dissolving like a river into the six-pointed delta of Broad Street. There was goodness in the world, I knew. I would help Hannafey, and at some point in the future a reformed Hannafey would help others, and one day the world would be something good. We stood clutching one another on the corner, next to a shabby credit union and a mesh sidewalk planter erupting with yellowed end-of-summer fronds, when Mildew Hannafey abruptly spun on his feet and shoved me to the ground.

"Get off of me!" he spat, enraged. "Just get the fuck off me!"

The sidewalk bruised my elbow, knocked my hip and knee. I was embarrassed to find myself on the stained pavement. Any passersby would have been confused to witness what had just transpired between me and this other man, we who had been locked arm in arm a moment before, but there was no passerby to do the witnessing. The sidewalk was empty on our side of the street. I scrambled to my feet and reached my hand into the space that Hannafey had recently occupied, but he was hurrying away up Broad.

"I'm helping you," I shouted after him. How had I been entrusted with the care of such an ingrate? Of all the happy, compliant drunks in the city. Of all the altruistic tasks. "I was helping you, you fuckhead."

"I don't need your help!" Mildew shouted back. "I don't know you!" He shouted louder, "I don't know him!"

I didn't follow after. Hannafey moved up the street at a near sprint, his hands jammed awkwardly into his pockets as though he were afraid of strangers reaching out and grabbing him by his fingers. But there were no strangers. The sidewalks were clear. The traffic thrummed atonally. I stood alone but for the ache of long-grown children galloping through the shoe-scuffed corridors of my heart.

YOUNG TIME

The Pope came to town late in September. It was thirty-six years since a Pope had last visited, and in their zeal to demonstrate that they were taking his security seriously, our temporal powers shut down Philadelphia like a city besieged. Ten-foot fences throttled the Parkway. They declared Center City a vehicle-free zone. They didn't want anybody to assassinate the Pope. We found out later a seventeen-year-old kid from Camden County was scheming to do exactly that: to waste the Pope right in the middle of the Mass on the Art Museum steps. They caught him when he tried to buy a sniper rifle from an undercover cop. He must have felt deeply aggrieved about something, or maybe he just wanted to make the news. There was widespread grousing about the Pope's visit among Philadelphians, who felt that their civil liberties had been curtailed, even if they couldn't articulate precisely how. "Fuck the Pope," they said, and left it at that. We were a post-Catholic city.

Even so, plenty of people still wanted to see the Holy Father, my cousin Matty among them. He wanted his sons to see the Holy Father too. The boys themselves—aged six and eight—were pretty agnostic about it.

"You guys really want to see the Pope?" I asked them. I was driving us all up Broad Street in Matty's Jeep Liberty on the Sunday of the Mass. The boys sulked politely in the backseat, dressed in cheery caps and t-shirts like they were going to a ball game. The older one, Gavin, ignored my query and continued to torture the Nintendo DS between his thumbs. The younger one, Brandon, had the courtesy to lift his stare from his own DS and fix it on my reflection in the rearview mirror, his baby teeth lined up neatly in his flummoxed mouth.

"Course they want to see the Pope, right guys?" asked Matty, turning in the passenger seat to face them. His voice got slow and sprightly when he spoke to his sons. "Historic moment, right guys? Eyes on the road, Dennis."

I wouldn't be seeing the Pope myself, but since I was crashing on Matty's couch and endeavoring to be a better guest and a more grateful sort of person, I had offered to drive Matty and the boys as close to downtown as the barricades would allow. In exchange for this favor, Matty said I could borrow the Liberty in the hours between when I dropped them off and picked them up again. Matty had always been a generous guy, even when we were kids. He was six years older than me, which was enough of a gap that he never delighted in bullying or humiliating me, the way my cousins who were only three or four years older did. After I dropped him and the boys off, I planned to drive across the river to Camden to see Walt Whitman's grave, then head to the Cherry Hill Mall to buy some hiking shoes, an expense I justified to myself as an early birthday present. It would be a splendid little day.

There wasn't a ton of traffic as we drove up from deep South Philadelphia, but what cars there were rolled along at half-speed. National Guardsmen were posted like street signs at the end of every block. They reminded me of kids in Halloween costumes, loitering in pairs in the midday sun, their baggy fatigues failing to camouflage them against the brick walls and shop windows. Women from the neighborhoods brought them pieces of fruit and cans of soda. Some of the women stood half a block away while their children delivered the offerings. The Guardsmen thanked the children and waved to the women like it was a thing that happened every day.

"Do we have any snacks to give the soldiers?" asked Brandon.

"We'll get them on the way back, buddy," said Matty. He had the boys two weekends a month. If it hadn't been his weekend, I'm sure he would have left the city—his girlfriend had already fled down the shore to get away from all the Popery—but there he was trying to make the best of it. Matty was thirty-two. When he was my age, he'd already been a father for two years. I couldn't imagine it. "We'll bring 'em some post-Pope brewskis, what do you say, guys?"

"None for Cousin Dennis," said Gavin. I hadn't spent much time with Gavin prior to that weekend, but I'd already identified him as a pedant.

"Yeah, none for you either, Gavin," I said.

"I'm gonna drink *wine*," said Gavin with relish. He'd made his First Communion that spring. Alcoholics on both sides of the family. The kid was doomed.

I took them as far as South Street, where cops and saw horses barred the way forward. Cars deposited disoriented pilgrims along the curb. "Alrighty, buds," said Matty, "Pope Time." He turned to me and asked, "You'll head to Corinne's now?"

Corinne was Matty's girlfriend, the one waiting out the papal visit at her sister's place in Cape May. She'd left behind her parrot—a scarlet macaw—and it was Matty's responsibility to make sure the bird didn't starve to death. As a second term of my car-borrowing contract, the responsibility had passed to me, though I'd never been to Corinne's house before and had very little experience with birds.

"I got it," I said. "Don't worry about it."

"You're not going to be able to drive on her street," said Matty, stepping squint-eyed into the sunlight. Corinne lived on an old, expensive block of Society Hill. The vehicle-free zone had swallowed her neighborhood. "You probably won't be able to get anywhere near it, so just park where you can and walk. And be chill around the bird. And, you know, don't mess with anything."

I'd only met Corinne once, a few days earlier. She had not struck me as a bird person, even if I had only a vague idea of what characteristics such a person might present. She had, however, struck me as the sort of person to get pissed if her directions were not followed to the letter.

"I have to pee," said Brandon from down near Matty's hip.

"Pee in your pants," said Gavin.

"Don't do that, buddy," said Matty, taking Brandon's hand in his own. "Just get in and get out, Dennis. Really, it's only me that's supposed to be in there."

They vanished into the crowd of pilgrims at the highest speed Brandon's short legs could manage. It was a two-mile walk to the Art Museum, and I didn't know how either of the boys would make it all the way there on foot. Exasperated honks sounded behind me, so I turned right on South and drove toward the river.

It had been a while since I'd had a car to myself. The Jeep was newish and quiet and comfortable, and I had the wild urge to get on the highway and speed west until its front tires were spinning in the surf of the Pacific Ocean. But I would follow the rules. I would feed Corinne's parrot, then genuflect at the mausoleum of the Bard of Democracy, which I had only just learned was located in a rambling cemetery on the outskirts of Camden. Then I would head to one of the region's historic malls to buy the most ergonomic hiking shoes available in my price range. Such were the sort of sedate, practical activities I was learning to enjoy as my sobriety approached its eleventh month. Like Cousin Matty, I was settling comfortably into adulthood.

Between the barricades and the one-ways and the pedestrians wandering wherever they wanted, the city had collapsed into a languorous maze. I had no idea where I could park to get anywhere near Corinne's house. Every legal space within fifteen blocks had almost certainly been nabbed by a Pope-watcher. I took turn after turn and spent a manic twenty minutes inching around Queen Village before I headed north again. I crept up 5th Street, anticipating roadblocks would bar me from crossing South, but I found the way unexpectedly clear. The cop at the intersection allowed the black SUV in front of me to roll across the border into the vehicle-free zone. I followed, impetuous, sure the officer would stop me, but he waved me right along.

Above South, it was a whole different streetscape. There was no car in sight other than the SUV, which soon disappeared down an alley. I drove to Spruce. I had never seen it so denuded of vehicles. There wasn't so much as a Vespa parked beneath the white oaks and stately brick facades. No people paced the sidewalks. Those who hadn't wanted to see the Pope had left town for the weekend. I felt a slight thrill at being somewhere I wasn't supposed to be.

I couldn't turn onto Corinne's block of 7th—the city had dropped two concrete Jersey barriers right in the middle of the road—so I parked on Spruce and hoofed it around the corner. The green of Washington Square was visible at the end of the street, and every window on every house was framed in the heavy, neatly painted shutters that distinguished the self-impressed row homes of Society Hill from those of the rest of the city. Corinne's house fit right in: three stories built before the Civil War, with white marble steps and an antique fire insurance plaque fixed beside the bright red door. Matty was a lawyer and made decent money, though most of it went to his ex-wife, which was why he lived in a three-bed-one-bath 1960s shoebox down by the stadiums. Corinne was a fancier kind of lawyer and made quite a bit more money. Her ex-husband was the fanciest and best-compensated lawyer of them all. Corinne got the Society Hill house in the divorce. No offer had yet been tendered, but it had occurred to me that Matty or Corinne might be able to find me a job in one of their offices or the other. If they did, I could quit washing dishes at the banquet hall. Hell, maybe I'd have an aptitude for the law. Maybe I'd end up in law school.

I unlocked the door with the spare key on Matty's 76ers bottle-opener keychain and stepped into the foyer. The house was narrow but the ceilings were high. It was all white—the walls, the wainscoting, the banisters, the window frames. A well-lit kitchen gleamed at the end of the long hallway. Right away, I heard the whistling of the unseen parrot.

I poked my head through the first doorway and there it was, in the corner of the living room, staring at me from its swing in a cage the size of an elevator. I'd been expecting something roughly the dimensions of a pint glass, but the creature roosting on the swing was at least two feet tall. Three, if you included the tail. Its feathers were a rowdy shade of red. They winked to yellow and then to blue as they rippled down its wings, bright and delineated as the stickers on a Rubik's Cube.

I approached the cage hesitantly, saying soothing, nonsensical things like, "Hello bird, hello gentle bird." Matty had forgotten to tell me the parrot's name and it hadn't occurred to me to ask. I didn't even know if it was a boy or a girl. I unlatched the cage and opened the door, ducking away in case the thing exploded out at me, a cyclone of beaks and claws. But the parrot only continued to sit on its swing, clicking softly. "It's lunchtime, my gentle, scarlet friend." I had never been so close to a bird so large. It was almost as big as Brandon. I was tempted to stick out my finger to see if it would climb onto my arm, but I was afraid its talons might snap my bones.

After a moment of unobtrusive gawking, I left the parrot on its swing and went to the kitchen, where the cabinets and counter-tops were painted an unblemished white above the cold slate floor. Instructions for the parrot's dinner were laid out on the island beside a knife, a metal dish, and a cutting board. From a crisping tray in the massive stainless steel refrigerator, I retrieved an apple, a tomato, a cucumber, and a banana. I chopped them up and scraped them into the dish. As soon as the knife started to clack on the cutting board, I heard a thumping from the hall. The parrot swooped resplendently into the room. It landed on the island beside me and snatched up the chopped cucumber piece by piece, holding the slices to its open beak, its black tongue lapping at the fruit while its glassy eye tracked the movements of my hands.

I stood with it for a while, attempting to discern its mood. "Do you talk?" I asked. I'd been told it knew a few words. The bird looked back at me without an answer. "I—love—you," I said in a stilted par-rot intonation. Matty had told me it was the bird's favorite phrase. "I—love—you."

The parrot said nothing. I left it to its meal.

I then did what I always did when I found myself alone in a new house: I started looking for the liquor cabinet. Not to drink anything. Just to see what it held. I found it on my first try, beyond the refrigerator, behind a bright white wooden door: a cityscape of bottles, green and brown and blue and clear, mostly mid-shelf vodka and bourbon. My gaze landed magnetically on an unopened fifth of Dewar's. It looked just like the one my parents had kept in the cardboard box at the back of their hall closet, the same place they used to hide our Christmas presents. I took it out of the cabinet, just to feel its weight in my hand. Whiskey was the traditional holiday tip for a mailman, and my father accumulated quite a few different brands over the years from the people on his route. He was not a whiskey drinker and neither was my mother, and the bottles collected dust beneath the winter coats until I came along and took an interest in them. I liked the Dewar's before I ever drank it, the tapered silhouette of the clear glass, the texture of the paper, the highlander on the label in his outlandish regalia. I drank most of the bottle in the fall of my senior year of high school, one sip at a time, seven o'clock on weekday mornings, steeling myself for first-period French where Madame Palmisano-Duffy taught us the language of love with an incorrigible Philadelphia accent. It seemed troubling, in retrospect, that I would take a swig of scotch so early in the morning, a clear warning of things to come, but at the time I really believed it helped me speak better French. Without it, I was too stiff, too unsure. I would clam up whenever Madame addressed me. The liquor unlocked my facility for language, even English. Only when I'd had a drink did I ever feel like I could articulate what I thought about anything. Since I'd gotten sober, I felt like I'd been recovering from a stroke, my words unrecognizable through the fog of aphasia, grammar embarrassed, sentences abandoned half-finished, all the while knowing that somewhere in every house, in the back of a closet or cabinet, waited a few dusty bottles that contained within them the golden ability to make me myself again.

My reverie was interrupted by the whoosh of wings. The macaw dove at my arm, its feathers batting me so ferociously in the face that I did not see—but certainly felt—its beak sink into the meat between my thumb and index finger. I dropped the Dewar's. The bottle shattered on the slate floor. The bird flew away again as I shook my arm and wailed. I couldn't see where it went. I squatted down, my left arm curled protectively over my head, and I instinctively reached for the larger pieces of glass with my bleeding right hand. A musk of scotch filled the room. I pricked my thumb on a shard and started to bring it to my mouth, then caught myself. I panicked at the thought of the scotch entering my bloodstream through the cuts. I stood up and ran to the sink to wash my hands. I threw open a window to fumigate the kitchen. There was blood all over the white window frame. I was getting blood on everything. My cuts were bleeding quite a lot. I wrapped my right hand in the white dish towel dangling from the oven door.

I was at a loss, for a moment, of what to do. The dish towel was ruined, soaked through with my blood. It would have to be thrown out. It was a blank, cotton thing, probably expensive but likely just one of a set. I needed a bandage before I stained every white surface in the house. I crept cautiously down the hall to the stairs, hunched over in case the parrot should dive-bomb at me through one of the doorways. In a mirrored cabinet in the second-floor bathroom, I found a large box of Band-Aids of different sizes and used three or four of them to patch up my hand. I squat-walked back downstairs, hoping I wouldn't find the parrot on the kitchen floor, lapping up the puddle of scotch. I didn't want to be responsible for poisoning the thing. The scotch appeared unmolested. I grabbed a roll of paper towels from a cupboard and spent a third of it sopping up the liquid. The smell was marvelous and terrible. I swept the whole wet mess of paper and glass into a trash bag, splashed water across the floor and used another third of the roll to soak it up. I cleaned up the blood where I could find it. I wondered if Corinne was the sort of drinker to notice a missing bottle of Dewar's. I could buy a replacement. But I wouldn't. I didn't go into liquor stores.

I needed to get the parrot back in its cage. I was hoping it might have gone there on its own, consumed with guilt for attacking me, its human feeder, but the giant wire box stood empty in its corner of the living room. Taking the broom in case I needed to shepherd it along, I tiptoed from room to room. "Good bird," I called. "Friendly bird." It wasn't on the first floor. I checked the second. All the doors in the house seemed to be open, even those leading to bathrooms and closets, and after searching the second floor I ascended to the third. "Nice bird, gentle bird." I looked on top of bookcases and behind curtains and under beds, though I didn't know if a parrot would hide so low to the ground. I searched the whole house, bottom to top, and did not find it, so I searched again, top to bottom. I was more frustrated than concerned—I didn't understand where such a behemoth could have gotten to—until I came back into the kitchen and saw the window I'd opened above the sink.

To be fair, it wasn't open very wide. And there was a screen in it—no, there was no screen. The screen had popped out of its frame and was lying on the walk outside. But could the parrot really have popped it out? For all I knew, the screen might have lain like that all summer.

I shut the window. I wondered, though, if the parrot was outside, maybe I should leave it open, so it could come back inside when it was ready? I opened the window again. But what if the parrot was still inside? I shut it again.

I started to freak out.

I ran out of the house. I stood in the middle of 7th Street scanning the blank sky for a bolt of red. There were clouds. A tiny, distant plane. No birds. No people around to ask if they had seen it. I turned and ran down narrow Manning Street, skimming the treetops, chimneys, fire escapes. There were no birds at all, not even pigeons. When had there ever not been pigeons? It was awkward to run with my wounded right hand still stinging beneath its bandages. I held it ineffectually to my chest, feeling slightly off-balance. I sprinted down the block, the ionic columns of St. George's Greek Orthodox Church rising skyward at the end of it, my eyes rising with them, hunting for fugitive rainbow wings. I ran past the last house, and as 8th Street opened up, I heard a shout and caught a blur out of the corner of my eye as it barreled into me.

For the first half of my journey to the ground, I was occupied with the following incredulous thought: *Did this son of a bitch really just hit me with his bicycle?*

Something hard smacked me in the eye, and I felt a searing jolt up and down my right calf, followed by a scorching in my palms. A second later the pain radiated from my hip and side. I wondered, momentarily, if a handlebar had punctured my abdomen.

"Are you fucking kidding me?" I cried, writhing on the asphalt. It felt like several of my organs had detonated. I tried to stand, winced, and lay back down again.

"Are *you* kidding *me*?" screamed a woman. The cyclist was also on the ground, a dozen feet away from her fallen racing bike. She grabbed at her knee, which I supposed to be the thing that had struck me in the face.

"You crushed me," I shouted back. As I felt around my torso, I realized that the bandages on my hand had come loose. The cuts were bleeding again, and there were scrapes along the palm where it had dug into the asphalt.

"You came out of nowhere," she said. "What the fuck were you doing?" She rose slowly to her feet. She was compact, sticklike, wearing an elongated helmet and one of those USPS cyclist jerseys.

"Fuck," I said again.

"Are you hurt?" she asked.

"You were going too fast." I sat up. "I could have been a child. Or a senior citizen."

"I didn't know you would be there," she said. "How could I know you would be there?"

"You were riding like a lunatic," I said. The city should have known this would happen if they closed the streets to cars. The cyclists would go mad with power.

"You came out of nowhere," she repeated, as though I had violated some law of the physical universe. She wobbled over to her bike and picked it up. "There was no way for me to know you would be there."

The searing pain in my gut subsided a bit. It didn't feel like I had ruptured anything, just mashed the skin over my hip. I got to my feet and felt a throb in my left leg. I looked down and saw that my jeans had torn below the knee. The skin beneath it was raw and wet.

"Do you need an ambulance?" asked the woman.

"No," I said, still smarting. "Have you seen a big red parrot?"

"A what?" she asked.

"I lost a scarlet macaw. It's really big. You'd know it if you saw it."

The woman looked at me with concern. "I think you need to go to a hospital."

"No," I said. "I don't need that." I stood up straight. I raised my hand to my forehead. There was blood on my fingers when I looked at them, but I wasn't sure what wound it had come from. "I have things to do."

The woman seemed to consider whether it was in her best interest to let me leave. "Should we exchange information?"

I waved her away and took off in a half-jog, half-limp down 8th Street, my right hand tucked under my left armpit. My jeans were ruined. My shirt, too. It wasn't that much blood, all things considered, but enough that it wouldn't come out in the wash. I turned down Spruce and headed back toward the house, thinking I needed more bandages before I could look for the parrot. The street was empty, not a car or a person in sight, just beautiful old brick houses and white oak trees. I was halfway down the block when I realized what was missing.

\\\\\\

The city must have scooped up Matty's Jeep while I was searching under beds for Corinne's macaw. I'd left it parked illegally for almost an hour. It was the second car I'd let get towed that summer. It was the first bird I'd ever lost. I'd allegedly let Cathy Tomlinson's cat escape one time while I was drunk, and something killed it, a dog maybe. That was the beginning of the end with her. I'd never gotten hit by a bicycle before, though once while riding up 12th Street, I steered my front tire into the cleft of the old trolley track and sailed over the handlebars and chipped a tooth. I fucked up the tire, but it wasn't my bicycle. I couldn't remember whose bicycle it was. I was drunk for that, too.

I staggered up 7th Street to Washington Square, hoping to find a cop to ask about the car. Just inside the brick gates of the park, I spotted a stocky, frowning officer on a mammoth white horse. I kept my distance, wary of the animal's maw.

"Excuse me, officer," I called up to the woman. "I had my car parked on Spruce Street—"

"If your vehicle was parked in the vehicle-free zone, it has been towed," she said. She glanced down at me, her eyes pausing on my forehead. I reached up and felt the sting of my fingers on the tender skin of my eyebrow. There was a cut there from the cyclist's knee, right where I'd gotten stitches after Cudahy kicked me.

"Sorry, towed where?"

"Could be a courtesy tow to a different block," she said, looking past me down the street. "But probably it's impounded."

"How would I know if it was one or the other?"

The horse revved its nostrils and took a step to the right. The officer yanked it back to its former spot. "The owner of the vehicle can call the Philadelphia Parking Authority, eight-thirty to four, Monday through Friday."

It was Sunday. "I'm not the owner of the vehicle," I said. "I need to get the car back to the owner today."

The officer projected her voice as though a gaggle of more important people waited several yards behind me. "The owner of the vehicle can call the Philadelphia Parking Authority, eight-thirty to four, Monday through Friday."

"There's nothing I can do right now?" I asked.

"Monday through Friday, sir."

"What about reporting a lost bird?"

She glanced down at me and met my gaze for the first time. "A bird?"

"A parrot," I said. "A scarlet macaw. A pet bird."

"Was the bird stolen, sir?"

"It escaped. I think." I touched the cut on my forehead again, pressing down until the sting subsided. "It's a very large bird."

"I suggest you contact local animal shelters, sir."

I knew that would lead absolutely nowhere. I wondered how far away the parrot might fly on its own, and if it would know how to find its way back when it wanted more cucumbers.

"There's a medical tent set up outside City Hall," the officer added. The horse let loose another mechanical sneeze.

I stepped away and took out my phone to call Matty. He wouldn't be happy to hear about any of this. The Jeep wasn't gone forever, but the impossibility of its immediate retrieval would complicate his life. Matty was supposed to drive the boys back to their mother's house in West Chester that night. He would have to call his ex, a woman named Tiff, and ask her to come back to the city and collect their sons because his Jeep had been towed because his live-in cousin had parked it illegally outside of his girlfriend's house in the vehicle-free zone. He wouldn't enjoy making that call. Matty had already opened himself up to rebuke just by letting me crash at his house. To Tiff, I was still a blackout drunk. It would take me a while to shake that reputation.

That was the Jeep. The parrot, well. I could offer to tell Corinne how I'd lost the parrot, and that would spare Matty a second awkward phone call, but I was sure he'd still catch some blame. And Corinne would assume I stole the scotch, if she noticed it was gone, and she would tell Matty, and everyone would think I was drinking again.

Staring at my phone in my bloodied hands, I decided to wait to talk to Matty in person. If he saw me standing there before him, lacerated and bruised, it might take some of the sting off his anger. I texted him, "Decided to come to Mass, where are you guys?" and limped through the square toward Walnut Street.

There were people on Walnut, pairs and trios trickling west from Old City. Soon there were larger parties in matching t-shirts, round people with broad, naive faces looking happily up at the buildings. I looked up with them. I knew Walnut, its busy honk-filled blocks. I was once nearly plowed over by a taxi outside the Irish Pub. Another time, before I totaled my Dynasty, I'd come within inches of pancaking a couple and their tiny dog at the crosswalk on 12th Street. I could still picture the guy screaming at me through the windshield while the woman clutched the dog to her chin. Now Walnut was open only to foot traffic. The restaurants spilled their tables into the thoroughfares.

At Broad I joined a denser crowd of pilgrims streaming up the wide avenue, thousands of people carrying signs and banners, messages of praise in different languages. Some wore flags draped over their shoulders, flags from all over the world. A kind of mindless joy crackled in the air. The procession swelled past City Hall to the lower, unbarricaded portion of the Parkway, thronged with tens of thousands of people. They milled about between food trucks and canvas tents. Vendors hawked merchandise—bobbleheads, baseball caps, mugs, rosaries—stamped with the Pope's avuncular portrait. There were prayer booths, prayer stations, candles, relics, holy water. I didn't look out of place, even in my bloodied state. I saw people with worse afflictions than mine, scars and deformities, milky eyes and wires twisting from hidden holes. A nun washed the feet of a man with empty shirt-sleeves. A fleet of pilgrims in mobility scooters crossed themselves before a statue of the Infant Jesus of Prague. It seemed, for one day on the Parkway, the relief of any ailment could be attained through prayers directed at some recipe of saints and angels.

My phone vibrated with a text from Matty. "We're all the way at the front. Bird fed?"

\\\\\\

The Pope Fence rose up beneath the Basilica on 18th Street in the form of ten-foot interlocking black mesh panels. The crowd funneled toward the security checkpoint on Cherry Street, along a serpentine path of waist-high steel barricades. The line moved slowly. In front of me, a small contingent wore red t-shirts with the Pope silk-screened on the front and Our Lady of Guadalupe on the back. Two of them carried guitars, and every few minutes they joined together in a Spanish hymn. One of the guitarists wore a scarlet mariachi jacket embroidered with gold thread. When he noticed me behind him, he reached into his pocket and pulled out a cornflower blue bandana. He handed it to me, gesturing to my forehead. I took it, thanking him, and dabbed my eye-brow. I wrapped the bandana around my bitten hand. I couldn't bring myself to look at my throbbing shin, which was probably best left covered by my shredded pant leg.

We made it through the checkpoint, our pockets emptied, our bodies scanned, our intentions deemed pure. Beyond the gates, the traffic circle of Logan Square had transformed into a festival lawn. A breeze blew above our naked heads as people milled around, searching for gaps among the congregated bodies. I realized it would take a miracle to find Matty and the boys in that sea of people. Chairs and coolers and blankets filled every available tract of ground. Massive television screens broadcast a feed of the distant altar, which sat on a stage built in front of the Art Museum at the far end of the Parkway. We would soon see the Pope on the screens, his face magnified to godly size. The sun shone down so bright I had to keep my wrapped hand raised to shade my eyes.

It had been a while since I'd gone to Mass. Longer since I'd gone to Confession. I'd quit the latter around age thirteen, once I was confirmed and no one forced me to do it anymore. I don't know how much I ever believed in penance, but it had felt good to be absolved by Father Gerard, to stride out of our parish church into a rejuvenated world. It always felt less like the priest had purified my soul than he had somehow purified time itself, had wound it back and made it young again. For a few hours, I would get to live in that young time—hours when, if I died, I could go straight to heaven—until I did something I wasn't supposed to do and tripped forward into sin.

But it was easy to say what my sins were when I was a kid. I'd disobeyed my parents, I'd hit my brother, I'd lied to my grandmother about breaking her Waterford vase. My later sins, my blackout sins—it was harder to confess what I didn't understand. I was aware that I had committed sins, but I didn't know what they were, not all of them, not unless someone was there in the morning to tell me. I didn't know their number or severity or cause. I always pretended I knew why someone was mad at me, even when I didn't, and I always denied doing whatever they were mad about, even if I had no idea whether or not I was guilty. I left the door open and Cathy's cat escaped, the one that was killed by a dog, and I woke up to her screaming at me. The cat's name was Skunk. Cathy called me a monster, but I loved Skunk, just like I loved her, and I didn't understand how someone who loved people could be a monster. I didn't know if I was a bad person, or an unlucky person, or what precisely I was. If I had sinned because I'd been corrupted by a chemical, or if the sin had always been in me, waiting for its moment of eruption. Any idea I might conceive of myself necessitated a swarm of asterisks, buzzing with doubt and guilt and shame. And so I didn't confess to anything, even after I got sober. I walked the city in a state of not-knowing, and I met people, and I presented myself to them, and I tried over and over to explain myself without the words to explain myself, without the truth of myself. *My name is Dennis*, I said without saying, *and I lived years of my life in the dark, cursing and swatting at shapes in the dark. My name was Dennis and it's still Dennis, and I don't know if that first Dennis is different from this one or if it's all just the same Dennis and always will be.*

An idea struck me there on the Parkway surrounded by those God-loving people, the whole city oriented like an arrow toward a stage where an old man would soon be offering us forgiveness. If I could get to the front of the crowd, if I could stand beside Matty and the boys and stare up into the small, wrinkled face of the Holy Father, if I could look him in the eye, perhaps I could wordlessly explain myself to him, and he might understand me, and through his intercession God might forgive me, and my time could be made young again.

Even limping as I was, I thought I could maneuver myself to the stage through the unwieldy family groups with their children and grandparents. Already the croon of the choir rose in the speakers. It filled the Parkway like music from deep in the earth. The Mass was beginning. I still had blocks to go. The Pope was on the screens now, leading the crowd in prayer. Around me, the masses stirred in soft recitation. *"I confess to You, Almighty God, and to you, my brothers and sisters, that I have sinned through my own fault."*

A woman on the screens sang in Latin. I saw the stage in the distance, occupying the space where the Art Museum normally hovered above the street. I moved up the right side of the Parkway where the worshippers had left the sidewalk mostly clear. A new woman on the screens spoke in Spanish. Another spoke in Vietnamese. More singers, more prayers. I reached the lawn of the Barnes Foundation where people stood on every scrap of grass, their eyes shut, their heads bowed or raised heavenward. The Pope began his homily. I paused a moment to listen with them.

I did not understand the Pope's words. He spoke in Spanish. The people around me spoke a dozen languages, a hundred. They had come from all corners of the world, a thousand far-flung places. Many had traveled farther than if they'd gone to Rome itself, just to stand on the Benjamin Franklin Parkway, surrounded by the museums of my childhood field trips. For a day, Philadelphia was not in America, but some other, holier place. I felt my exterior dissolve in the unintelligibility of it all.

Beyond the baseball field on 22nd Street, the crowd grew denser than before. I swam into it, felt it on my skin, placed my hands on people's shoulders as I moved through them. Some turned and smiled. Some patted my arm. None recoiled at my bloody head. Their silent faces said, *Welcome, Dennis, you've finally come home.* I'd been months away, years away, crashing on cots and floors and couches and in strange beds, in rooms that weren't the shape of my room, in houses where I did not live. No more. I was almost there. I could imagine myself at the foot of the stage, staring up at the cross above the altar like I had when I was a kid, when faith seemed accessible if only I could deserve it. Before I started drinking in the mornings I had French. Before I lost my words. I have sinned. It is my fault. Forgive me.

As I got near the front, I reached another Pope Fence, a second layer of interlocking black mesh panels. I looked for a way around, but it rose up to the left and right of me without a corner or a gate.

"Is there a way to get closer?" I asked the woman beside me. She was a nun, the full habit and everything, a rosary dangling from her fingers. "Is there a way to get to the stage?"

"For ticket holders," she said.

"Ticket holders?" I realized I was in a different enclosure than the one that contained the stage. The ticket holders for the Mass—the well-to-dos and clergy of the Archdiocese—must be cordoned off in another, separate zone, with a second fence and a second round of security, inaccessible to me and the public at large. Of course. They'd never let so many people get that close to the Pope. From where I stood, the altar was blocked from view by the small amphitheater of seats. Even the amphitheater was rendered mostly invisible by tall, wide-topped chestnut trees. I could see a sliver of heads where the dignitaries sat, a wall of cloth that might have been a section of the choir. A pyramid of flowers. That was all.

On the screen above the amphitheater, half within my field of vision, the Pope levitated in his green vestments. He consecrated the Host for the Eucharist, a wafer held in both hands above his head, a solar disk. A single bell sounded in the Parkway's artificial valley. Around me, no one spoke. Heads bowed in deference. The Pope prayed over the Host in a voice no louder than a whisper. Wind audible in the microphone, ghostly in the trees. Another clang of the bell.

"Dennis!" I heard.

I turned and there was Matty, thirty feet away, hand cupped around his mouth. Waving. Smiling. Gavin and Brandon loitered beside him. Both wore new, ill-fitting Pope t-shirts. "What the hell happened to you?" asked Matty as I wove my way to him through the crowd.

"You're bleeding!" shouted Brandon, pointing at my head.

"I got hit by a bicycle." I assured them several times that I was okay.

"Well, looks like we're not going to see the Pope after all," said Matty. "I should have read the website more closely." He laid his hand on Brandon's hair. "But we're still having fun, right guys?"

The boys faced forward even though there was nothing to see, fingers clenched on the fence, noses pressed into its diamonds. Mouths open as though ready to answer an as-yet-unposed question. They waited. Watched. Expected, reasonably, that something yet would happen. There's nothing else, I wanted to tell them. We've gone the whole way, and this is what there is. Fences. Screens. Chestnut trees.

The Lord's Prayer whimpered from the crowd. The Pope recited the embolism in cautious English: "Deliver us, Lord, we pray, from every evil. Graciously grant us peace in our days."

"Will we get Communion, Dad?" asked Gavin, the little wino.

"They'll just give it to the people right around the stage," said Matty. It would be impossible to offer the sacrament to the tens of thousands assembled on the Parkway. The rest of us would wait to be dismissed, then return to our pre-papal lives. Fly home to Manila, to Oaxaca, to Cincinnati. Catch a bursting subway car to South Philadelphia. The stage would be torn down, the fence packed away. Vehicles would race back into the avenues of Center City like wolves reintroduced into a wilderness.

I looked for disappointment on the boys' faces. I could not tell if it was there. They looked like boys. Slightly agitated, slightly bored. What was this day, to them, in an endless series of days?

"The Jeep got towed," I said. "And the parrot is gone. It flew away."

Matty looked as though he hadn't heard me. "What's that about the Jeep?"

"I parked it illegally, and it got towed," I said. "And I broke a bottle of scotch in Corinne's kitchen, and I opened a window and her bird flew away, and I don't think it's ever coming back."

\\\\\\\

Then they appeared, floating through a newly opened gate in the fence: yellow umbrellas, a procession of them, like bulbs on a wire. Votaries in white albs carried patens of the Host, each paired with a helper tied up in a yellow sash, a yellow parasol held high to mark them in the crowd. A long column of them, a golden ribbon threading itself along the Parkway, back to where I had started, unraveling and embroidering each patch of crowd as it went. It was like the broken Host had multiplied exponentially, like every mouth in the world might be fed. It went on for minutes, another pair appearing, another, another, twinned believers beneath yellow half-moons.

It wasn't a miracle, those umbrellas. They didn't mean anything more than what they were: a final bit of pageantry. A climax to a show that had been going on longer than good taste or patience should have allowed. I knew that Philadelphia was in America and that God did not live there.

But as we watched those umbrellas, the people around us started weeping. They made no sound, the sun glistening down their cheeks. Gavin noticed it, and he began to cry himself, wiping at his tears with the collar of his shirt. Brandon looked up at his brother, horrified, and he cried as well. They were too young to understand the things they felt. Matty wept. I wept with them. My God, what else was there to do?

HISTORIES

The house was next door to a sex club. The two buildings shared a wall. Wednesday, Friday, and Saturday were club nights, and at seven o'clock, the vast gravel lot beneath the I-95 overpass began to fill up with black Mazdas and motorcycles. From then until closing, a revolving coterie of sex-weary visitors shared cigarettes ten feet from our garage. At first I found it strange, walking past them on my way to and from the house, but the novelty soon grew routine. That Wednesday, I nodded to the group when I got home with my groceries, as one does to his neighbors.

It was nearly a year since I quit drinking. My anniversary was a couple of days away. October found me, unexpectedly, paying rent for a room. The house was a few exits north of downtown, in a thin triangle of the River Wards that hadn't yet taken off. The elevated interstate rumbled night and day fifty feet from my bed, eight lanes of cars zipping through the air like they meant to ascend into heaven. On the far side of the highway there was nothing but a skinny belt of woods, a graffiti-coated pier, and the vegetable stink of the Delaware.

Three months earlier, I'd given up meat. Two months earlier, I'd given up cigarettes. I might start again with either of them. It was impossible to know. I'd just turned twenty-seven.

I walked through our garage, through our backyard, into our kitchen. Dave Deane was dressing a free-range chicken on the counter. He bought it on a farm in Upper Makefield. He cooked it with garlic and rosemary, ate it with cauliflower rice. Dave Deane didn't do grains. He was in the Nutrition Sciences Ph.D. program at Drexel. He didn't do sugar. He supported the city's soda tax. He ran five miles every morning. Dave Deane wanted to live forever.

"Look at this." He took a bottle of milk from the refrigerator, held it toward me with his vascular arm. "Completely raw. My chicken guy hooked me up." The milk looked like milk. "Pasteurization kills the good bacteria. This is the way our great-grandparents drank it."

I passed on the raw milk. I said yes to the fresh eggs. I cooked my eggs with garlic and rosemary, ate them with grilled tomatoes and plantains. Dave Deane and I sat at the table like we were having a family dinner. We plugged in the strand of LED lights wrapped around the potted fig tree beside the front door. The bulbs were encased in plastic jack-o'-lanterns. From a distance, they looked like luminescent fruits dangling from the branches.

I was grateful for Dave Deane. He was not at the top of my list when I needed a place to stay, but after parting ways with Matty last month, I'd given him a call. He owned the house. He said I could rent a room and pay for it like an adult. I was going to tell him never mind—I didn't care for his tone, the judgment it implied—but it had been late in the day, late in the year, and I was tired of asking people for favors. I figured I could make it work.

After dinner, we drank coffee. Dave Deane drank his with a dash of raw milk. I drank mine black. I-95 rolled and receded on the far side of our garage. Dave Deane told me about the driverless trucks that would soon revolutionize our highways.

"I almost crashed your car one time," I told him. "That Saturn you had. This was a couple years ago. I went out one night in Northern Liberties with Seamus and Conn and Hector, and we borrowed your car. I fell asleep at the wheel on the way home, right on Delaware Avenue. I'd had a few, obviously. Almost killed us all." I laughed. I didn't know if Dave Deane would find it funny. "I woke up just in time."

"I used to eat their food when I lived with those guys," admitted Dave Deane. "I would eat it and play them off each other. Eat Seamus's pasta and blame it on Conn. Eat Conn's pizza and blame it on Seamus. They never suspected me. That was before I gave up grains."

I laughed at the notion of Dave Deane as a thief. I should give up grains myself, I thought. I could give up sugar. I could give up eggs if I had to. Tropical fruit. Apples from Chile, avocados from Mexico. I could give up imported cheeses, desert-grown almonds. I could live off local produce, Jersey tomatoes, Pennsylvania mushrooms.

We cleared our plates. I did the dishes. Dave Deane retired to his bedroom to study trophological texts. I consulted his small living-room library, selected a John le Carré novel. I read it beneath the strands of pumpkins glowing with their hermetic inner light.

\\\\\

My bedroom shared a wall with the sex club. Club nights weren't as raucous as you might expect. I lay on a foam mattress as thin as my palm, listening for the moans of strange encounters, the squeals of jostled furniture. I never heard these things. Only a dull, percussive house beat, like an overexerted heart.

I thought of Maeve Slaughtneil. She often came to mind as I lay in bed. Not in an erotic way, though she was the only person I'd slept with since I got sober. If my imagination started to wander in a certain direction, I would hear my mother's voice—*Maeve Slaughtneil is disturbed*—and that would ruin everything. There were other, baser thoughts I could conjure up when needed, of other women from longer ago or never at all. No, when I thought of Maeve, I thought of the little dab of blood above her eyebrow, the look she gave me as I got dressed to go. *So leave, then. You can leave if you want.*

People liked to ask me about the day I quit drinking. The why and how of it. As the anniversary dawdled toward me, I'd been wondering the same thing. The truth was that I could hardly remember it, the day I quit. Really, I'd quit at night, since night was when I mostly did my drinking. All I remembered about that particular night was that I couldn't be in my apartment—being in my apartment made me want to drink—so I'd ridden buses around the city. The Night Owls ran till four or five in the morning, and I'd ridden them with no aim other than to kill time. But knowing I'd done something wasn't the same as remembering it. My brain had switched into survival mode. It wasn't taking notes.

The afternoon I slept with Maeve Slaughtneil, though—I could remember that. The particulars of it. The smell of the stale carpet in the public library, the papery must of its shelves. The chilled, sour air. The heft of Herodotus's *Histories* in my hand, and Maeve Slaughtneil who I had known since we were little kids now lean and tall, her hair glowing, her face glowing, the whole classics aisle glowing with late-spring light from the high windows. And I was glowing, too. I swear I glowed every day back then, in those first six months that I was clean. I was thinner than I'd been, and my skin was better, and my eyes were clearer. I'd gotten a handle on my thirst, but I hadn't stopped wanting things. Truly, I wanted far more than I had when I'd been drinking, wanted all the things the drinking had kept from me. I wanted Maeve Slaughtneil. Maybe I'd always wanted her and hadn't known it, and maybe she'd always wanted me. Maybe neither of us had ever been good enough for one another, but on that day, in that chance moment, we were the exact right thing. There are all kinds of reasons someone might want to sleep with somebody, or not want to, or want to at one time but not later. I wanted it at the time and later I wished I hadn't, but maybe a part of me was still glad that I did.

Now I had my own room, even my own bathroom, in a house, in the city. The sex club's electronic beat thudded beyond my plaster. The walls of my room were Navajo white. The floor was hardwood, though not original. The boards were the modern snap-in kind. I had an unpainted pine twin bed frame. I had an unpainted pine table that I used as a desk. I had an unpainted pine chair. I had a particle board dresser that fit snugly into my closet. My walls were blank, devoid of distraction. It took a long time to learn to sleep after I got sober. It had been years since I'd fallen asleep on my own, since I hadn't gone to bed drunk. Suddenly I'd needed to sleep like a normal person, and I couldn't remember how. But I learned again. Eventually, I learned to do everything again.

\\\\\\

I woke to the scrape of trowels on bricks. I stepped onto the roof deck that extended behind my third-floor bedroom and peered down into the backyard, a tight square hemmed in by our house, our fence, our detached garage. Dave Deane was down there with his friend Ranim. They were excavating a corner of the brick-paved yard to clear space for a vegetable garden. They wore surgical masks over their mouths to protect their lungs from whatever mold might lie beneath the century-old pavers.

"Hey, those are antiques," I called down.

Ranim placed a hand to her forehead, peered up at me through the sunlight. "There are no antiques on this continent." Her voice echoed against the walls of her enclosure. Ranim was born in Aleppo, one of the oldest cities in the world.

"Monk, I put tea in the fridge," called Dave Deane. "Bring us some?"

On the stairs, I passed their bicycles hanging from wall-mounted racks. Dave Deane and Ranim biked everywhere. They tried to keep their carbon footprints small. I had yet to get a bike, but I didn't have a car either. I could give up cars, I thought. I could give up riding in other people's cars. I could give up buses. I could give up the subway. I could give up any place that I couldn't reach on foot. I could walk wherever I needed to be. I could weigh the value of every step, every minute of travel.

A pitcher of black tea cooled on the refrigerator shelf next to Dave Deane's raw milk. I poured the tea into three ice-filled glasses and carried them out to the patio table, catty-corner from the spot where the diggers extracted their bricks.

Ranim held up a paver for Dave Deane's appraisal. "What do you think, David? Is this Roman or Assyrian?"

Dave Deane removed his mask, wiped the sweat from either side of his nose. "We'll call the Penn Museum. Have them send an archeologist."

They rested on chairs beside the table. I sat on the step leading into the house. The tea was cool and unsweetened. "What are you going to do with these bricks?" I asked.

"We can put one in each toilet tank," said Dave Deane. "It saves water."

"How?" asked Ranim. "That's ridiculous."

"It takes up volume. So less water fills the tank."

"And you've done this before?"

"Of course," said Dave Deane. "Only one brick, though. You can't use two. It won't flush if you use two. You want one for your bathroom, Monk?"

"Sure." Every day, Dave Deane showed me how easy it was to be less wasteful. Place a brick in a toilet tank, compost my biodegradables. Bring my own bag to the supermarket, never turn on the heat. I could wear a sweater indoors in winter. I could cover the roof with plants to cool the house in summer.

"You're both nuts," said Ranim.

Ranim was short and slim with eviscerating eyes. She was in the pharmacology program at Drexel. She and Dave Deane were in the tense, flirtatious period of a new romance. When she spoke to me, she was normally making eye contact with him. "Do I look like a Syrian rebel, Monk, with my mask and my bricks? Do I look like a dangerous refugee?"

"You're not a refugee," said Dave Deane, uncomfortable with the joke. Ranim left Aleppo before the war to do her undergrad at Penn. She spoke flippantly about her devastated city. I assumed it was because people were always asking her about it. Aleppo had been in the news for years. I wanted to ask her about it, too. I wanted to know what it was like to leave your city intact, then find out it was destroyed while you were living half a world away.

"I'm an expat," she said. "Just like . . ."

"Paul Bowles," I said. "And Jane Bowles. In Tangier."

"That's right," she said. "I'm an exile for my art."

"And that art is . . . ?" asked Dave Deane.

"I'm a brick model." Ranim held her bricks like they were luxury items. "I'm something of an icon in the brick community."

I was envious of the way she looked at Dave Deane, like he was the final, unexpected piece she needed to make her life good. But I dismissed my envy. I could be happy for Dave Deane, happy that he inspired passion in a woman like Ranim. I could be happy for Ranim, that she found fulfillment in a guy like Dave Deane. Other people's love did not indict me. I could root for it and admire it. I could be uplifted by it.

"When can you start planting?" I asked.

"There's too much lead in the soil," said Dave Deane. "We need to make our own dirt. We can compost over winter and maybe have enough in time for spring."

"Lead makes you crazy," said Ranim.

"We don't want that," I said. "I used to be crazy."

"Not anymore?" asked Ranim.

I shook my head. "I quit."

"You're lucky," she said, looking always at Dave Deane. "Most madness can't be quit."

We sipped our tea. The sun was bright and the city was peaceful. I could give up coffee, I thought. I could make do with tea.

\\\\\\

I used the torn-up bricks from the backyard to build myself a bookcase. Dave Deane helped me lug them up the stairs. I washed the bricks in bleach, dried them in the roof-deck sun. Later, I salvaged boards for the shelves from under I-95, where all sorts of discarded things lay coated in grime. I carried them under my arms like a young Ben Franklin with his three loaves of bread on his first day in town. I brought them in through our back door just as the sex club patrons were arriving for their Friday bacchanal. It was different people all the time. I'd yet to recognize a regular. They never smiled or spoke to me, but they always made eye contact. I supposed sex club people were confident people. Assertive people. I wondered what would happen if one night I followed them inside. If they would let me. If they would welcome me, caress me, pull me into their piles of limbs. Or if I would simply order a club soda and sit by myself on a couch, timid and ignored.

I erected the bookcase against the wall that I shared with the club. There were three shelves—unpainted wooden boards—but I had no books for them at the moment. I lay on my bed and stared at my handiwork, such as it was. There was an imbalance in the bricks somewhere. The shelves rattled from the bass next door.

The sound of night music used to make me wish I had somewhere to go, people to go with. I didn't feel that way anymore, not really. I valued my solitude, my early evenings, my sleep. Dave Deane and I were private people. We kept mostly to our rooms, to our work. I had a freelance gig writing practice materials for standardized tests. SAT, ACT, GED. I spent my weekends asking hypothetical high school students to choose the best definition of *reinvigorate*. To explain the difference between average and marginal productivity. The pay wasn't good, but it was enough.

It was not such a difficult thing, if I thought about it, not to drink. To get up and only do the things that normal people did, in the normal way. I rose early. I ate consciously. I walked to the store. I did my work. When nighttime came, I was usually tired. Sometimes I lay in bed and stared at the blankness of the ceiling, wondering what the rest of my life would entail. Sometimes it seemed wide open—obscenely so, like I was standing on a rooftop with the city spread before me, the horizon line low, the sky as big as people were always insisting that it was. But other times the future seemed so compact, condensed to fit within the four walls around me, as though my entire life would be improvised solely from the objects in my room. I didn't know which vision to believe. I didn't know if those two lives looked so different from each other, in practice. A big life. A small life.

I could give up sex, I thought. I'd never had a lot of it, was never any good at it. I could give up dating. Avoid any hurt feelings. I could give up friends. I had friends and I couldn't say it helped too much. I liked Dave Deane because he wasn't a close friend, just a guy I'd known for a while. His life with Ranim was siloed off from mine. I could give up people, I thought. I could keep my own company. I could give up masturbation. I could give up hot showers. I could give up caffeine. I could give up tea. I could drink turmeric or ginger dissolved in hot water, with lemon juice, unsweetened. I could get a flip phone, or have no phone at all. I could get by with less. I could need almost nothing.

\\\\\\

I came home one night with my groceries—a shaker of turmeric, a finger of ginger root, a bag of lemons—and found Dave Deane and Ranim loitering by the garage with a bald man. It was Thursday, not a sex club night, but the man was a sex club man. He was stocky and middle-aged and looked thoroughly relaxed in his black t-shirt and sweatpants. He smoked a cigarette, forcing Dave Deane to weave this way and that in order to dodge his desultory plumes.

"This is Rick," said Dave Deane. "He owns the club."

"You just missed the tour." Rick shook my hand. There was concrete in his grip, and in his voice. "Should we run it through again?"

Ranim laughed to herself. I tried to catch her eye, but she turned her face into Dave Deane's shoulder.

"I'm trying to convince Rick to go in on some solar panels with me," said Dave Deane. "He's got the better roof for it."

"Just have to run the numbers on my end," said Rick. He gestured toward the club's black door. "You want to see the place? We can go up again."

"I should get dinner started," said Dave Deane. I knew he wouldn't subject his lungs to the club's tobacco-laced air a second time. I was surprised he'd risked it even once.

"You should go in, Monk," said Ranim. "It's quite a space. A lot of . . . features."

"So much room up there," said Dave Deane. "You could fit fifty panels up there easily."

"Maybe not right now," I said. I lifted my grocery bag to prove that I was occupied. Dave Deane snagged the rim of the canvas with a finger and peeked inside.

"Well, some other night," said Rick. "Drinks on the house. I'm the bartender."

Ranim laughed again and looked at the ground. Dave Deane pulled the sack of lemons from my grocery bag. There were a dozen of them. Too many. I hadn't known how many to buy.

"I'm not a drinker," I said to Rick. "But thanks."

"Oh, I don't drink neither," answered Rick. "Haven't had a drink in twenty years."

I told Rick I was impressed by any alcoholic who could still tend bar.

"I'm not an alcoholic anymore," said Rick, as though I hadn't understood what he said.

"Any sober person, I mean."

"Like AA and all that?" asked Rick. "I don't worry about that. I just pour drinks and make sure everybody's having a good time. You should come by, have a cranberry juice."

Ranim was still laughing. I wasn't sure if she was laughing at Rick or at me or at something she had seen inside. Dave Deane removed the twist tie from the bag of lemons.

"I went to a meeting, once, twenty years ago," said Rick, waving his cigarette in the air. "People talking about, *oh, I did this, I did that, I hurt her, he hurt me.* Depressive shit. Me, I look to the future. We're open tomorrow night. Halloween weekend is always a blast. You should all come by. Real friendly people, real accepting of everybody."

Dave Deane pulled a lemon from the bag and spun it in his fingers. He brought it to his mouth and took a bite, rind and all, as though it were an apple.

Rick flinched. Ranim smacked Dave Deane's arm, a startled grin spread across her face.

"The peel's got all the nutrients," said Dave Dean, lemon juice running in rivulets down his chin.

\\\\\\

It was hard to know what I really remembered and what I had filled in later, based on other attempts, other bus rides. The Night Owls had heaved and slowed, wheezed and started up again, through neighborhoods with working streetlights and neighborhoods confined to the dark. Whitman Plaza to Olney Terminal. Frankford Transportation Center to the Neshaminy Mall. Port Richmond across the Badlands to East Falls. My fellow riders were cooks and janitors and nurses, people sleeping on the way to the late shift or the way back home, heads tilted against cold window glass or the hard fabric of their seats. I rode with them for hours, one route then the next, spine straight, fists jammed into my pockets, until the sun came up and I realized I was on a bus full of people in khakis and dark green polos. Everyone was dressed the same except for me. Who were these people, so alike one another? Clearly I was not meant to be among them. Or maybe I was, I thought in my madness, maybe these were my new people. The bus pulled up to a stop on Girard Avenue and they all got off. I got off too. I followed them down the street until we came to a wrought iron gate stretched between two ornate Victorian huts. There was a sign built into the top of the gate, its letters sharp and black against the waxy sky: *Garden, Zoological Society*. The men and women strolled beneath it, like they were right where they should be. Zookeepers, I realized. They had brought me to the zoo.

I sat there on a curb in the parking lot for two hours before the place opened to the public. I was the first visitor of the morning. Once inside, I tried to look at the animals, but they held no interest for me. Instead, I just wandered the twisting paths, monstrous ferns poking out at me, children shrieking and darting and flailing, around and around and around, until I threw up near the penguin tank. When the zoo closed for the day, I rode buses again to wherever they would take me: the urine-soaked shed at 69th Street and the wind-blasted loop above Penn's Landing, across the rattling Passyunk Avenue drawbridge to the floating blinkers of the airport and over to bombed-out Chester and back, dead-eyed through the dead-of-night city, until the subways started running at quarter to five the next morning, my second morning, and I caught a train home and fell asleep.

I didn't know why sobriety stuck that time and not any other time. I had ridden the buses other nights to stay sober. Maybe the zoo made the difference. I'd never tried the zoo before.

\\\\\\

My brother, Owen, paid me a visit from the suburbs. I opened the front door and there he was on the stoop in a tattered felt hat and a long fake beard. Beneath his jacket was a frayed plaid shirt with the front pocket half-torn off. His slouched, bashful posture helped to sell the costume. He was headed to a Halloween party in Fishtown and figured he'd check in on me while he was in the neighborhood.

"Gandalf?" I asked him.

He held up an empty pewter beer mug. "Rip Van Winkle."

I hadn't seen him since my parents kicked us out in May. He was still living in Bucks County in an apartment with his friend Logan. He'd found work as a barback. "It sucks," he said, when I asked him how he liked it.

He set the beer mug on my kitchen countertop. I poured us glasses of ginger tea from the large carafe in the refrigerator and took him up to see the roof deck. The door to the deck was across the landing from my room on the third floor, and though technically it was one of the house's common areas, I tended to think of it as my private space. There were two chairs out there, a small tiled table. A potted laurel tree with a skinny, straight trunk and a globe of tapering leaves. I hoped the roof deck would impress Owen, who had always taken pleasure in my lack of success, even if the deck only overlooked I-95 and the riverine woodland beyond. The overpass was walled in, so we couldn't see the cars, just the boxy tops of tractor trailers.

"This is nice," said Owen, brushing his hand against the laurel's leaves. I expected him to complain that I had no beer to offer him, but he said the tea, too, was nice. His beard rested below his face to keep his mouth unobstructed.

"Have you actually read 'Rip Van Winkle?'" I asked him.

"We read it in high school," he said. He pulled the beard off his ears, rolled it up, and shoved it in his pocket. "You're not the only one who's read stuff."

"Are you high?"

"Barely," he mumbled. In the absence of the beard, the redness of his eyes was conspicuous. "I get anxious driving on the highway. It takes the edge off."

We looked over the deck's railing to the new compost bin that sat in a corner of the backyard.

"Dave Deane and his girlfriend made that," I told him. "They're starting a vegetable garden. She's from Aleppo, do you believe that?"

"It's quiet," said Owen. "Considering Ninety-Five is right there."

I suspected he'd only come because my mom asked him to check in on me, but that was all right. I was actually glad Owen had stopped in. I'd just that morning decided on a course of action, and I was excited to tell somebody about it. I'd read about a mountain in the west of Ireland, rising along the shore of a shallow bay. It was a holy mountain, with no trees, just broken rocks and gravel all the way to the top. People climbed it with bare feet. They climbed it because Saint Patrick had climbed it long ago. Even before Saint Patrick, people had climbed it for eons and eons. Climbers stopped at three holy cairns on the way to the top and walked around them sunwise praying Hail Marys and Our Fathers. On the summit, there was a little chapel where a priest said Mass twice a year, once on Easter Sunday and once on the Feast of the Assumption. I'd decided that some year soon, maybe even next year when I'd saved up some money, I was going to climb that mountain, on one holy day or the other. I would slide off my shoes and socks, and pick my way up the stones, and circle the cairns, and at the top I would step into the chapel and stand there before whatever spry priest the parish sent up to say the Mass. I would take the host and decline the eucharistic wine, and I would walk back down the mountain with my bloody feet, and I would go to one of the restaurants in the nearby town to eat some of the oysters that they caught in the shallow bay, just a few, just to taste them. And that would be the end of it. I'd forget about my drinking life after that. I'd move on and think about something else.

"Do you have Maeve Slaughtneil's number?" I asked Owen.

He frowned at me like he was expecting a trick. "Why?"

"I wanted to text her but I don't have her number." I sat down in one of the chairs by the table. They had no cushions, just flat, cold metal. "Do you have it or not?"

"I don't have it," said Owen. "I know Mom already sent a card."

"Why would Mom send a card?" For an irrational moment I worried my mother had written Maeve to apologize for how I'd treated her.

"Her and Mrs. Slaughtneil were pretty close at one point," said Owen. He shrugged. "What else do you do when something like that happens? You send a card."

"Something like what?" *I was so sorry, Maeve, to hear that Dennis took advantage of you in your disturbed state.*

My brother leaned against the railing, still looking at me like he couldn't tell if I was fucking with him. He'd been looking at me like that for most of our lives. "Do you not know?"

"Know what?" I felt a shiver in the muscles of my back. It was chillier on the deck than it had been lately. "Owen, what the fuck are you talking about?"

Owen ran his finger around the rim of his tea glass. "I don't really know how to say this politely. Maeve set herself on fire."

"She what?" I asked. It sounded like a euphemism. "What do you mean?"

"I mean she set herself on fire. With, like, gasoline. She lit herself on fire. This was like a week and a half ago."

A car horn sounded somewhere down the highway. We stared at each other for the length of its two desperate bleats. "On purpose?" I asked.

"I think." He picked at something on the railing with his thumb nail. "Or lighter fluid, maybe? I don't know."

"Well is she okay?" I asked. "Is she . . . ?"

"She's alive. But she's, you know. She's in pretty bad shape."

I was having difficulty keeping a grip on my glass. The muscles in my arms had tensed up. I set it down on the table and crossed my arms over my stomach, newly aware of my skin bristling beneath my clothes.

"She's supposed to recover," continued Owen. "But, yeah, she's burned very badly over most of her body."

A horrific image barged into my head, but I refused to look at it straight on. I willed it into the corner of my mind.

"Why did she do that?" I asked.

Owen moved his hat farther back on his head. The brim formed a sort of rumpled halo around his face. He squinted up at the sun suspended over the wide sex club roof, where there weren't any solar panels yet to catch the light.

"I don't know," he said at last. "Probably a suicide attempt, right? Why else would someone do that."

"But why?"

"She's bipolar," he said. "That's what Mom told me. Diagnosed a couple years ago. You know about her manias and all that?"

"No."

"You know how she dropped out of school, and she was touring around with that band?"

"No. I don't know anything about it."

Owen set his glass down on the railing and stuck his hands in his pockets. He pulled one hand back out again and looked down at what it held. It was his false beard, balled up like a scared animal. He slipped it back in his pocket, picked up his glass, and came to sit beside me.

"I saw her one time at Temple," he said, crossing his legs. "I was still in high school. I was down there with Logan, at the rugby house, and the rugby guys were buying ketamine off this wook. The guy looked like he lived in a car, with the dreadlocks and the poncho and the crazy eyes. But he had a woman with him, this smokeshow wook girl that all the rugby guys were eyeing because she was barely wearing anything. It took me a minute to recognize her."

When Maeve saw my brother, she ran over and threw her arms around his neck in a way that made the whole rugby team jealous. She led him to the beer-smelling couch and told him how she'd toured all up and down the East Coast playing tambourine in a jam band. The band broke up after a festival in the Everglades, but Maeve was still getting paid to dance at shows, a glowstick ballerina. Owen was shocked by all of it. Maeve had always been a serious girl, and here she was with henna tattoos down her wrists and owl feathers in her hair, telling him she ate a mushroom cap every morning to keep her chakras unclouded. Then the wook and the rugby guys got in an argument, and the wook left, and Maeve left with him.

"She had already tried to kill herself at that point," muttered Owen, looking down at the deck boards beneath his shoes. "I found that out later, from Mom. A few months before I saw her at the rugby house, Maeve swallowed a bottle of sleeping pills, somewhere in Florida. She had to have her stomach pumped. Her parents only learned about it because she sent them the hospital bill." He took off his hat and set it on the table beside our glasses. "We don't have to keep talking about this."

"No," I said. "I want to know."

"You saw her this summer, right? Mom mentioned it."

"At the library," I said.

"How'd she seem?"

I shrugged. There was too much to get into. "You never can tell with people."

"That was the last time I saw her," said Owen. "I rode around looking for her one time, though, after that. You know how Maeve disappeared for a while?"

I leaned back in my chair and clasped my hands behind my head.

"After I saw her at the rugby house, she went fully AWOL. Like, milk-carton-kid vanished. Nobody heard from her for like three years. Then one day, her parents got a call from a jail in Colorado. Maeve had been arrested for breaking into somebody's apartment. She was methed out, picked up with some other people who were methed out. Her parents worked it so that they could bring her back to Pennsylvania. She went into some kind of facility in Warminster where they put her on antidepressants, but the antidepressants induced a mania, and she walked out of the place. I'd heard about all this from Mom—"

"How often do you talk to Mom?" I asked. "It sounds like you're always talking to Mom."

"I don't know," he said, tilting his head. "Every few days?"

"That often?"

"Yeah, just about. I mostly call her. She doesn't call me too much." Owen paused like he expected me to ask another question. "Anyway, Mom told me Maeve was missing, so I went looking for her. Me and Morgan, we skipped class that day and drove around Bucks County. The cops found her late in the afternoon. She'd walked all the way to Bensalem for some reason. But nobody told us the search was over, so we were still driving around in the dark. That was maybe a year and a half ago."

I pictured Owen riding in his friend's car, slumped in the passenger seat with his knee up on the dashboard, the way he'd sat whenever I'd driven him to the bars. I pictured the evening glare angling in through the windshield, the sun low and useless in the sky as they passed by softball fields and big-box stores. I pictured Owen looking over himself in the side-view mirror, attempting to pick out Maeve's silhouette in the bus shelters and parking lots. I pictured, too, the scene that Owen must have had in his head as they drove: the small thrill of that college party when he was still in high school. Not one of the shitty ones in my dorm to which I'd reluctantly admitted him, but the one at the rugby house where Maeve Slaughtneil strolled improbably out of the night and rested her painted hands on Owen's shoulders.

I wondered if he'd always loved her. Not love-loved, but the kind of love you feel for an older girl when you're a kid, a girl you'll never get a chance with because she's always in a different phase of life. For a moment at the rugby house, Maeve's long elliptical orbit had brought her back from the farthest reaches and placed her next to Owen on a cigarette-burned couch. Then the spheres had shifted and she'd spun away again. I could see him sitting in Morgan's darkening car as they drove around Bucks County looking for a girl that had already been found, wishing he would have held onto her, years before, on the couch.

I could see him wishing it again now, sitting next to me on the deck.

Owen rubbed his eyes with the heels of his hands. "As far as I knew she was doing well since then. Living with her parents. And then this happened. She did it in the field behind their house."

It was wrong, him sitting there telling me these things I should have known myself.

"How come," I started to say, but I needed to clear my throat. "How come she didn't die?"

"They think she changed her mind after she started. She rolled. Put herself out. Some people walking their dog through the field saw the whole thing."

He sighed and ran his hands in circles over the caps of his knees. He had little cuts on his fingers, the kind I got when I was washing dishes, when the hot water cooked my skin so soft that even the spoons could tear it open. He caught me looking at them and stuffed them back in his pockets.

"She's still at the hospital," he said. "They think she'll probably live. That's what's important, right? She'll live."

I nodded. Has lived. Will live.

\\\\\\

And then what?

Look. Look the whole world over, and never find a place for yourself. Leave your home, chase your madnesses, hook your fingers around the far edges of life. Press up against every warm body you meet, try your hand at every trade, make offerings to every god and saint, and still— the days. The days. On the peaks of holy mountains, in the mood-lit dens of sex clubs, they are counting their days.

\\\\\\

Owen pulled his jacket tighter around his shoulders. That afternoon was colder than others had been lately. Too cold for iced tea. The traffic rattled on I-95. Beyond the overpass, the trees had browned. It was Halloween. Tomorrow, I would be one year sober.

"Anyway," said Owen, rising to his feet. He looked especially tall standing beside me on the deck. He'd turned twenty-three that summer. I was sure I'd texted him, if not on the day, then the day after. He'd been taller than me since he was seventeen. He looked capable of anything.

I used to want to be something. Just what that was, I was never sure. Something different than the people I knew, maybe, something outside of the lives they lived. But I gave that up. It seemed like a thing for a kid to want. A silly, entitled thing, to want something special for yourself.

Later, I felt entitled to a stable job, but I didn't feel that way anymore. I had given up stability. I had given up a living wage. I could give up retirement, if I had to. I could work till I died.

"There's more trees down here than I would have thought," said Owen, stepping over to the railing. "More color."

I could give up health insurance. I could give up medicine. I could give up the function of some or all of my limbs. I could lie in a hospital bed, maybe. I could live in a chair. People made it work. I thought I could, too.

"Hey Dennis," said Owen over his shoulder. "Maybe I'll move to the city, huh? Plenty of bars in Philadelphia."

I could give up a year. I could give up a few. I'd lost a few already. I could lose a few more. Here—take my years. Dole them out to the others. Share them with Dave Deane and Ranim and Owen. With Maeve Slaughtneil. Make their lives long, if you can't make them good.

Take my years. Just leave me my days. Leave me tomorrow, at the very least. An addict only ever wants tomorrow. Tomorrow, I can make it work. Give me tomorrow to splash across my face, to muss into my hair. Let me walk around in it, watch the compost molder in the yard, smell the season on the river. Let me show you how okay I am, how good, how sorry. How easy to love. I have to be inflexible on this. I can't compromise any further. I'll cry and yell and plead. I'll beg you on my knees.

Just give me one more day.

\\\\\\

Owen wandered the perimeter of the deck, his shoulders hunched up toward his chin. He looked like he wanted to go back inside but didn't want to be the one to suggest it. I knew I should get up and open the door, but I didn't move. I sat, and he shuffled back and forth, and the traffic rolled on past us, and I wondered how long we might stay like that. He kept glancing at me as if he wanted me to say something. Finally he stopped pacing around and just stood there.

"Hey Dennis?" he asked.

"I'm thinking about going to the zoo tomorrow," I said to him. "Would you want to go to the zoo with me?"

My brother nodded and picked his hat up off the table. "Sure, let's go to the zoo."

ACKNOWLEDGMENTS

I'd like to thank the many people who helped me make this book, whether directly or indirectly, particularly Deborah Ghim, Samantha Shea, Ansa Khan Khattak, Lauren Grodstein, Lisa Zeidner, Paul Lisicky, Gregory Lee Sullivan, Sophia Starmack, Matthew Neill Null, Jaimy Gordon, Leila Chatti, Abe Murley, Tom Macher, Christine Sneed, Andrew Ervin, Brandon Som, M. Callen, Marie Kane, Aimee Bender, Danzy Senna, Maggie Nelson, Dana Johnson, Percival Everett, Hilary Schor, Risa Takeuchi, Chris Beha, Sally Toborowski, Melissa Hughes, Daniel Pieczkolon, Charley Birkhead, Marc Sammartino, Hunter Baskerville, Tom Nunn, Sean Howe, Shain Wancio, Kyle Dougherty, Jason Woodring, Dylan Raisner, and Snake McColligan, as well as all the teachers, writers, journal editors, coworkers, relatives, roommates, friends, friends of friends, and patient strangers whose kindness I've imposed upon over the years. Thanks, also, to Central Bucks High School West, the Pennsylvania Governor's School for the Arts, Temple University, the Kimmel Harding Nelson Center for the Arts, the Fine Arts Work Center, and the creative writing programs at Rutgers University-Camden and the University of Southern California. Thanks to all my co-fellows and workshop-mates in Doylestown, Erie, North Philadelphia, Camden, Provincetown, and Los Angeles. Thanks to Rob Volansky and Isaac Blum. Thanks to Sean Hoffman, Joe Manno, and Ken Krell. Thanks to Marissa Gawel. Thanks to Daniel, Carol, and Laura Deagler most of all.

Credit: Marissa Gawel

ABOUT THE AUTHOR

Michael Deagler was raised in Bucks County, Pennsylvania. He lives in Los Angeles, where he is pursuing a PhD in creative writing and literature at the University of Southern California. This is his first novel.